'I have the f███████████n, that one is ████████████fe around yo███████████at deal without ever giving the appearance of actually looking. That makes you dangerous.'

'Only to those with something to hide. The innocent have no reason to fear me.' His eyes found hers and held them captive. 'I trust *you* do not find me dangerous, Lady Annabelle?'

Author Note

It's always a treat when an idea for a new story comes out of a book I haven't even finished writing. And that's exactly what happened with BRUSHED BY SCANDAL.

Lady Annabelle Durst and Sir Barrington Parker both made their debuts in COURTING MISS VALLOIS, and although they never met I knew they would be drawn to one another. After all, they were both intelligent, attractive people, who liked nothing better than to help others get out of or avoid potentially embarrassing or damaging situations.

But what if that potentially damaging situation happened to one of *them*? How would they feel about being investigated by the other person? Worse, could they ever bring themselves to *love* that other person if the crime they threatened to expose had the power to destroy everything they held most dear?

I hope you enjoy Barrington and Anna's love story. I had great fun writing it.

BRUSHED BY SCANDAL

Gail Whitiker

All the characters in this book have no existence outside the imagination of the author, and have no relation whatsoever to anyone bearing the same name or names. They are not even distantly inspired by any individual known or unknown to the author, and all the incidents are pure invention.

First published in Great Britain 2011
by Mills & Boon, an imprint of Harlequin (UK) Limited,
Eton House, 18-24 Paradise Road, Richmond, Surrey TW9 1SR

© Gail Whitiker 2011

ISBN: 978 0 263 88793 8

Harlequin (UK) policy is to use papers that are natural, renewable and recyclable products and made from wood grown in sustainable forests. The logging and manufacturing process conform to the legal environmental regulations of the country of origin.

Printed and bound in Spain
by Blackprint CPI, Barcelona

Gail Whitiker was born on the west coast of Wales and moved to Canada at an early age. Though she grew up reading everything from John Wyndham to Victoria Holt, frequent trips back to Wales inspired a fascination with castles and history, so it wasn't surprising that her first published book would be set in Regency England. Now an award-winning author of both historical and contemporary novels, Gail lives on Vancouver Island, where she continues to indulge her fascination with the past, as well as enjoying travel, music, and spectacular scenery. Visit Gail at www.gailwhitiker.com

Previous novels by this author:

A MOST IMPROPER PROPOSAL*
THE GUARDIAN'S DILEMMA*
A SCANDALOUS COURTSHIP
A MOST UNSUITABLE BRIDE
A PROMISE TO RETURN
COURTING MISS VALLOIS

*part of *The Steepwood Scandal* mini-series

To Mum and Dad, who continue to be an ongoing source of love and support in so many areas of my life. Thank you for always being there.

And to my good friend Lynne Rattray, who inspires me with her *joie de vivre* and her unflagging sense of humour.

Chapter One

It was a perfect night for sin. The mid-May evening was deliciously warm, the air sweet with the fragrance of rosewater and violets, and the attention of one hundred and forty-nine of the guests moving slowly through the overheated rooms of Lord and Lady Montby's palatial London house was focused on anything *but* the young lady slipping furtively through the French doors and onto the dimly lit balcony beyond.

Fortunately, as the attention of the one hundred and fiftieth guest had been fixed on that silly young woman for some time, the chances of *her* making a clean escape were never very good. Over the course of the evening, Lady Annabelle Durst had watched the exchange of smiles and glances passing between Miss Mercy Banks and a certain red-coated officer, and, given that the gentleman had recently left the room by the same doors through which Miss Banks now passed, Anna had no doubt that a clandestine rendezvous was planned. A rendezvous that could only end in disaster for one or both of them.

'Mrs Wicks, would you please excuse me,' Anna said quietly. 'I've just seen someone I really must speak with.'

'Why, of course, Lady Annabelle, and I do apologise for having taken up so much of your time, but I really didn't know who else to turn to. Cynthia simply refuses to listen and I was at my wits' end, wondering what to do next.'

'I understand perfectly,' Anna said, endeavouring to keep one eye on the French doors. 'Cynthia has always been the most stubborn of your daughters and if you force her to spend a month in Scotland with her grandmother while her sisters are allowed to go to Bath, she *will* rebel. However, I believe the compromise I've suggested should help to alleviate the tension and make everyone feel better.'

'I don't mind saying it's made *me* feel a great deal better,' Mrs Wicks murmured. 'You're an uncommonly wise young woman for your age, Lady Annabelle. Your father must be very proud.'

Aware that her father would have been a great deal more proud had he been sending word of her upcoming engagement to *The Times*, Anna simply inclined her head and moved on. There was no point in telling Mrs Wicks that her unwed state was an ongoing source of consternation to her father or that he had offered to settle not only a handsome dowry, but one of his smaller, unentailed estates on her the moment she announced her engagement. Why bother when there was absolutely no one in her life for whom she felt even the slightest attraction?

As for being deemed a very wise young woman, Anna supposed it could have been worse. She might have been called studious or obliging—agreeable, even—none of which truly described her character. Yes, it was true, she had been dispensing an inordinate amount of advice to wilful young ladies and their frustrated mothers of late, but what was she to do when they kept coming to her for answers? Their problems were relatively easy to understand and comparatively simple to fix, even if the parties involved thought otherwise.

As to the hapless Miss Banks, that was clearly a situation Anna was going to have to deal with personally if she hoped to ward off imminent disaster.

The balcony, illuminated by multiple strands of brightly coloured lanterns strung from one end to the other, ran almost the entire length of the house, but one glance in either direction was enough to show Anna that her quarry had already vanished into the gardens. Foolish girl. Did she really believe that the gardens were empty? That no one else had sought privacy in the shadowy follies and Grecian temples sprinkled throughout the trees?

Obviously not or she wouldn't have allowed herself to be led astray—and Anna had no doubt the girl *had* been led. Mercy Banks was as green as a leprechaun's jacket. Barely seventeen, she was in London for her first Season, so it was only to be expected that, upon meeting a young man who looked at her as though she were Aphrodite reincarnated, she would mistake attraction for something deeper.

Anna had been seventeen once, too. She remembered all too well the excitement of looking up to find a handsome gentleman watching her; the exhilaration of his hand casually brushing hers when they drew close enough to converse, followed by the warmth of his breath as he leaned in close to whisper a compliment.

Oh, yes, she knew well the lure of those forbidden bowers. But *because* she had been prevented from making a mistake by someone who had noticed her infatuation and taken the time to intervene, Anna now recognised the importance in doing the same for others. Unfortunately, as she walked down the stone steps and into the garden proper, she realised she was not the only one intent on locating the wayward Miss Banks. Marching with grim resolve along the gravel path ahead of her was the young lady's mother, determined to find her errant daughter before some dreadful misfortune could befall her.

Obviously, more desperate measures were now called for.

'Mrs Banks,' Anna called in a pleasant but carrying voice. 'What a pleasure to see you again.'

Mrs Banks, a small, rotund lady wearing a dark green gown and a headband adorned with flowers and fruits of an exotic hue, paused to glance over her shoulder; upon seeing Anna, she stopped, her expression of concern changing to one of pleasure. 'Why, Lady Annabelle, how nice to see you again. It must be nearly a month since we last had an opportunity to chat. Lady Falconer's musicale, wasn't it?'

Anna inclined her head. 'I do believe it was.'

'I thought so. Dreadful soprano. I vow my ears rang most painfully for the rest of the night,' Mrs Banks said with a frown. 'But what are you doing out here all on your own?'

'The house was so warm, I thought to enjoy a quiet stroll through the gardens,' Anna said, keeping her voice light and her words casual. 'But where is Mr Banks this evening? I take it he did come with you.'

'Oh, yes, albeit reluctantly. He's not much into these society affairs, but I told him we must make an effort if we hope to settle Mercy in an advantageous marriage.' Mrs Banks sighed. 'For his sake, I hope she finds a husband sooner rather than later. He's that anxious to get back home.'

'I'm sure it will be sooner,' Anna said, heart jumping as she caught sight of a red coat just beyond Mrs Banks's right shoulder. 'But I wonder, Mrs Banks, if you've seen the new fountain Lady Montby recently had installed over by the reflecting pool? It really is quite spectacular.'

'I'm sure it is, but at the moment, I am more concerned with finding Mercy.'

'Really?' Anna affected a look of confusion. 'I am quite sure I saw her inside the house.'

'You did? Where?'

'Heading in the direction of the music room.'

Mrs Banks rolled her eyes, but Anna noticed a definite softening in the lines of tension around her mouth. 'I might have known. Someone told Mercy that Lady Montby had recently acquired a new pianoforte and naturally she was anxious to see it. The child is quite musically gifted,' her mother confided proudly. 'And while I take care not to compliment her too much, I am hopeful it will help in the quest to find her the right kind of husband.'

'I'm sure she will do you both proud,' Anna said, slipping her arm through the older woman's and turning her around. 'But as long as we're heading back inside, why don't we take a peek at the fountain? It will only take a moment, and then you can carry on and look for your daughter.'

Obviously deciding it was a good idea, Mrs Banks made no demur as Anna led her in the direction of the fountain, which was indeed a spectacular affair, and which, more importantly, was located at the opposite end of the garden from where Anna suspected Mercy and her officer were hiding. Once there, she introduced Mrs Banks to Mrs Wicks, who immediately launched into a diatribe about the difficulties of presenting ungrateful daughters to society, whereupon Mrs Banks said how thankful she was that she only had one daughter to marry off, rather than three.

Anna left the two women happily commiserating with one another and quickly retraced her steps. She was almost at the far end of the path when Miss Banks stepped out, her cheeks flushed, her blue eyes wide with apprehension. 'Lady Annabelle!'

'Miss Banks. Enjoying a few minutes *alone* in the garden?' she asked pointedly.

'Yes! That is…no. That is…oh dear.' The girl looked up and the expression on Anna's face turned her cheeks an even brighter shade of red. 'Please tell me Mama didn't know where I was.'

'She did not, but only because I suggested you were still inside the house,' Anna said. 'If she had caught you and your young man out here together, the consequences would have been dire!'

The girl's pretty face fell. 'I know. And I promise I won't do it again. It's just that…'

When she broke off blushing, Anna prayed the silly girl hadn't done anything irredeemably stupid. 'It's just that what?'

Mercy sighed. 'He said it would be all right. He told me… he loved me.'

Of course he had, Anna thought drily. Was a declaration of love not the most common justification for inappropriate behaviour on a young man's part? 'Then I take leave to tell you that he had a very poor way of showing it. Has he secured your father's permission to speak to you?'

Miss Banks looked even more miserable. 'We have not even been formally introduced. We first saw one another in Hyde Park a week ago, then again at a masquerade two nights past.'

'At which time he suggested a rendezvous for this evening,' Anna surmised.

The girl nodded.

'Then you must not see him again until a formal introduction has been made. Whatever his feelings, asking you to meet him alone in a secluded garden demonstrates the worst kind of judgement,' Anna said firmly. 'He must seek a proper introduction and when the time comes to speak of his intentions, he must approach your father and ask permission to call upon you. Please believe me when I say that what he did tonight was *not* an indication of love, Miss Banks, no matter how much you would like to believe otherwise.'

The young girl bit her lip. 'No, I don't suppose it was. But I did so want to see him again…even if only for a few minutes.'

'A few minutes are more than enough to ruin a lifetime,' Anna said more gently. 'You must guard your reputation as fiercely as you would your most precious possession, because right now, it *is* your most precious possession. Once lost it can never be regained and no one will suffer more for its absence than you. So, no matter what *any* gentleman says to you, or how sweetly he says it, do not let yourself be tempted into such an indiscretion again.'

'Yes, Lady Annabelle.'

Anna could see from the expression on Mercy's face that she had learned her lesson and that the episode would not be repeated. Nor did Anna expect that it would. It wasn't that Mercy was bad. She was simply young and impetuous, as were so many girls her age.

As Anna herself had once been.

'And now, we shall return to the house and you will find your mother and endeavour to set her mind at rest,' she said, leading Mercy back along the gravel path. 'As for your young man, you are not to look for him again, and, if he seeks you out, you are to tell him you will not speak to him until the two of you have been properly introduced…which I shall endeavour to do later this evening.'

Miss Banks gasped. 'You would do that for me?'

'I would, but only if you give me your promise that you will never see…' Anna paused. 'What is the officer's name?'

'Lieutenant Giles Blokker.'

'Fine. That you will not see Lieutenant Blokker again without suitable chaperonage. I may not be around to save you the next time.'

'You have my promise, Lady Annabelle. And thank you! Thank you so very much!'

Upon returning to the ballroom, Miss Banks did exactly as she had been told. When Lieutenant Blokker tried to approach her, she treated him to a look that would have done her crusty old grandmother proud and then went in search of her mother. The young man looked understandably crushed, but Anna hoped it had taught him a lesson. If he truly cared for Miss Banks, he would do whatever was necessary in order to further the connection in the manner of which society approved. If not, he wasn't worth having in the first place.

'Do you attempt to save them all from themselves?' asked an amused masculine voice close to her ear. 'Or only the ones who don't know any better?'

Anna turned her head and found herself looking into the face of a stranger. A very handsome stranger, but a stranger none the less. 'Were you speaking to me, sir?'

'I was. And pray forgive my boldness, but I happened to be in the garden when you came upon the young lady, and such was my timing that I was privy to most of your conversation with her just now. She is indeed fortunate to have you as her champion.'

His voice was velvet over steel. Resonant, powerful, the kind of voice that held audiences spellbound and sent impressionable young women swooning. Anna could imagine him reciting Shakespeare on the stage at Drury Lane, or reading love sonnets by Bryon or Wordsworth, those low, sensual tones sparking desire in any young woman's breast.

But was their meeting now entirely coincidental? While she thought him too old for Miss Banks and too casual in his addresses to her, the fact he had been in the garden at the same time as they had, and that he just happened to be standing next to her now, left her wondering.

'I only attempt to save the ones I deem worthy of saving,' she replied carefully. 'The rest I leave to their own devices.'

'Just as well,' the gentleman said. 'Most people sin for the fun of it and wouldn't welcome your intervention, no matter how well intentioned. Unlike Miss Banks, whose romantic heart would likely have got the better of her had you not stepped in to save the day.'

Anna caught an undertone of amusement in his voice and, despite her natural inclination to be wary, found herself smiling back at him. He was certainly an attractive man. His face was long rather than square, his jaw angular, his cheekbones high and well formed. Intelligence gleamed in the depths of those clear grey eyes and his lips, curved upwards in a smile, were firm and disturbingly sensual. His clothes were expensive, his linen impeccable, and while his hair shone black in the light of a thousand candles, the tiny lines at the corners of his eyes put him closer to thirty than twenty.

No, he definitely wasn't after Miss Mercy Banks, Anna decided. He could have eaten the silly little chit for dinner and still gone away hungry. But neither was this a casual conversation, of that she was sure. 'I am undecided as to whether I should be flattered by your comments or offended by them,' she said. 'I had no idea my actions were being so closely observed.'

'A gentleman should never make his attentions too obvious, Lady Annabelle. I pride myself on my ability to observe without *being* observed—a quality necessary to those who involve themselves in the convoluted lives of others. Wouldn't you agree?'

Anna's eyes widened. So, he knew who she was and what she was about. That alone should have put her on her guard, yet all it did was make her more curious. She liked a man who didn't play games; Lord knew, London society was all too full of them. 'I fear you have the advantage of me, sir.

You obviously know a great deal more about me than I do about you.'

'Only because you are more visible in society,' he murmured. 'And as much as I regret the inequity of the situation, we both know it would be ill-mannered of me to introduce myself, so I shall wait for the thing to be done properly as you have so kindly offered to do for Miss Banks.'

His words abruptly called to mind the promise Anna had made earlier and her brows knit in consternation. 'An offer made impetuously at best, I fear. Apart from the officer's name, I know nothing about the man and have no idea if he is even *worthy* of an introduction.'

'Then allow me to set your mind at rest. I happen to know that Lieutenant Giles Blokker is an amiable young man who, despite having behaved with the decorum of a rambunctious puppy, is an excellent catch. His father is Major Sir Gordon Blokker, who distinguished himself with Wellington on the Peninsula, and his mother is the former Lady Margaret Sissely. The boy was educated at Eton, went on to read English and history at Oxford, and, as his father's only son, he is heir to a considerable estate. More importantly, I believe he is the kind of man of whom both Miss Banks's mother and father would approve.'

Surprised by the extent of the man's knowledge and by his willingness to share it, Anna inclined her head. 'I am grateful for your recommendation, sir. How fortunate that you are so well acquainted with the officer.'

'In fact, we've never met. But one hears a great many things during the course of one's social day, and if I feel it is information that may be of use to someone else, I am happy to pass it along. I trust that, in this instance, it serves you well. Good evening, Lady Annabelle.'

With that, he bowed and walked away, leaving Anna with a host of unanswered questions tumbling around in her brain.

Who was he, and why did his sudden appearance at her side not seem as coincidental as he might like her to believe? By telling her all he had about Lieutenant Blokker, he'd put her in the enviable position of being able to make the promised introduction, aware that not only might she be introducing Miss Banks to her future husband, but that he was a gentleman worthy of the role. Had he known more about the predicament in which she'd landed herself than he had chosen to let on?

Not surprisingly, Anna found herself watching the handsome stranger as he moved around the room. She noticed that he did not linger with any one person or group for any length of time, but that his gaze touched on every person there, his expression unreadable as he took note of who they spoke to and with whom they danced. Even when he stopped to speak to an upright older gentleman who was clearly intent on engaging him in a serious conversation, his eyes continued in their restless study. Was he was a private investigator of some kind? He looked too aristocratic for such an occupation, but then, perhaps a man who didn't *look* the part was *exactly* the sort of man who should be doing that kind of work.

He'd certainly made an impression on her. For once she'd actually *enjoyed* having a conversation with a gentleman newly met at a society function. Normally, she was quick to wish them over, knowing all too well what they were really all about.

Is this someone with whom I have anything in common? Do I feel a connection strong enough to spend the rest of my life with him? And, of course, what do we each stand to gain by aligning our families in marriage?

They were all questions Anna had asked herself in the past. And with that one unfortunate exception where the marriage *would* have been a disaster, the answers were always the same.

No, not likely, and nothing.

But this gentleman intrigued her. She found herself watching for him in the crowd, curious to see how he acted with other people, anxious to catch just one more glimpse of him. Wanting to know if he might be looking back at her.

And when he did and Anna felt her gaze trapped in the soft silver glow of his eyes, she knew it was too late to look away. She had carelessly exposed herself, allowing her interest in, and her curiosity about, a stranger to be revealed. Was it any wonder that when he tipped his head and slowly began to smile, she felt the heat rise in her cheeks and the breath catch in her throat?

Goodness, who would have thought that with just one look, he could make her feel as awkward as a schoolgirl, as young and as gauche as Miss Mercy Banks. Surely as a mature woman of twenty-four, she knew better than to encourage the attentions of a man she'd only just met…

Anna dipped her head and boldly returned his smile. No, clearly she did not. But as she opened her fan and reluctantly turned away, the knowledge that a handsome man whose name she didn't know still had the power to make her blush was more than enough to keep the smile on her face for the rest of the evening.

'Parker, have you heard anything I've said?' Colonel Tanner demanded in a harsh whisper.

'Every word, Colonel.' Sir Barrington Parker's expression didn't change, though he was careful to pull his gaze from the face of the exquisite young woman who had just smiled at him across the room. No small feat for a man who appreciated beauty as much as he did. 'You wish me to investigate the disappearance of your mistress—'

'I never said she was my mistress!' the older man blustered.

'There was no need. Avoiding my eyes while you described her told me all I needed to know,' Barrington said smoothly. 'She is approximately twenty years old, slim, with dark brown hair and rather startling green eyes. The last time you saw her she was wearing a pale blue gown with a white shawl and a bonnet with either blue or black ribbons.'

The older man grunted. 'Apologies. Just don't like blathering on to a man who doesn't appear to be listening.'

'I wouldn't accomplish much if I didn't listen, Colonel,' Barrington said, though in truth he hadn't been paying as much attention as he should. Through the mirror on the wall behind Tanner, he had been watching Lady Annabelle Durst attempt to play matchmaker. She had waited until Lieutenant Giles Blokker was in the midst of a small group of people with whom she was obviously acquainted and had sought the necessary introduction. Then, as the other couples had drifted away, she had engaged Lieutenant Blokker in conversation, no doubt with the intent of bringing Miss Banks's name into the discussion.

At that point, Barrington had seen a look of cautious optimism appear on Blokker's face, followed moments later by one of genuine happiness. When Lady Annabelle turned and started in the direction of Miss Banks and her mother, the young pup had fallen into step behind her, clearly delighted that he was on his way to being formally introduced to the young lady who had captured his heart.

'Where did you last see Miss Paisley, Colonel?' Barrington asked, reluctantly dragging his attention back to the matter at hand.

'Hogarth Road. I keep a house there. Nothing elaborate, you understand,' the Colonel said gruffly. 'Just a place for friends to use when they come up to London.'

Barrington nodded. He knew exactly what the house was

used for and it certainly wasn't the convenience of friends. 'I shall make enquiries. Where can I reach you?'

'Best send a note round the club. Wouldn't do to have anything come to the house.'

Barrington inclined his head. Though most wives knew about their husbands' affairs, none wanted proof of them showing up at their front doors. 'As you wish.'

'Look here, Parker, it's not what you think,' the Colonel said, clearing his throat. 'Eliza's not like the rest of them. She worked as a lady's maid in a respectable establishment until the eldest son took a fancy to her. When she was turned off without references, one thing led to another until she ended up in a brothel. That's where I met her,' he said, again not meeting Barrington's eyes. 'She told me her story and naturally I felt sorry for her, so I asked her if she'd like to come and work for me. I knew Constance was looking for a new maid and I thought it might be a way of getting Eliza back into respectable employment.'

Barrington's smile was purposely bland. 'And did your wife agree to take Miss Paisley on?'

'She did, but it wasn't long before she realised there was something going on and I had to let Eliza go,' the Colonel said regretfully. 'Felt so damned guilty, I offered to put her up at the house on Hogarth Road until she was able to find something else.'

With the small stipulation, Barrington surmised, that she become his mistress while she was there. A gentleman's altruism only extended so far. 'It would seem Miss Paisley has much to be grateful to you for, Colonel.'

'I thought so, which was why I was so surprised when she left without telling me,' the Colonel said. 'Bit concerned, if you know what I mean.'

Barrington did know and he wasn't surprised. Tanner was a decent chap, somewhere in his mid-fifties, with four married children and eight grandchildren. His wife had been in poor health for the last five years and, though he was devoted to her in every other way, her ill health had prevented them from enjoying a normal marital relationship. So he had turned, as so many men did, to the ranks of the *demi-monde* and there he had encountered Miss Elizabeth Paisley, the young woman for whom he had developed an unfortunate affection. Now she was missing and the Colonel was worried about her.

Probably with good reason, Barrington thought as he shook the man's hand and walked away. It was a simple fact that women of Miss Paisley's ilk were concerned with one thing and one thing only. Survival. It wasn't easy making a living on the streets of London. A woman never knew if the man who pulled her into a darkened alley and threw up her skirts was going to be a paying customer or the last man she ever saw alive. Being a prostitute was not without its risks. But being the mistress of a wealthy man took away those risks and gave a woman security. It put a roof over her head and kept food on her table. So why would someone like Miss Paisley walk away from all that if she'd had any other choice?

It was a question Barrington couldn't answer. And as he prepared to leave Lady Montby's reception—after deciding it was best that he not stop to engage the delightful Lady Annabelle in conversation again—he realised it was one that would trouble him until he did. To that end, he made a mental note to ask his secretary to make some initial enquiries into Elizabeth Paisley's whereabouts. Sam Jenkins had been with Barrington long enough to know what kind of questions to ask and who to ask them of. Then, depending on what he turned up, Barrington would either call upon one of his extensive network to continue the investigation or delve into the matter himself.

He wasn't sure why, but as he climbed into his carriage for the short ride home, he had a feeling there was more to the disappearance of Miss Elizabeth Paisley than met the eye.

Chapter Two

$Anna$ pulled her dapple-grey mare to a halt by the base of a large oak and waited for Lady Lydia Winston to catch up with her. The two had made a point of riding together on Tuesday and Thursday mornings, and these rousing canters had become one of the highlights of Anna's week. Lady Lydia, daughter of the Marquess of Bailley, was by far one of the most amusing and interesting people Anna had ever met.

'Goodness!' Lydia said as she drew her spirited Arabian bay level with Anna's mare. 'I was sure I had you at the big tree, but you sprinted past me as though I was standing still!'

'I suspect Danby put oats in Ophelia's bucket this morning.' Anna reached down to give the mare's glossy neck an affectionate pat. 'She's not usually that quick off the mark.'

'Nevertheless, I had enough of a lead that it shouldn't have made a difference. Tarik isn't used to being left behind.' Lydia's ready smile flashed. 'I won't be so easily fooled the next time.'

Anna laughed, pleased that her little mare had done so well. She nudged her to a leisurely walk, content to enjoy the glorious morning sunshine and the relative emptiness of the park. During the fashionable hour, the avenue they were now travelling would be crowded with elegant carriages and their equally elegant passengers, but at this time of day it was the perfect place to enjoy a brisk canter.

'By the by, have you heard the news?' Lydia enquired.

'That depends. All I heard at Lady Montby's reception last week was that Cynthia Wicks had threatened to run away if her mother forced her to spend a month with her grandmother in Scotland.'

'Good Lord, so would I,' Lydia declared. 'Lady Shallerton is a cold fish with whom I wouldn't wish to spend an hour, let alone a month. But it wasn't Miss Wick's escapades I was referring to. It was the Baroness Julia von Brohm's.'

'Baroness von Brohm,' Anna repeated slowly. 'Should I know her?'

'La, Anna, where have you been? It is all about town that the Viennese baroness has come to London to find a new husband.'

'Why? What happened to her old one?'

'He died. Almost two years ago now, leaving her a very lonely but extremely wealthy young widow. Apparently, he showered her with the most glorious jewellery and she was heartbroken when he died. Not because he gave her jewellery,' Lydia was quick to say, 'but because they were genuinely in love. But she is finished with her mourning now and has come to London to start a new life. I understand she's taken a very fine house in Mayfair and is in the process of redecorating it from top to bottom.'

'I'm surprised she would have chosen to leave Vienna at such a time,' Anna remarked. 'One would think she would prefer to stay with her family and friends.'

'Friends I'm sure she has, but again, rumour has it that her only brother moved to America when she was quite young and hasn't been heard from since. And both of her parents are dead.'

'How tragic. What about her late husband's family?' Anna asked.

'Apparently, they were never close. Difficulties with the mother-in-law, from what I hear.'

'So Vienna is full of unhappy memories and the arms of her family hold no welcome. No wonder she decided to come to London,' Anna said. 'Has she any close friends here?'

'I don't believe so. Society is wildly curious about her, of course, but it hasn't exactly thrown open its doors in welcome.'

'Then we must be the first to do so,' Anna said without hesitation. 'I suspect once people see the daughters of the Marquess of Bailley and the Earl of Cambermere welcoming her, the rest of the doors will open soon enough. All it takes,' she added with a knowing smile, 'is that first little push.'

Barrington's sword flashed once, cutting a smooth silver arc through the air and echoing down the length of the long gallery. Metal slid along metal as the two men moved through the orchestrated dance of extend, lunge, parry and retreat, and while concentration was etched on the faces of both men, only Barrington's brow was dry. He feinted to the left, drawing his brother-in-law's blade wide and ultimately opening him up to defeat.

'Damn it!' Tom Danvers snapped as the point of Barrington's sword flicked his chest for the fifth time. 'You've beaten me again!'

'And I will continue to do so if you do not apply yourself more keenly to the sport,' Barrington said, drawing back. 'You won't stand a chance if you keep both feet firmly planted on the ground, Tom. You need to keep moving. Dance on the balls of your feet.'

'Oh, yes, that's easy for you to say,' the other man complained good-naturedly. 'I've three stone and five years on you and it's not so easy being nimble when you've more weight below your waist than above it!'

Barrington laughed. 'Then tell that pompous French chef of yours to start preparing less fattening meals.'

'What? And have him quit because *I* had the audacity to tell him what to cook! Jenny would have my head. Monsieur Etienne is the finest French chef in London!' Tom exclaimed.

'Be that as it may, he is not doing *you* any favours by serving all those heavy sauces and rich desserts,' Barrington pointed out. 'If you wish to be quicker on your feet, the weight will have to come off. In fact, I have a solution.'

'I'm not sure I wish to hear it,' Tom muttered.

'Of course you do. I shall take Monsieur Etienne off your hands for a few weeks and you can have Mrs Buckers. I guarantee your clothes will fit better after only three days.'

'Perhaps, but I won't care because Jenny will have left me.'

Barrington clapped his brother-in-law on the back. 'A man must sacrifice for his sport. Ah, there you are, Sam. Has my two o'clock appointment arrived?'

'Not yet, Sir Barrington,' the secretary said, 'but another gentleman has and is asking to see you. I put him in your study.'

Barrington nodded. A visitor in his study meant one of his network had come in with information. Friends he welcomed in the gold salon. Any one else was made to wait in the hall until he had ascertained the nature of their business. He did not purport to be a private investigator, but, because of his past successes, there were those who sought him out regardless.

'Thank you, Sam. Tell the gentleman I shall be there directly.' He turned to smile at his brother-in-law. 'Sorry to cut it short, Tom…'

'No need to apologise. You're a busy man, and, in truth, I've taken all the humiliation I can for one day,' Tom said good-naturedly. 'Before I go, however, Jenny wanted me to find out if you were available for dinner one night this week. She misses you dreadfully and even young George was heard to say it has been a great deal too long since his Uncle Barr came to play with him.'

Barrington's pleasure was unfeigned. 'Tell my sister I shall make a point of coming one evening this week, and then inform my nephew that I shall be sure to arrive early enough to play two games of hide and seek with him.'

'He will not sleep for the knowledge,' Tom said, starting for the door. 'By the by, I should warn you that you won't be the only guest.'

Barrington groaned. 'Don't tell me Jenny's matchmaking again?'

'I'm afraid so.'

'Who is it this time?' He sighed.

'Lady Alice Stokes.'

Barrington dug into his memory. 'Lady Alice—?'

'Stokes. Eldest daughter of the Earl of Grummond,' Tom supplied helpfully. 'Beautiful, cultured and an heiress in her own right. Jenny thinks she would be perfect for you.'

'That's what she said about the last three ladies she introduced me to and they were all unmitigated disasters.'

'True, but at least you wouldn't have to worry about Lady Alice marrying you for your money. Or for your title,' Tom pointed out.

True enough, Barrington conceded. An earl's daughter could do much better than a baronet, and if she had her own money, his wouldn't be as much of an attraction. 'Very well, you may tell my sister I shall come on Friday. That should give her ample time to put everything in place.'

'You're a brick, Barrington,' Tom said in relief. 'I was afraid you'd bow out if I told you the truth, but I didn't like the idea of you being caught off guard.'

'Rest assured, I shall be the perfect guest,' Barrington said. 'And you need not fear retribution from my sister. I shall act suitably surprised when the beautiful Lady Alice and I are introduced.'

'You are a gentleman in every sense of the word.'

'Just don't let me hear any mention of the words *engagement* or *marriage* or I shall be forced to renege on my promise,' he warned.

Tom grinned. 'I shall do my utmost to make sure you do not.'

They parted on the best of terms; Tom to return to his happy home, Barrington to return to his study to find out what new information had come to light. While there might be more comfort in the former, he was not of a mind to complicate his life by taking a wife. Investigating the underhanded dealings of others was hardly conducive to forming intimate relations with gently reared young ladies. It was neither the occupation of a gentleman nor what he'd planned on doing when he'd returned to London after his father's death.

However, when an unfortunate set of circumstances involving two of his father's friends and a large sum of money had forced him into the role, Barrington had discovered a unique talent for uncovering the hidden bits of information others could not. His carefully cultivated network of acquaintances, many of whom held positions of power and even more who held positions of knowledge, made it easy for him to find out what he needed to know and, over time, he had established himself as a man who was able to find solutions for people's problems.

Naturally, as word of his reputation had spread, so had his list of enemies, many of them the very men he had helped to expose. Beneath society's elegant and sophisticated façade lurked a far more dangerous element—one comprised of men to whom honour and truth meant nothing. Men who were motivated by greed and who routinely committed crimes against their fellow man.

Hence Barrington's wish to remain single. While he could be reasonably assured of his own safety, he knew that if his enemies tried to get to him through the woman he loved, he would have no choice but to comply with their demands. The unscrupulous did not trouble themselves with morals when it came to getting what they wanted.

That's why he had taken to avoiding situations that might place him in such an awkward situation. He existed on the fringes of society, close enough to be aware of what was going on, but far enough away that he wasn't seen as potential husband material. So far it had worked out well, much to the annoyance of his happily married sister. He was able to assist the people who came to him with problems, while avoiding the complications that came with marriage.

Now, as he headed to his study, Barrington wondered which of the sins was about to be revealed and who would be thrown out of Eden as a result. Paradise was sometimes a very difficult place in which to live.

'Ah, Richard,' he said, opening the door to see his good friend, Lord Richard Crew, standing at the far end of the room, his attention focused on a particularly fine painting by

Stubbs that covered a large part of the end wall. 'Still hoping I'll sell it to you?'

'Hope has nothing to do with it,' Crew murmured. 'Eventually, I'll name a price you won't be able to refuse.'

'Don't be too sure. I've rejected every offer you've put forward so far.'

'Fine. I'll make you another before I leave today.'

Barrington smiled as he moved towards his desk. Lord Richard Crew was an ardent lover of horse flesh and owned more paintings by Stubbs, Tillemans and Seymour than any other gentleman in London. Quietly picking them up as they came available for sale, he had amassed an impressive collection—with the exception of *Whistlejacket*, a magnificent painting of a prancing Arabian thoroughbred commissioned by the Marquess of Rockingham and acknowledged by many to be one of Stubbs's finest. *That* was the piece of work currently hanging in Barrington's study, and the fact that he owned the *one* painting his friend wanted more than any other was a constant source of amusement to him and an ongoing source of irritation to Crew.

'Did it ever occur to you,' Barrington asked now, 'that money doesn't enter into it?'

'Not for a moment,' Crew said, finally turning away from the canvas. 'Every man has his price and it's only a matter of time until I find yours. But rest assured, I *will* find it. And I know exactly where I'm going to put *Whistlejacket* once I finally wrest it from your iron grip.'

Barrington smiled. 'And where might that be?'

'In my study, opposite my desk. That way I'll see it when I'm working.'

'I would have thought you'd want it in your bedroom.' Barrington moved to the credenza and poured brandy into two glasses. 'That way, you'd see it most of the time.'

'True, but I would only be paying it half as much attention.' Crew's smile widened into a grin. 'After all, there are so many *other* pleasurable things to occupy oneself with in the bedroom, wouldn't you agree?'

The question was rhetorical. Lord Richard Crew's reputation as a lady's man was honestly come by because, in point of fact, Crew adored women. He had ever since a buxom dairy maid had introduced him to the pleasures of Venus in the loft of his father's barn, followed in quick succession by three of the housemaids, two of the village shop girls, and a married woman Crew had steadfastly refused to name.

As he'd grown into a man, his appreciation for the fairer sex had not waned, but out of respect for his parents, he'd left off tupping the household servants and moved on to ballet dancers and actresses. He had steadfastly avoided marriage and refused to trifle with virgins or débutantes, saying it was a matter of pride that he had never deflowered an innocent or given false hope to a well-born lady. And once it became known that he preferred his women uncomplicated and experienced, the list of married ladies willing to accommodate his voracious appetite grew.

Hence Barrington's surprise when, during the investigation of the Marchioness of Yew's infidelity, he'd learned that his good friend was finally in honest pursuit of the lady's very respectable and exceedingly lovely nineteen-year-old daughter, Rebecca.

'Sexual conquests aside, dare I hope you've come with news about the identity of Lady Yew's alleged lover?' Barrington enquired.

'Nothing alleged about it.' Crew strolled towards the desk and picked up a glass in his long, slender fingers. 'I happened to be in the lady's house on the occasion of the young man's last visit and saw them acting very lover-like towards one another.'

'How convenient. Were you there in hopes of seeing the lovely Lady Rebecca or to question the mother?'

'Most definitely the former.' Crew raised the glass to his nose and sniffed appreciatively. 'Unlike our young Romeo, I have no interest in romancing ladies over the age of thirty. The bloom has long since gone from that rose.'

'But with maturity comes experience,' Barrington said, reaching for his own glass. 'A gently reared miss of nineteen will know nothing of that.'

'Fortunately, I am more than willing to teach her all she needs to know.' Crew swallowed a mouthful of brandy, pausing a moment to savour its flavour before sinking into a chair and resting his booted feet on the edge of the desk. 'However, returning to the matter at hand, the gentleman in question is not our typical Lothario. I've never heard his name mentioned in association with lady *or* ladybird; in truth, I'd never heard of *him* until his arrival in London just over a month ago. So the fact he has chosen to dally with a marquess's wife is somewhat unusual.'

'Are you sure they *are* lovers?'

Crew shrugged. 'Lady Rebecca confided her belief that they are. She told me she's seen the gentleman enter her mother's private quarters on more than one occasion, and, as I was leaving, I saw them myself going upstairs together hand in hand.'

'Damning evidence indeed,' Barrington said. 'And reckless behaviour for a man newly arrived in London. Does he suffer from a case of misplaced affection or unbridled lust?'

'Knowing the marchioness, I suspect the latter,' Crew said in a dry voice. 'It's well known she favours younger men because her husband is a crusty old stick twenty-five years older than she is.'

'Still, she has charmed a legion of men both younger *and* older than herself, and, up to this point, her husband has always been willing to turn a blind eye,' Barrington said. 'For whatever reason, he is not inclined to do so this time.'

Crew shrugged. 'Perhaps he fears a genuine attachment. It's all very well for a woman to take a lover to her bed, but it is extremely bad taste to fall in love with him. People have been known to do abysmally stupid things in the name of love.'

'Too true. So, who is the poor boy Lord Yew is going to flay?'

'His full name is Peregrine Tipton Rand.'

'Good Lord. *Peregrine Tipton*?'

'A trifle whimsical, I admit, but he's a country lad visiting London for the first time. Apparently, his father owns a farm in Devon. Rand's the oldest of four brothers and sisters but he hasn't shown much interest in taking over from his father. Seems he's more interested in books than in bovines, so when the mother died, the father shipped him up here to stay with his godfather in the hopes of the boy acquiring some town polish. Unfortunately, all he acquired was an affection for Lady Yew.'

Barrington frowned. 'How did a country boy come to be introduced to a marchioness?'

'Through the auspices of Lord Hayle, Viscount Hayle.'

'Hayle?' Barrington's eyebrows rose in surprise. The beautiful Lady Annabelle's *brother*? 'I wouldn't have thought the Earl of Cambermere's heir the type to associate with a country gentleman of no consequence.'

'I dare say you're right, but as it happens, he has no choice.

Rand is *staying* with the family. Cambermere is the man reputed to be his godfather.'

'Reputed?'

'There are those who say the lad bears a stronger resemblance to the earl than might be expected.'

'Ah, I see.' Barrington rapped his fingers on the desk. 'Wrong side of the blanket.'

'Possible, though no one's come right out and said it.'

'Of course not. Cambermere's a powerful man. If he did father an illegitimate child years ago and now chooses to have the boy come live with him, no one's going to tell him he can't. Especially given that his own wife died last year.'

'But there are other children living in the house,' Crew pointed out. 'Legitimate children who won't take kindly to their father foisting one of his by-blows on them.'

Especially the son and heir, Barrington reflected grimly. Viscount Hayle was not the kind of man to suffer such a slight to his family name. If he came to suspect the true nature of Rand's paternity, he could make things very difficult for all concerned. So difficult, in fact, that Rand might hightail it back to the country, and that was something Barrington had to avoid. He needed to find out as much as possible about the young man *before* news of his liaison with Lady Yew went public—because there was no doubt in Barrington's mind that it would. The marchioness wasn't known for being discreet. Her list of lovers was a popular topic of conversation at parties, and the fact that *this* time, her husband had chosen to make an example of the young man would definitely make for scintillating conversation over wine and cards.

'You've gone quiet,' Crew said. 'Mulling over how best to break the news to dear Peregrine's unsuspecting family?'

'As a matter of fact, I was.' Barrington got to his feet and walked slowly towards the long window. 'I met Lady

Annabelle Durst at Lady Montby's reception the other week.'

'Ah, the beautiful Anna,' Crew murmured appreciatively. 'Truly one of society's diamonds. I cannot imagine why she's still single.'

Barrington snorted. 'Likely because she's too busy trying to prevent silly young women from ruining themselves.'

'An admirable undertaking, though knowing how many silly young women there are in London, I don't imagine it leaves much time for looking after her own future.'

'Virtually none,' Barrington said, his thoughts returning to the lady whose existence he had first learned about during an investigation he'd undertaken the previous year. It had not involved Lady Annabelle directly, but had focused instead on the uncle of one of the girls she had been trying to help. As a result of that investigation, however, Barrington had become familiar with her name and with her propensity for helping naïve young girls navigate their way through the choppy waters of first love.

Always from a distance, of course. Given his own self-imposed boundaries, Barrington knew better than to risk getting too close to her, but he was strongly aware of her appeal and smart enough to know that she could be dangerous for that reason alone. He'd met a lot of women in his life, but there was something about Lady Annabelle Durst that set her apart from all the rest. Something rare. Something precious. Something indefinable...

'Well, if you're going to sit there all afternoon and stare into space, I'm leaving.' Crew drained his glass and set it on the desk. 'I am expected for tea with Lady Yew and her daughter; if you have nothing more to tell me, I may as well be on my way.'

'Fine. But while you're sipping tea and whispering endearments in Lady Rebecca's ear, see if you can find out anything else about her mother's relationship with Rand,' Barrington said. 'The more I know about the situation, the better off I'll be when it comes time to confront him with it.'

Crew unhurriedly rose. 'I'll ask, but, given the extent of the marquess's displeasure, I doubt you'll hear Rebecca *or* her mother mention the name Peregrine Rand with favour again.'

Anna was reading Shakespeare when the door to the drawing room opened. Leaving Hamlet on the page, she looked up to see their butler standing in the doorway. 'Yes, Milford?'

'Excuse me, my lady, but a gentleman has called and is asking to see Mr Rand.'

Anna glanced at the clock on the mantel. Half past eight. Somewhat late for a social call. 'Did you tell him Mr Rand was from home?'

'I did, but he said it was a matter of some urgency and wondered if you knew what time he might be home.'

'Lord knows, I certainly don't.' With a sigh, Anna set her book aside. 'Did the gentleman leave his card?'

Milford bowed and silently proffered the tray. Anna took the card and read the name. *Sir Barrington Parker.* How strange. She knew the man by reputation rather than by sight. A wealthy baronet with an impressive home, he was, by all accounts, a cultured, educated and exceedingly charming man who was also reputed to be one of London's finest swordsmen. The story went that he'd spent several years in Paris training under a legendary French master; when his father's death had compelled him to return to England, Sir Barrington had been besieged by the pinks of society asking him to teach them his skills. With very few exceptions, he had refused every request.

Why, then, would he be here now, asking after a man with whom he was unlikely to have even the slightest acquaintance? 'Ask him to come in, Milford. Then inform my father that we have a visitor.'

The butler bowed. 'Very good, my lady.'

The wait was not long. Moments later, the door opened again and Milford announced, 'Sir Barrington Parker.'

Anna rose as the butler withdrew, but the moment the baronet arrived she stopped dead, totally unprepared for the sight of the man standing in her doorway. *'You!'*

'Good evening, Lady Annabelle.' Sir Barrington Parker strolled into the room, as impeccably turned out as he had been the night of Lady Montby's reception. His dark jacket fit superbly across a pair of broad shoulders, his buff-coloured breeches outlined strong, muscular thighs and his cravat was simply yet elegantly tied. 'I told you an occasion would present itself whereby our introduction could be made in a more acceptable manner.'

'You did indeed,' Anna said, struggling to recover from her surprise. She'd thought about him several times since meeting him at Lady Montby's, and, while she'd found him a powerful presence there, he was, in the small confines of the drawing room, even more compelling. 'I simply did not think it would be in my own home or that the illustrious Sir Barrington Parker would turn out to be the gentleman with whom I exchanged opinions the other night.'

'Illustrious?' His beautiful mouth lifted in a disturbingly sensual smile. 'I fear you are confusing me with someone else.'

'On the contrary, rumour has it that you are an excellent fencer and an unparalleled shot. *And* that you've uncovered more than your fair share of secrets about those who move in the upper reaches of society.'

His smile was indulgent, much like that of a teacher addressing an errant pupil. 'You and I both know how foolish it is to put stock in rumours, Lady Annabelle. One never knows how or why they start and most often they are proven to be wrong.'

'Do you deny that it was you who exposed Lord Bosker as an embezzler?' Anna said. 'Or that you just *happened* upon that letter naming his fine, upstanding cousin, Mr Teetham, as his accomplice?'

'I tend to think the timing was, for the most part, coincidental,' Sir Barrington said, careful to avoid a direct answer. 'Their crimes would have come to light soon enough. They grew careless, too confident in their own ability to deceive.'

'But *you* were the one who drew attention to what they were doing,' Anna persisted. 'Had you not, they would most likely have continued in their games and who knows what other crimes they would have perpetrated. But forgive my manners, Sir Barrington. Pray be seated.'

'Thank you. And while your confidence in my ability is flattering, I should tell you it is entirely misplaced.' He glanced at the chairs arranged in front of the fireplace and settled into the wingback chair opposite the one upon which her book lay open. 'There were other people involved in their arrest and to a far greater extent than myself. But, as we are talking about other people's affairs, how did matters proceed between Miss Banks and Lieutenant Blokker after you and I parted company the other night?'

Surprised he would even remember the conversation, Anna managed a smile. 'Remarkably well, all things considered. Lieutenant Blokker turned out to be a delightful young man and I realized, after speaking with him, that while the manner of his approach to Miss Banks left much to be desired, his intentions were strictly honourable.'

'Ah yes, the ill-fated rendezvous in the garden,' Sir Barrington mused. 'Not the best thought out of plans, but thanks to you no harm came of it.'

'And thanks to you, the two are now formally introduced and eager to begin a courtship,' Anna said. 'But I don't suppose Miss Banks's romantic escapades have anything to do with your reason for being here this evening.'

'Regrettably, they do not. I was actually hoping to speak to your house guest, Mr Rand, but I understand he is from home.'

'Yes, he is.' Anna gazed at him, surprised to feel her heart beating a little faster than usual. Obviously she wasn't used to being alone with such a disturbingly handsome man. 'I wasn't aware the two of you were acquainted.'

His dark brows arched ever so slightly. 'Are you acquainted with *all* of Mr Rand's friends and associates, Lady Annabelle?'

'As a matter of fact, I am. Peregrine has only recently come to stay with us, and, given how anxious my father was that he become known in society, I took the liberty of including him in all of *my* social activities,' Anna said. 'That being the case, I think I can safely say that I *do* know with whom he is and is not acquainted. I have never heard him speak of you.'

Briefly, the gentleman smiled, but while it softened the lines of his face, it did nothing to lessen the intensity of the expression in his eyes. 'I am not acquainted with Mr Rand, Lady Annabelle, nor is he with me,' he said quietly. 'I've come here at the behest of another, on a matter of extreme urgency to both.'

'An urgent matter?'

'Yes. One I would prefer to discuss in private with the gentleman. Or, failing that, with your father, if he is at home.'

'He is, Sir Barrington,' Lord Cambermere said, walking into the room. 'But if Edward has done something that warrants discussion—'

'It is not Edward Sir Barrington wishes to speak to you about, Papa,' Anna said calmly. 'It is Peregrine. And there is no point in my giving you privacy since we both know Peregrine will tell me everything the three of you say the moment Sir Barrington leaves.'

'He may not wish to tell you this,' Sir Barrington said, slowly getting to his feet. 'And I would prefer to speak to you about it in private, my Lord.'

Cambermere frowned. He was a tall, solidly built man with warm brown eyes, a ruddy complexion and dark hair that was just beginning to show signs of grey at the temples. His clothes were more suited to a country gentleman than a man about town, but now that his year of mourning was over, Anna was hopeful he might once again take up an interest in socialising, and, by necessity, his appearance.

'Yes, I'm sure you would,' the earl said. 'But I have no doubt Anna speaks the truth about the boy's repeating everything we say. He's my godson, you see, and the two have become as thick as thieves in the short time they've been together. I'm surprised he's gone out without her tonight. Still, he's a quiet enough lad. I can't imagine him doing anything that would be inappropriate for Anna to hear about.'

Anna could tell from the look on the baronet's face that he was less than pleased with her father's decision. Equally aware that trying to force the earl into a private interview was not the conduct of a gentleman, Sir Barrington merely shrugged those broad shoulders and said, 'Very well, though you may wish to change your mind once I begin to relate the details of the situation. You see, not long ago, a titled gentleman came to see me with regards to a personal matter concerning his wife.'

'His wife?' The earl looked decidedly confused. 'What has this to do with Peregrine?'

'The gentleman suspected his wife of having an affair,' Sir Barrington continued. 'Naturally, he asked me to make enquiries as discreetly as possible and to keep the results similarly confidential. He knew I'd had some success in this area and I agreed to look into the matter for him and see what I could learn. Now, having discovered the identity of the gentleman, I felt it behoved me to hear his side of the story. That's why I'm here. I regret to inform you, Lord Cambermere,' Sir Barrington said quietly, 'that the gentleman guilty of having an affair with the wife of a highly placed nobleman is none other than your godson, Mr Peregrine Rand.'

Chapter Three

'Peregrine!' Anna said on a gas. 'You think *Peregrine* is having an affair with a married woman? But that's impossible!'

'The facts would indicate otherwise,' Sir Barrington said. 'But perhaps you would care to explain why you believe it to be so unlikely?'

'Because he isn't the type to get involved in something like that. In fact, I don't think he's ever even been involved with a woman. He is…a student of history,' Anna said, needing to make him understand why his accusation was so totally misplaced. 'Old bones and ancient ruins hold far more appeal for Peregrine than would the charms of the most practised seductress.'

At that, Sir Barrington's mouth lifted in a smile. 'I doubt Lord Yew would appreciate his wife being referred to as a practised seductress, but—'

'Lord Yew!' Cambermere interrupted. 'Dear God, don't tell me you're talking about the marchioness?'

'I am.'

'Damn!' The earl muttered something under his breath,

then abruptly turned to his daughter. 'I think under the circumstances it would be best if Sir Barrington and I were to continue this conversation in private, Anna. There's nothing here you need to be involved with.'

'But why not? I already know the worst,' Anna said. 'And I stand by my claim that Peregrine is innocent of the charge.'

'Unfortunately, I have evidence to the contrary,' Sir Barrington put in. 'And I do not intend to reveal *that* in front of you, no matter what your father says.'

'Of course not,' Cambermere mumbled. 'Not fit for a lady's ears, I'm sure. But I will have the details of it before the lad comes home.'

'But, Papa—'

'No, my dear. Sir Barrington and I will discuss this alone,' her father said firmly. 'When Peregrine gets home, have Milford send him straight to my study. And you are *not* to speak with him beforehand.'

Anna said nothing as the two men left the room because, in truth, she didn't know what *to* say. Peregrine involved in a scandalous affair with a married marchioness? Impossible! Even if he were to lift his head out of his books long enough to look at a woman, it certainly wouldn't be to one married to another man. He had a stronger moral code than that, of that she was sure.

And yet Sir Barrington Parker claimed to have proof of the affair. What kind of proof could he have, and how had Peregrine come to be accused of this wretched undertaking in the first place? Had Lord Yew a grudge against him? Perhaps as the result of a card game or a wager? Had they had words over some political issue, or a difference of opinion over the current government's handling of some matter of concern to both of them?

There had to be *something*. Anna refused to believe that

Peregrine would ever stoop to something as shoddy as an affair. He might have been raised in the country, but everything about his behaviour thus far convinced her that his parents had instilled good moral values in him.

Why should that change simply because he was visiting London for the first time?

'And you are quite sure of your facts?' Cambermere said unhappily.

'Quite.' Barrington walked unhurriedly around the earl's study. It was a comfortable room—masculine yet not oppressively so, with large leather chairs, several glass-fronted bookcases and a large mahogany desk, the surface of which was covered with papers and estate ledgers. Tall windows bracketed a portrait of the fifth Earl of Cambermere, the present earl's father, and on the wall opposite hung one of a lady Barrington suspected of being the late Lady Cambermere.

Obviously, the earl liked looking at his wife's portrait. Perhaps she'd spent time with him here, keeping him company while he worked on the complexities of estate business. Certainly there was evidence of a woman's touch in the room: the brass candlesticks on the side table; the throw cushions that picked up the dark blue of the curtains; the warmth of the Axminster carpet. All the small, homely things that turned a house into a home. All the things his own house was so noticeably lacking.

'I never lay charges without being sure, my Lord,' Barrington said. 'It wastes time and inflicts unnecessary pain on the innocent. Mr Rand's activities were confirmed by a family member who saw the two enter Lady Yew's chamber and by a friend of mine who happened to be in the house at the same time as Rand. He was quite specific about the details of Mr Rand's visit, right up until the time he and the lady went upstairs arm in arm.' Barrington turned to face the older man. 'And regardless of whether or not what took place upstairs was of an intimate nature, you know as well as I do that his being alone with the marchioness is more than enough to convict him.'

'Damn!' the earl swore again. 'I never expected behaviour like this from Peregrine. Edward's always been one for the ladies. God knows how many have lost their hearts to him. But he's a good-looking lad and as charming as they come.'

'Has he shown no interest in marrying?'

'No, and at almost twenty-six, he's of an age where that's exactly what he *should* be turning his mind to,' the earl said testily. 'I've told him as much, but he doesn't pay heed to me. Says he'll marry when he's good and ready and not a moment before.'

'So he likes to play the field,' Barrington said.

'Always has. But Rand isn't inclined that way. In the time he's been here, I don't think I've ever heard him *talk* about a woman, let alone embroil himself in a sordid affair with one. My daughter was right in that regard.'

Barrington didn't bother to offer a reply. Family dynamics were neither of importance nor of interest to him. Emotion had to be kept separate from fact or everything risked drowning in sentimentality. Some might consider him cold for harbouring such a belief, but as far as he was concerned, it was the only way to do business. 'My Lord, I trust you appreciate the gravity of the situation,' he said bluntly. 'Lord Yew is understandably angry that his wife entered into an intimate relationship with another man; while it is correct to say that the lady is equally to blame, it is the gentleman the marquess intends to punish.'

'Of course,' Cambermere agreed. 'Men are always at fault in these situations. Well, what do you propose we do about it?'

Barrington was about to answer when the door to the room burst open and Lady Annabelle swept in, all blazing eyes and righteous indignation. 'Forgive me, Papa, but I simply *cannot* stand by and allow Sir Barrington's accusation to go unchallenged. Peregrine would *never* do something like this. It runs contrary to everything he stands for—which leads me to believe that it must be Sir Barrington's information that is in error.'

Barrington stared at the woman standing just inside the door, aware that she truly was magnificent. The candlelight deepened her hair to a rich, burnished gold and, in the dim light, her eyes shone a clear, deep blue. She was like a golden lioness protecting her cub. He almost hated having to be the one to prove her wrong. 'I have someone ready to swear that Mr Rand spent time alone with the marchioness in her private rooms, Lady Annabelle,' he said quietly. 'I need not tell you how damaging such a disclosure would be.'

He saw her eyes widen and knew that she did indeed appreciate the gravity of what he'd just said. But it was equally clear that she still didn't believe him. 'How do you know your witness was telling the truth, Sir Barrington? You have only his word that what he claims to have happened really did. I know Peregrine and I can assure you that he is not the type of man—'

'Anna, please,' her father interrupted. 'If Sir Barrington says he has proof of Peregrine's guilt, we must believe him.'

'But why? If he only took the time to speak with Peregrine, he would know that what he is suggesting is quite impossible.'

Cambermere sighed. 'You must forgive my daughter, Sir Barrington. She has grown uncommonly fond of my godson in the short time he's been here and is clearly reluctant to hear ill spoken of him.'

'I understand,' Barrington said, wondering if the closeness between the lady and Mr Rand had anything to do with the fact that they might well *be* brother and sister. 'Is Mr Rand spending the rest of the Season with you?'

The earl nodded. 'That was the plan. His father and I are… old friends. We were…at school together,' he said, glancing at a file on his desk. 'Haven't seen him in years, of course, but I was at his wedding and agreed to stand as godfather to his firstborn.' He turned towards the window, his face half in shadow. 'A few months ago, I received a letter from him, telling me that his wife had died and asking if I'd be willing to take Peregrine for a few months. Show him the sights of London, that sort of thing.'

'And you agreed.'

'I thought it the right thing to do.' The earl swallowed hard, his voice when he spoke gruff. 'He is my godson, after all.'

Barrington nodded, not sure whether it was grief or regret that shadowed the earl's voice. 'Are *you* aware of the company your godson keeps, Lord Cambermere?'

'Can't say that I am. His interests run vastly different to mine. He doesn't ride, he prefers not to hunt and I don't believe he's all that partial to moving in society. As my daughter said, he would rather spend his evenings with a book.'

Or in the marchioness's bed. 'Do you know where he is this evening?' Barrington enquired.

He saw the look that passed between Cambermere and his daughter, but wasn't surprised when the earl said, 'No. As I said, I don't make a study of the boy's comings and goings.'

'Yet you said Lady Annabelle usually goes with him to social engagements.'

'Yes.'

'Then why is she not with him tonight?' Barrington asked.

Barrington glanced at Lady Annabelle as he waited for a response. What little he knew of her encouraged him to believe that she would give him an honest answer. But when he saw her colour rise and her golden brows knit together, he suspected she already had. 'I see.'

'No, you don't see!' Lady Annabelle said quickly. 'Peregrine didn't ask me to accompany him because he was going to visit someone with whom he was already acquainted. It wasn't necessary that I go along.'

'Were you not surprised that you did not also receive an invitation to the reception?'

'Not at all. There are often events to which I am invited that other members of my family are not,' she explained. 'We may move in the same circles, Sir Barrington, but we do not have all the same friends.'

Barrington knew there was nothing to be gained in challenging the remark. Lady Annabelle was trying to defend Mr Rand—and failing badly in the attempt. 'Lord Cambermere,' he said finally, 'my client has made it clear that he intends to make an example of the man involved with his wife. However, for the sake of you and your family, I would prefer to see this matter settled quietly and with as little scandal as possible. If I could get Lord Yew to agree to it, would Mr Rand be willing to break off his association with Lady Yew and swear that he would never see her again? Perhaps be willing to write a letter to that effect?'

Cambermere nodded. 'I don't see why he would not—'

'But why *should* he write such a letter, Papa!' Lady Annabelle demanded. 'If he has done nothing wrong, surely there is no—!'

'*Enough*, Anna! If you cannot keep silent, I *will* ask you to leave,' her father said, displaying signs of impatience for the first time that evening. 'I don't know if you appreciate how serious a matter this is. In years gone by, Peregrine would have been called out for such an offence. In fact, I'm sure the thought crossed Yew's mind. He is not a man to be trifled with.'

'But you are condemning him without trial,' she persisted. 'Pronouncing him guilty without even giving him a chance to prove his innocence. All on the strength of *this* man's say so!' she added, her voice suddenly growing cold.

Barrington's eyes narrowed. So, the fair Lady Annabelle would defend her visitor to the last, blindly ignoring the evidence that he had put forward. Pity. While her loyalty did her credit, all it meant was that the outcome of the situation would be that much more painful for her in the end.

'If I may suggest,' he said slowly, 'I am well aware of how shocking this must sound and agree that Mr Rand must have his hearing and be given a chance to explain. But I do have an appointment with Lord Yew tomorrow afternoon and he will be looking for answers. So I would ask that you speak to Mr Rand as soon as possible and get back to me at the earliest opportunity.'

'I shall speak to him the moment he returns home this evening,' the earl said, 'and send word to you first thing in the morning.'

'Thank you. You have my card.' Barrington glanced at Annabelle, but wasn't surprised that she refused to meet his eyes. 'I regret, Lady Annabelle, that our introduction should have taken this form. It is not how I wished we might have started out.'

'Nor I, Sir Barrington.' She did look at him then and Barrington saw how deeply she was torn. 'If you knew Peregrine as I do, you would understand why I say that he is incapable of such a deceit.'

'Sadly, it is not possible for me to be intimately acquainted with everyone I am asked to investigate. Nor would it do me any good to encourage that kind of relationship. I must judge what I see without emotion clouding my vision. I trust the word of those who provide me with information and trust my own skills when it comes to assessing the value of what they've told me. I have no reason to doubt the source of this particular piece of information.'

'Yet who is to say that your source is any more honest than Peregrine?' she parried. 'He is as much a stranger to you as your source is to us. Does he even *know* Mr Rand?'

'By sight, and that is all that matters,' Barrington said. 'I deal in facts, Lady Annabelle. Not emotion. One dilutes the other to such an extent that the truth is often unrecognisable.'

She shook her head. 'I'm not sure I like your truths, Sir Barrington. You presume a great deal without being personally involved.'

'It is *because* I am not personally involved that I am able to reach the conclusions I do.'

'Then I sincerely hope that when we come to you with proof of Peregrine's innocence, you will offer him as sincere an apology as he deserves,' she said.

Barrington inclined his head. 'I will be happy to offer an apology if such is warranted. But if he is guilty, I expect the same courtesy from you. I'm good at what I do, Lady Annabelle—and I haven't been wrong yet.'

Her chin rose and he saw a flash of defiance in her eyes. 'There is a first time for everything, Sir Barrington. And in this instance, I will enjoy being the one who points it out to you.'

Barrington stared down at her, aware that while she frustrated him to the point of distraction, she also aroused in him feelings of an entirely different nature. In fact, he was finding it harder and harder to look at her and not imagine how she would feel in his arms. How the softness of her body would fit into the hard angles of his and how sweet the taste of her lips would be.

And that was the problem. While he admired her more than any woman he'd ever met, the fact that he wanted her in his bed was an unforeseen and unwelcome complication.

'I expect time will provide the answer to that,' he said, offering her a bow. 'My lord,' he said, turning to her father, 'I look forward to your visit on the morrow.'

'I will be there, Sir Barrington.' The earl's face was set in grim lines. 'Of that you can be sure.'

In the weighted silence that followed, Anna restlessly began to pace.

'You don't like Sir Barrington,' her father said flatly.

'It is not so much the man I dislike as his attitude,' Anna muttered, her eyes on the faded pattern of the carpet. 'I am as deeply convinced of his error as he is of mine, yet he is intractable.'

'And you are not?' her father retorted. When she said nothing, he continued, 'What of his claim that he has never been wrong?'

'A man may make whatever claim he likes, but we have only his word that it is the truth. And regardless of what he says, I will *not* believe Peregrine guilty of this.' Anna stopped and looked at her father. 'You know what kind of man he is, Papa. You've spent time with him. Talked with him at length.'

'Yes, I have, but women can make fools of us all. And sometimes circumstances compel us to do things…to *be* things…we would not normally do or be,' her father said.

Anna shook her head. 'That may hold true for some men, but *not* Peregrine. He is a good and honest man. I would stake everything I own on that.'

'Then I would advise you to be careful, my dear. Sometimes what we believe in our hearts is as far from the truth as it is possible to be. And that which we say will *never* happen, happens with alarming regularity.'

'You're speaking in generalities,' Anna said. 'I'm talking about Peregrine, and I know him a damned sight better than—'

'Annabelle!'

Anna sighed. 'A great deal better than does Sir Barrington Parker. Besides, if Lady Yew *is* having an affair, it is only what her husband deserves, cold, unfeeling man that he is.'

'Nevertheless, she is his wife and it is her duty to remain faithful to him,' the earl said.

'Even though he has kept a score of mistresses since the day they were married?'

The earl's face flushed. 'You should not be speaking of such things!'

'Why not? It isn't as though Lord Yew makes an effort to conceal his activities. He is constantly seen at the theatre with one or other of his mistresses. I'm surprised he hasn't invited them home to dine—'

'Enough! I will not hear you speak of such things, Anna,' the earl said harshly. 'Go back to the drawing room and continue with your needlework. I shall deal with Peregrine when he comes home and then we will settle this matter once and for all!'

It was well past midnight by the time Peregrine finally came home. Lying awake in bed, Anna heard the front door open, followed by the sound of muffled conversation. No doubt Milford telling Peregrine that the earl wished to see him. She heard footsteps, the sound of another door opening and closing, and then silence.

How long would the interview take? Would her father give

Peregrine a chance to explain himself? Or would he assume, as Sir Barrington had, that Peregrine was guilty and demand that he make amends at once?

It did not make for pleasant contemplation and, irrationally, Anna wished it had been anyone *but* Sir Barrington Parker who had brought forward the accusation. Because despite what she'd said to him tonight, she *was* attracted to him, more than to any man she'd ever met. She felt surprisingly at ease in his company, even though the sight of him set her pulse racing and her thoughts whirling. She enjoyed his sense of humour, admired his intellect and sensed that beneath that cool and controlled exterior beat the heart of a strong and passionate man.

But how could she be attracted to *any* man who wilfully intended to persecute a man whom she considered as practically a member of her family? Their formal introduction had been made as the result of his coming here to investigate Peregrine's behaviour. An *erroneous* investigation, Anna assured herself. Because if she allowed herself to believe that Peregrine would indulge in such a pastime, it could only mean that she didn't know him as well as she'd thought—and she liked to believe that being able to read people on an intuitive level was something she did well.

It was what enabled her to offer advice to confused young women who came to her, and to their equally confused mothers. By cutting through the layers of emotion, she was able to see down to the bones of the situation. And yet, was that not the very justification Sir Barrington Parker had used for his conduct tonight?

'*...I deal in facts, Lady Annabelle. Not emotion. One dilutes the other to such a degree that the truth is often unrecognisable...*'

Perhaps, but in this case, emotion was all Anna had to go on. Emotion and trust. She had to believe in the integrity of her family and all they stood for. For where would she be—indeed, where would *any* of them be—if she could not?

Anna awoke to the first rays of sunshine slanting in through her bedroom window and realised that she had fallen asleep without ever having heard Peregrine come upstairs. Bother! Now she had no way of knowing what the result of his conversation with her father had been. Nor could she just barge into Peregrine's room and ask him. He might be her father's godson, but he was still a young, single male and it would be inappropriate for her to go to his room alone, even under circumstances like these.

With that in mind, Anna quickly rang for her maid and set about getting dressed. Peregrine was normally an early riser, but if she could catch him before he set off, she might have a chance of finding out what she needed to know. Unfortunately, though she hurried her maid through her preparations, it wasn't timely enough. By the time she reached Peregrine's room and knocked on the door, there was no answer and she could hear nothing from inside. He must have already gone down for breakfast. Perhaps he'd passed a poor night after the interview with her father.

Given how angry her father had been, Anna knew that to be a definite possibility.

In the breakfast room, however, she was disappointed to find only her brother seated at the long table. Edward looked up at her entrance, his greeting somewhat reserved. 'Good morning, Anna.'

Anna inclined her head as she made her way to the sideboard. 'Edward.' Though only two years separated them in age, they had never enjoyed a close relationship. Edward tended to belittle her efforts at helping others, while she couldn't understand his cavalier treatment of friends and servants alike. She had once seen him cut a good friend dead when word of the fellow's marriage to a lady of lesser standing had reached him, saying that anyone who associated with rubbish was like to be tainted by the smell. And when his valet had come down with a fever, Edward had dismissed him, saying he couldn't abide to be in the same house as a sick man. Her father had offered to reassign the poor man to the stable, but not surprisingly, the valet had chosen to leave.

Now, as Anna helped herself to a slice of ham, a piece of toast and a boiled egg, she was thankful the rest of the staff were in such excellent health. 'Have you seen Peregrine this morning?' she asked, sitting down across from her brother.

Edward didn't look up from his newspaper. 'No.'

'What about Papa?'

'Out.' He turned the smoothly ironed page. 'Said he would be back in an hour.' He glanced at the clock. 'That was half an hour ago.'

So, her father had already left to meet with Sir Barrington Parker. That meant she *had* to speak to Peregrine as soon as possible. But where was he? And if he'd gone out, when might he be back? If she could talk to him, find out what had really happened, she might be able to speak to Sir Barrington on his behalf.

Leaving her plate untouched, she got up and headed for the door.

'What, no breakfast?' Edward enquired. 'Cook will be displeased.'

'I haven't time. I have to find Peregrine.'

'He's probably still in his room,' Edward said, turning another page. 'I understand he was drinking quite heavily at the Grundings' soirée last night.'

Anna stilled. 'Where did you hear that?'

'From someone who was there.' He finally looked up and smiled. 'It seems our country guest is finding London very much to his liking.'

Pursing her lips, Anna left the room. Edward hadn't meant the remark kindly. For whatever reason, he'd taken an instant dislike to Peregrine and had taken to making snide comments about his appearance, his manner of dress, even his accent. Anna had taken him to task about it several times, but it hadn't made any difference. The sniping continued and Edward made no attempt to hide his feelings when Peregrine was around.

Fortunately, Peregrine knew how Edward felt about him, but he refused to make an issue of it, saying it likely stemmed from the difference in their upbringings. Edward had been raised in a nobleman's house and was heir to an earldom, whereas Peregrine had been raised on a farm with parents who, though comfortable, were neither titled nor gentry.

Still, he was a guest in their home and he deserved better. Anna liked him very much. Despite his obvious lack of sophistication, he was good natured and quick to laugh and didn't belittle her efforts the way Edward did. He admired her for caring enough about the welfare of others to get involved and he also liked many of the same things she did, so they frequently found themselves laughing together at the various social events they went to.

Edward, on the other hand, was never to be found in the same room as Peregrine. Supremely conscious of his own position in society, he sought the company of those equal to him or blessed with a higher status. If there was a snob in the Durst family, it was definitely her brother.

Reaching Peregrine's door, Anna raised her hand and knocked. 'Peregrine?' When she heard no response, she waited a moment and then tentatively pushed it open.

He wasn't there. Worse, his bed hadn't been slept in.

Anna felt a knot form in the pit of her stomach. *Where had he spent the night and where was he now?* Equally important, what kind of mood was he in? Peregrine was an uncommonly sensitive man. If her father had falsely accused him of having an affair with Lady Yew, Peregrine might well have left the house angry and embarrassed that his godfather would believe such shameful lies about him. But where could he have gone?

There was only one way to find out. Heading to her bedroom, Anna fetched her bonnet and gloves. Returning to the hall, she rang for Milford and asked to be told where Sir Barrington Parker lived.

'Lady Annabelle Durst, Sir Barrington,' Sam said quietly.

Barrington looked up from the deed of land he had been perusing and saw the lady standing in his doorway. She looked like a breath of summer in a gown of pale yellow silk trimmed with deeper yellow ribbons, an elegant wide-brimmed bonnet perched atop her golden hair. Her lips were a soft dusky rose, but her blue eyes appeared unusually bright against the pallor of her skin. She was distraught and, recognising that, he rose at once. 'Lady Annabelle.'

'I hope my timing is not inconvenient, Sir Barrington.'

'Not at all. Pray come in. Bring your maid, if you wish.'

'No, I would rather speak to you privately.' Lady Annabelle waved the girl into a chair outside his study. 'I cannot bear not knowing.'

So, it was curiosity that had compelled her to come. Obviously, she hadn't spoken to her father yet. Barrington indicated the high-back chair in front of the fireplace. 'Won't you sit down?'

She did not. Visibly upset, she began to pace. Barrington understood the compulsion. He had been a pacer once himself. 'May I ring for tea?'

'Thank you.' This time, she did look at him. 'That would be most welcome.'

He glanced at Sam, who nodded and quietly withdrew.

For a moment Barrington said nothing, more interested in studying her than he was in initiating a conversation. She was as beautiful as ever, but this morning she looked to be drawn as tight as a finely strung bow. He had a feeling that if he pulled too hard, she would snap. 'What did you wish to ask me, Lady Annabelle?' he said softly.

Her head turned towards him, her blue eyes filled with misgivings. 'Have you seen my father this morning?'

'I have.'

'And? Did he speak to you about Peregrine?'

Barrington nodded, aware that he was far more in control of his emotions than she was of hers. 'Are you sure you won't sit down?'

'Please…just tell me,' she implored. 'I wanted to ask Peregrine myself, but he wasn't in his room this morning; by the looks of his bed, he hadn't slept there at all.'

'I suspect he did not,' Barrington agreed. 'Lord Cambermere informed me that after his conversation with Mr Rand last night, the young man left the house without any indication as to where he was going or when he might return. Apparently he was in a state of considerable distress.'

He saw her eyes briefly close. 'Did he admit to…what you accused him of?'

Barrington wished he could have said otherwise, but he wouldn't lie. Not even when he knew the boy had. 'No.'

With a soft cry, Lady Annabelle sank into a chair. 'I knew it! I *knew* he was innocent.' When Barrington made no response, she raised her head, her eyes narrowing at the expression on his face. 'You don't believe him.'

'It takes more than a man *saying* he didn't do something for me to believe him innocent when the evidence speaks so clearly of his guilt.'

'But why would he lie?' she protested.

Barrington gave a non-committal shrug. 'Why does anyone

lie? To protect themselves or to protect someone else. I'm sure you've had dealings with young women who told you one thing, yet did another.'

'Yes, because they had no wish for their misdemeanours to become public.'

'Exactly. Mr Rand is likely embarrassed by what he's done and hopes to convince others that he is not at fault.'

He saw her stiffen. 'Peregrine has *never* lied to me.'

'Perhaps there has not been enough at stake for him to do so,' Barrington said quietly. 'Now there is.'

The door opened again and Sam walked in, carrying a silver tea service. At a nod from his employer, he set the tray on the small table beside the desk and then quietly withdrew. Barrington crossed to the table and picked up the milk jug. 'Milk and sugar?'

'Just milk, thank you.'

He poured a drop into one of the cups, then filled both cups with hot tea. Accepting hers, Lady Annabelle said, 'I still think you're wrong, Sir Barrington. If Peregrine said he is not involved with Lady Yew, he is not. Why can you not accept that as truth?'

'Because the rest of his behaviour leads me to believe otherwise. How do you explain the fact that he chose not to stay home last night?'

'I suspect he was deeply embarrassed by my father believing him capable of such reprehensible conduct. Would *you* not wish to avoid someone who had accused you of doing something you had not?'

'Maybe. But I also like to think I would be mature enough to admit my mistakes, if I were so foolish as to make them.'

'And I repeat, I do not believe Peregrine has made a mistake.'

He heard the quiet certainty in her voice and was moved to

smile. He, too, had once been so trusting; so willing to believe in the goodness of others. When had he lost that *naïveté*?

'The attraction between a man and a woman is one of the most powerful forces on earth, Lady Annabelle,' he said. 'You have no idea how many crimes are committed, and how many lies are told, in the name of that attraction.'

'Not perhaps as well as you do,' Lady Annabelle agreed, 'but we are talking about Peregrine's character and of that I believe I *can* speak with authority. If he told my father he is not having an affair with Lady Yew, he is not.'

'Then it would seem we have reached an impasse,' Barrington said. 'There is nothing more to say.'

She looked somewhat taken aback by his easy acceptance of her statement, but, equally willing to accept it at face value, she finished her tea and then set the china cup and saucer back on the table. 'What will you tell Lord Yew?'

'I don't know,' Barrington said honestly. 'But I have between now and two o'clock to work it out.'

'Then I shall leave you to your deliberations.' She stood up and offered him her hand. 'Thank you for seeing me, Sir Barrington.'

'My pleasure.' Barrington felt the softness of the glove in his hand, the slenderness of the fingers within. 'I'm sorry that circumstances are such that you leave believing the worst of me. Again.'

'Actually, I don't. We each have our own ways of involving ourselves in other people's lives, Sir Barrington,' Lady Annabelle said. 'I tend to think the best and assume people innocent until proven guilty, whereas you believe the exact opposite.'

'Not at all. I simply strive to uncover the truth,' Barrington said. 'That is why people come to me. And experience has taught me that if the truth is not immediately discernible, it *will* come out in the end.'

'Then at least you and I are able to part knowing that the truth of *this* matter has already been established,' she replied. 'Goodbye, Sir Barrington.'

Barrington inclined his head, but said nothing as she left the room. He stood by his desk until he heard the sound of the front door close before letting his head fall back and breathing a long, deep sigh.

So, the lovely Anna thought the matter closed. Wrong. Peregrine Rand *was* guilty. The fact he had chosen not to *confess* his sin meant absolutely nothing. In his heart, he knew what he'd done and, if Peregrine was as noble as Lady Annabelle made him out to be, guilt would eat away at him until he had no choice but to make a clean breast of it. Either way, the young man was doomed to failure.

As it seemed was he, Barrington reflected, when it came to securing the good opinion of the lovely Lady Annabelle Durst. If it turned out that his accusations were correct and Rand was guilty of having an affair with Lady Yew, she would resent him for having proven her wrong. On the other hand, if Rand was telling the truth, she would resent him for having doubted his integrity in the first place. In short, they had reached a stalemate. And contrary to what either of them might wish to believe, in a situation like this, there was simply no way one or the other of them was going to win.

Chapter Four

Anna finally caught up with Peregrine later that afternoon. She had been resting in her room, nursing the megrim she'd had for the better part of the day, when she heard the heavy thump of footsteps in the hall and realised he was finally home. Pushing the lavender eye pads aside, she quickly got up and went to the door. 'Peregrine!'

He clearly wasn't in the mood for conversation. Dressed in boots, hacking jacket and breeches, he didn't stop when she hailed him and was almost at the bottom of the stairs before she finally caught up with him. 'Peregrine, wait! I need to talk to you.'

'I haven't time.' His voice was unusually brusque. 'I'm going riding with friends and I'm already late.'

'Then you'll just have to be a few minutes later,' Anna said, putting her hand on his arm and turning him around. 'Where were you last night? I was worried about you.'

'You had no reason to be. I simply went out.'

'But not until *after* you spoke to Papa. Why did you leave again? And why didn't you come home?'

He flicked the hard leather crop against the top of his

boot. 'I lost track of time. When I realised how late it was, I decided it was best I just stay out.'

'Why? Because of something Papa said?'

Peregrine was a good-looking young man with a shock of thick, black hair, deep brown eyes and a wide, generous mouth. A mouth that suddenly narrowed in anger. 'I don't care to talk about it.'

'But you don't have a choice, Peregrine. There's a rumour going around town that you are having an affair with Lady Yew,' Anna said, needing him to understand the gravity of the situation. '*I* know it isn't true, but you can't simply pretend the rumour doesn't exist.'

'As a matter of fact, I can. I told your father as much when he questioned me about it last night and I certainly don't intend to stand here and justify my behaviour to you!'

Stung by the vehemence of his reply, Anna said, 'I'm not asking for justification. I just told you I don't believe what people are saying. But a meeting is being held this afternoon between Lord Yew and the man he asked to investigate his wife's infidelity and your name is going to come up—'

'Damn it, Anna, did I not just say that I don't want to talk about it?'

'But you must! Your reputation as a gentleman is at stake, don't you understand?'

'What I understand is that a man's private business is not his own,' he snapped. 'Do you know why I jumped at the chance to come to London? Because I was tired of having to listen to my father's sanctimonious preaching. Of being told what I could and could not do. I thought that by coming here, I would finally be able to lead my own life. Yet now I find that every move I make is watched and criticised by people I don't know, and that even you and your father have no qualms about intruding into something that is none of your business.'

'None of our business?' Anna repeated in astonishment. 'How can you say that? You are my father's godson. We *care* about you.'

He had the grace to look embarrassed. 'I'm not saying you don't.'

'Then why are you being so defensive? I know you didn't have an affair with Lady Yew,' Anna said. 'For one thing, she's already married. For another, she must be at least fifteen years older than you.'

'Since when did either of those things matter to the fine, upstanding members of society?' Peregrine shot back. 'Half of London seems to be involved with people other than their wives or husbands. Why should Susan and I be any different?'

'Susan?' Anna interrupted, shocked. 'You call her *Susan?*'

'Yes.' He raised his chin in defiance. 'What else would one call a good friend?'

'Given that she happens to be someone else's *wife*, I would have thought Lady Yew the more appropriate form of address,' Anna said, concern lending an edge to her voice.

'You're being stuffy, Anna. I didn't do anything wrong,' Peregrine said. 'She gave me leave to speak to her in such a manner.'

'Really? And what else did she give you leave to do?'

The tips of Peregrine's ears flamed red. 'Nothing.' But when he refused to meet her eyes and began fidgeting with his crop, Anna knew he was lying to her—and she felt the foundations of her world tremble.

So, it *was* all a lie. Peregrine *was* involved with Lady Yew. Worse, he was *in love* with her. He'd given himself away when he'd spoken her name. His mouth had quivered and his eyes had softened, the way a person's always did when they referred to the man or the woman they cared about deeply.

And she, stupidly, had believed him. She had defended him to both her father *and* to Sir Barrington Parker, a man she had charged with making a false accusation, when all the while it was Peregrine who had been telling lies.

Needing to regain a measure of calm, Anna turned her back on him, clenching her fists at her side. 'Since you obviously did not see fit to inform my father of the truth last night, I will have it now,' she said, fighting to keep her voice steady. '*Are* you having an affair with the Marchioness of Yew?'

'Anna, *please*!'

'Don't Anna me! I want the truth, Peregrine. People's reputations are at stake here. Mine included.'

'Nonsense! This doesn't concern you!'

She whirled to face him. 'Of course it concerns me! I spoke up on your behalf,' she cried. 'I defended you to someone who was ready to think the worst of you. And I refused to believe them when they told me what you were supposedly guilty of.'

Footsteps on the stairs alerted Anna to the fact that they were standing in a place where anyone might hear them, prompting her to grab Peregrine's arm and pull him into the drawing room. 'Furthermore,' she said, closing the door behind them, 'I assured Father and this…other gentleman that you couldn't possibly have been guilty of having an affair with Lady Yew because you didn't even *know* her.'

'But I did know her,' Peregrine admitted.

'How? *I* didn't introduce the two of you.'

'No. Edward did.'

'Edward?' Anna repeated, confused. 'But…when were the two of you ever at a society function together?'

'It wasn't at a society function we met.' Peregrine ran his fingers through his hair, hopelessly dishevelling it. 'Edward had been on at me, saying that if I had any hopes of becoming a gentleman, I needed to educate myself in gentlemanly ways.

That meant knowing how to shoot, how to ride and how to fence. Since I'm already a good rider and I can handle a gun, that only left fencing, a sport to which I've had absolutely no exposure. Edward offered to take me to Angelo's and I met the Marquess of Yew there.'

'That doesn't explain how you met his wife,' Anna pointed out.

'She was waiting for him outside in their carriage,' Peregrine said. 'Edward pointed her out to me when we arrived. When I commented on how beautiful she was, he kindly offered to introduce us.'

Kindly? Anna doubted her brother had *ever* had a kind thought in his head when it came to Peregrine. 'All right, so you were introduced. If you knew Lady Yew was married, why did you pursue her?'

'Because on the way home after the match, Edward told me about their marriage. He said it was a loveless union and that Lady Yew was desperately unhappy because Yew paraded his mistresses right under her nose and didn't give a damn as to what she thought.'

'Be that as it may, she *is* his wife and you were wrong to interfere.'

'But she doesn't *love* him!' Peregrine said, his voice rising. 'She told me that what she feels for me is the most wonderful, the most exciting feeling she's ever experienced, and that when we finally are able to be together—'

'Together?' Anna interrupted incredulously. 'Are you telling me that Lady Yew said she was going to *leave* her husband?'

'Not in so many words, but—'

'Don't play games with me, Peregrine. Did she or did she not *say* that she was going to leave her husband?'

'Not exactly, but—'

'So she made you no promises that she would run away with you,' she said flatly.

'Well, no, but—'

'There are no buts, Peregrine. Lady Yew has been playing with you.'

'She wouldn't do that!' he said hotly. 'You don't understand how it is between us! She *loves* me!'

'Love? I doubt the woman knows the meaning of the word,' Anna said dismissively. 'In fact, I can give you the names of at least ten other young men with whom she claims to be in love. Men with whom she has flirted and danced and driven nearly insane with jealousy. It's what she does.'

'I don't believe you,' Peregrine said, stubbornly clinging to his beliefs. 'She said nothing to me about other men. And even if there were, it doesn't signify. What she felt for them could be nothing compared to what she feels for me. She said she's never met anyone like me before.'

Anna sat down, aware that Peregrine was no more educated in the ways of love than poor Mercy Banks. 'I'm sorry, Peregrine, but Lady Yew is *not* going to run away with you. Her husband is one of the richest men in England. He owns properties in four counties and his personal worth is staggering. As his wife, Lady Yew is one of the most influential women in society. If you think she would risk throwing that all away to run off with the penniless godson of the Earl of Cambermere, I would advise you to think again.'

'But Edward said—'

'I don't care what Edward said,' Anna said, though she damn well did care and she intended to talk to her brother at the first opportunity. 'Tradition is the foundation upon which society is built. Noble families marry into noble families, thereby ensuring that the tradition carries on. Casting discretion to the wind and haring off because you believe yourself in love with someone else's husband or wife is destructive to the fabric of society—and nobody knows that better than those who occupy its uppermost rungs. I'm sorry, Peregrine, but the kindest thing you can do for yourself is to get over this as quickly as possible and then move on with your life.'

Anna knew it was a sobering speech, but she also knew it was one Peregrine needed to hear. He had to understand that his hopes were futile, that whatever dreams he harboured were as insubstantial as fairy dust.

'But I *love* her,' he whispered, misery inflecting every word. 'How am I supposed to get over that? I've never felt this way about a woman before.'

'You get over it by waking up each day and telling yourself that she is married to a man who will *never* divorce her… even if she wished him to.'

Anna said the words as gently as she could, but she still saw Peregrine wince and felt her heart go out to him. It was never easy hearing that the person you loved didn't love you in return. In fact, finding out that you were little more than a source of amusement, whether it be for an hour or a day, or even a year, was the most devastating thing imaginable. It destroyed your confidence and tore at the very foundation of who you were.

Having been through it, Anna knew exactly how injurious it was to one's sense of well-being.

For a few minutes, Peregrine just sat there, his brow furrowed, his eyes bleak with despair as he struggled to come to terms with everything she had told him. It was hard waking up from a dream, but he had been indulging in an impossible fantasy; for his own good, Anna knew he had to come back to reality.

He finally stood up and slowly began to walk around the room. 'Part of my reason for staying out last night,' he said slowly, 'was because I was embarrassed. I never expected your father to find out what was going on. I thought it was just between Sus—between Lady Yew and myself.'

'Yes, I'm sure you did,' Anna said. 'But while London might seem like a big city, never forget that there are eyes and ears everywhere. When you play with fire, you will eventually get burned.'

'I know, but you never really believe that. It's as though you're living in a bubble. You can see out, but no one can see in. But, of course, everyone can.' Peregrine dropped his head and breathed a long, deep sigh. 'Your father thought it would be a good idea if I were to…write a letter to Lord Yew, apologising for my behaviour. He said that if I promised not to see Lady Yew again, it might…smooth things over with him.' He raised his head. 'Do you think he's right?'

Aware that it was Sir Barrington Parker who had suggested writing the letter, Anna simply inclined her head. 'I think the letter a good idea, yes. With luck, it will set the marquess's mind to rest and persuade him to let the matter go. Because if he takes it into his head to persecute you, Peregrine, there will be no future for you in London.'

Peregrine nodded, and for a full five minutes he was silent, reviewing his options. Then, as if realising he had none, he said finally, 'Very well. I shall write the letter. But I'll give it to you, rather than to your father. I don't think he ever wants to see me again.'

'Don't be a goose, of course he wants to see you.'

'You weren't there,' Peregrine said ruefully. 'You didn't see the look on his face. Why do you think I lied to him, Anna? God knows I didn't want to. But when I saw how disappointed he was at even having to *ask* me if I was involved with Lady Yew, I knew I couldn't tell him the truth. So I lied. That's why I couldn't stay here last night,' Peregrine admitted. 'I was too ashamed to sleep under the same roof as him. He's been so good to me. I couldn't bear to repay him like this.'

'Oh, Peregrine,' Anna whispered. 'If Father was disappointed, it was only because he cares about you and wants you to do well in London. He knows how harsh society can be towards those who flaunt its rules.'

'Then society is a hypocrite!' Peregrine cried. 'I'm not the only man involved with a married woman. There are countless other such affairs going on and everyone knows it!'

'Yes, and they are tolerated as long as they are conducted discreetly and with neither party voicing an objection,' Anna told him. 'But for whatever reason, Lord Yew has chosen to object to the liaison and, as a gentleman, you have no choice but to withdraw.'

The gravity of her words must have penetrated his romantic haze, because for the first time Peregrine seemed to appreciate the magnitude of what he had done. He glanced down at his boots, his mouth working. 'Very well. I shall go for my ride as planned and while I am out I shall think about what I wish to say. Then, I shall come back and write a letter of apology to Lord Yew.'

Anna did a quick mental calculation. Sir Barrington had said he was meeting with the marquess at two. There wasn't a hope Peregrine would be back from his ride in time to have the letter finished and delivered by then, which meant she had no choice but to send word to Sir Barrington herself.

'Peregrine. Have I your word that you will stop seeing Lady Yew, that you will say as much in your letter to Lord Yew?'

Peregrine frowned. 'Have I not just said I would?'

'Yes, but I need to be very clear as to your intentions.'

'From where I stand, I don't think I have any choice.'

'Fine. Then off you go on your ride,' Anna said. 'I'll see you at dinner.'

'Not tonight.' Peregrine got up and slowly walked towards the door. 'Edward said he would be dining at home this evening and I have no intention of sitting at the same table and letting him humiliate me any further in front of your father.'

'Why would he do that?'

'Because I was foolish enough to confide my feelings for Lady Yew to him.' Peregrine looked at her and sighed. 'He knew exactly how I felt—and he said nothing at all about it being a hopeless quest.'

Anna needed no further explanation. How could she explain that it was just her brother being himself? 'I'm sorry, Peregrine. Really, I am. And I know how hard it is not to be with the person you love, but there will be others. You have only to open your heart and let love find you.'

His mouth twisted. 'I've been open to love a long time, Anna, but this is the first time it's come anywhere close to finding me. Infatuation is one thing, but true love doesn't come along every day.'

No, it did not, Anna reflected as she sat down to write the letter to Sir Barrington. True love was elusive: as fragile as a sigh, as mysterious as the night. It inspired placid gentlemen to write romantic poetry and sensible young women to lose themselves in dreams. For those lucky enough to find it, love could be a life-altering experience.

But falling in love could also be a painful and humiliating experience, one that shattered a person's belief in their own self-worth and that was best forgotten as quickly as possible. Her brief, ill-fated liaison with the Honourable Anthony Colder was a prime example of that, as was poor Peregrine's misplaced affection for Lady Yew. If anyone needed proof of the *destructive* power of love, they need look no further than that.

Lady Annabelle's note arrived well in advance of Lord Yew's visit and while Barrington was relieved that a solution had been found, her words did not make him feel better. Not when he knew what it had cost her to write them.

Sir Barrington,
As time is of the essence and Mr Rand is otherwise occupied, I thought it best to send word of his intentions as quickly as possible. I have been informed that he is indeed guilty of having an affair with the lady in question; however, he has assured me that he intends to end the relationship and that he is willing to confirm the same in a letter addressed to her husband. I hope you will convey these sentiments to the gentleman and that he will find it a satisfactory resolution to the problem.

    Neither my father nor Mr Rand has been made aware of this correspondence and I would prefer that it remain that way. As one who has been accused of 'involving herself in the convoluted lives of others', I think it the wisest course of action.

It was simply signed 'Annabelle Durst' in a clear and legible hand.

So, Mr Peregrine Rand had been unable to maintain his lies in the face of the lady's questioning. Good—because there was no doubt in Barrington's mind that Annabelle *had* questioned him. Profess to believe him she might, but she had still needed to hear from his own lips that he was innocent of the charge and that the rumours were not true.

How devastated she must have been to find out that they were…and how difficult for her to write this note. She had believed wholeheartedly in the young man's innocence, put trust in her intuition when it came to what he would and would not do—only to discover that her intuition was not strong enough to stand up against the wishes and desires of his own heart. Disillusionment was always a bitter pill to swallow.

He glanced again at the parchment in his hand. Closing his eyes, he raised it to his nose and gently inhaled. Yes, it was still there…a lingering trace of her fragrance, the scent sweet but sensually provocative. An echo of the lady herself. He set the parchment down and walked slowly towards the long window, his mind filled with thoughts of Anna.

It was a long time since a woman had affected him to this degree. Indeed, he wasn't sure one ever had. For the most part, he'd always believed aristocratic ladies to be like exotic birds: lovely to look at, but troublesome to own. They strutted around society's stage like the fragile, inconsequential creatures they were, generally offering nothing of substance beyond the ability to play the piano or paint pretty pictures. It was the reason he had found commitment so easy to avoid.

But Lady Annabelle was neither fragile nor inconsequential. She was intelligent. Passionate. The quintessential lady and beautiful beyond all. But beauty without soul had never appealed to him, and it was because she cared so much about other people that Barrington found himself so strongly attracted to her. She cared about Mercy Banks and the host of other silly young women who needed her help in extricating themselves from situations that could have ruined them. She cared about her country visitor, who might well be her half-brother, and about her father, who, with typical male arrogance, was ready to dismiss everything she said. Yes, admirable indeed was the Lady Annabelle Durst. A lady worth getting to know.

And yet, as a result of what had passed between them, Barrington doubted a deeper acquaintance was possible. In his hand, he held her acknowledgement that she had been wrong, and he right. That was the first strike against him. He had proven everything she had most desperately wanted not to believe. She had stood up for a man who hadn't deserved her loyalty, and she had been let down. Matters would never be easy between them now.

Still, now that he knew the truth about Rand, he would do everything he could to mitigate Lord Yew's anger and to settle the matter as humanely as possible. As for Rand, if he truly believed himself in love with Lady Yew, he was already suffering enough by having found out what she was really like. No point making it worse by dragging his name through the mud, and by association, the beautiful Lady Anna's.

The note Anna received from Sir Barrington later that afternoon was brief, but reassuring.

Your note was well timed. I met with Lord Yew, and after being assured of Mr Rand's willingness to see the error of his ways, the marquess is willing to let the matter go. He will settle for a letter and a promise of restraint on Mr Rand's part and shall consider the matter closed. I have not written to your father. I leave it to you to inform him of the outcome, and Mr Rand. I remain,
Your most humble servant
B.

Anna folded the letter and tapped it against her chin. So, the matter was resolved. The Marquess of Yew had been informed as to the identity of the guilty party and had been willing to accept an olive branch in the form of a promise and a written apology. Sir Barrington had handled the matter admirably. As long as the marquess honoured his word, Peregrine would be free to go about London without the finger of blame being pointed at him at every turn.

Just as well, since Anna was quite sure he would have bolted had such been the case.

Unfortunately, as she set out for her afternoon visit to the Baroness von Brohm, Anna realised that the entire affair had left a bad taste in her mouth. Not only were her feelings towards Peregrine affected by what she had learned, but her brief acquaintance with Sir Barrington Parker had been tainted by the events they had both unwittingly been drawn into. She had insinuated that he hadn't known his business, accused him of misjudgement and gloated when she'd believed him wrong. She owed him an apology.

But was he the type of man to whom apologising was easy? She remembered the way he had teased her over her steadfast belief in Peregrine's innocence, mocking her belief in the man's inability to tell lies. Would he be condescending of her apology now? Had he been waiting for just such a moment to say, 'I told you so'? Anna hated to think of him as being deliberately cruel, but, not knowing the nature of the man, she had little else to go on.

She was not at all surprised that thoughts of him occupied her fully during the carriage ride to Mayfair.

Julia von Brohm was not what Anna had been expecting. Thinking to see a pale, unhappy woman in her mid-forties wearing the unrelieved black of a widow still in mourning for her husband, Anna was surprised to be greeted by a slender and very attractive woman of no more than thirty, garbed in a stunning gown of rich burgundy satin. Her honey-brown hair was arranged in a simple but elegant chignon at the nape of her neck, and her eyes were a clear, bright blue that appeared even brighter against the translucent whiteness of her skin.

'Lady Annabelle,' the baroness said, extending both hands in greeting. 'I cannot tell you how pleased I was to receive your note.'

'And likewise, how pleased I was to receive your acceptance,' Anna said. 'I regret that my good friend, Lady Lydia Winston, was unable to come, but her mother was taken to bed with a terrible head pain and required her assistance.'

The baroness's pretty face softened in sympathy. 'Poor lady. Having had a mother-in-law who suffered with megrims, I know the role a daughter must play. But I am so pleased that you were brave enough to come on your own.'

Anna tilted her head to one side. 'Brave?'

'Come now, Lady Annabella. You must surely have heard the rumours—that I am a lonely widow who cannot stop crying for her late husband. That I am a beautiful woman whose company must be endured, but not enjoyed.'

The smile came easily to Anna's lips. 'I knew you were a widow, Baroness, and I assumed that you would be lonely. But I certainly did not hear that you were dismal company or someone to be avoided. And even if I had, I would have come anyway and drawn my own conclusions.'

'I am very glad to hear it,' the baroness said in her charmingly accented voice. 'And I think that you and I are going to become good friends. Ah, Smith,' she said to the young maid who appeared in the doorway. 'We shall have tea and a plate of pastries. Cook would be most upset if we did not offer our guest a sampling of her wares.'

As the maid curtsied and withdrew, the baroness turned back to Anna. 'I hired most of the staff upon my arrival, but dear Frau Hildenbaum has been with my family since I was a girl. She insisted on coming to London with me and when she heard I was having an English lady to tea, she set to work. She has been baking since early this morning.'

'How delightful, for I confess to a definite weakness for pastries,' Anna said as she sat down on a comfortable sofa across from the baroness. The room was quite beautiful, the walls papered in pale blue and gold silk, the shades of which were reflected in the carpet and furnishings. An exquisite medieval tapestry was suspended from a brass rod between the two long windows that gave view over the square below, and numerous other works of art adorned the walls. The baroness either had exceptional taste or the good fortune to have ancestors who did.

Even more stunning was her jewellery. Anna's eyes were repeatedly drawn to the brooch pinned to the bodice of her gown. It was shaped like a flower, with a single piece of amber in the centre and with petals made up of diamonds and rubies.

'You are admiring my brooch?' the baroness asked during a lull in the conversation.

Anna looked up, embarrassed to have been caught staring. 'Yes. Forgive me, but it is so beautiful.'

'My late husband gave it to me for my twenty-first birthday.' The baroness's face glowed. 'Ulrich spent a lot of time travelling and often came home with little trinkets like this. He had exceptional taste.'

'Baroness—'

'Please, won't you call me Julia?' she interrupted gently. 'I have no wish to be so formal with you.'

'Then you must call me Anna. And I was about to say that your husband must have loved you very much to have given you such an exquisite gift.'

As soon as the words left her lips, Anna regretted having uttered them. She had no wish to invoke unhappy memories for Julia and she feared that mentioning her late husband in such a way might be all that was required to bring them on. But apart from a delicate flush, Julia remained admirably in control of her emotions. 'He did love me. Ours was a true love match. Not common in our world, I suppose, but I was more fortunate than most.'

'So it wasn't an arranged marriage.'

'Oh, yes, but Ulrich and I fell in love shortly after we were introduced. That probably sounds ridiculous, but it is the truth.'

'I think you were indeed incredibly fortunate,' Anna said. 'I know of so many marriages that are arranged for the benefit of the parties involved and end up being the most dismal of relationships. That is why I always prefer to see marriages based on love. Have you any children, Bar—Julia?'

Where the mention of her husband had not brought tears to her eyes, the mention of children did. 'Sadly, no. Ulrich and I were not able to conceive a child together. Perhaps if we'd had more time—'

When Julia broke off, Anna leaned over to place her hand over the other woman's. 'I am so sorry for your loss, Julia,' she said gently, 'but you are young enough to marry again and to bear many healthy children.'

Julia nodded, her eyes glistening with unshed tears. 'I would like to think so, but if the difficulty in conceiving lies with me, it will not matter who I marry. I know that will serve as a deterrent to certain gentlemen.'

'Only those looking to set up a nursery,' Anna said, seeing no point in not stating the obvious. 'If we are being practical, there are many older gentlemen who would be happy to offer you marriage without children being a condition.'

'You are kind to say so, Anna, but, in truth, I do not long for a husband. The memory of Ulrich is enough.'

'But memories won't keep you warm at night and you are far too beautiful to spend the rest of your life alone,' Anna pointed out. 'You must get out in society and start mingling again.'

'I would like that,' Julia admitted, 'but in the three weeks I've been here, I have not received a single invitation.'

'Then we must start the ball rolling.' Anna smiled, convinced more than ever that she had done the right thing in coming to visit the baroness. She pulled an invitation from her reticule and handed it to Julia. 'This is from the Countess of Bessmel. It is an invitation to a soirée at her home the evening after next.'

'An invitation!' Barely managing to conceal her delight, Julia broke the seal and unfolded the invitation. 'But we have never met.'

'I know, but I chanced to be at a breakfast with the countess the other morning and told her I intended paying a call on you. She said she was planning to do the same, but that the pain in her legs was preventing her from getting around. That's when she asked if I would be good enough to deliver the invitation to you and to say how much she hopes you will attend.'

Julia read the invitation again and her smile brightened immeasurably. 'This is…so very good of you, Anna. And of Lady Bessmel, of course. I will write at once to accept.'

'Excellent, because she is looking forward to meeting you,' Anna said. 'Lady Lydia will also be there, and with three such highly placed ladies at your side, you can be assured that the rest of society will take notice.'

Julia's smile was as radiant as the diamonds pinned to her breast. 'Thank you, Anna. I feel better simply for having met you. And perhaps before you leave, you would like to see some of my other jewellery? I can assure you that a few of the pieces make this brooch look quite plain.'

Chapter Five

Though Barrington did not make a habit of attending all of the society functions to which he was invited, he recognised the wisdom of dropping in on certain, select events. Dark alleys and gentlemen's clubs were all very well, but he had learned long ago that most of the truly useful gossip was to be overheard in the drawings rooms and ballrooms of society. And given that Lady Bessmel was acknowledged to be one of the finest gossips in London, the thought of missing an event at her magnificent Park Lane mansion was tantamount to professional suicide. Now, as Barrington stood opposite the entrance to the grand ballroom, watching the parade of swirling dancers make their way around the room, he wondered how many darkly held secrets would be exposed tonight.

A quick sweep of the room revealed the usual attendees: blue-blooded aristocrats with their equally blue-blooded wives, a smattering of officers and politicians, some in the present government, some casualties of the last, as well as the miscellaneous collection of ladies and gentlemen who, though not titled, were well born enough to receive the much-coveted invitations. Colonel Tanner was standing at the far side of the room with his pale little wife, but, other than a brief nod in Barrington's direction, betrayed no sign of having seen him.

Barrington allowed his gaze to move on. He was used to being ignored by those for whom he worked, if one wished to call it that. It was a hazard—or a blessing—of the job, depending on how one looked at it.

Then, suddenly, there was a commotion as three ladies entered together. Lady Annabelle Durst, magnificent in lilac silk, Lady Lydia Winston, lovely in shimmering green, and a third, slightly older but equally striking woman with whom Barrington was not acquainted. She wore an elegant silver-grey gown, long white gloves and a diamond necklace that could have fed London's poor for a year. And when he heard whispers in the crowd and realised that most of Lady Bessmel's guests didn't know who the lady was, he put the pieces together. This must surely be the mysterious Baroness Julia von Brohm.

More importantly, however, it was also the first time he had seen Anna since the arrival of her note acknowledging Peregrine's guilt. How would she receive him? With haughty indifference or grudging acceptance?

Knowing that the question had to be asked, he crossed the room to where she stood and bowed in front of the three ladies. 'Good evening, Lady Lydia. Lady Annabelle.'

'Why, good evening, Sir Barrington,' Lady Lydia said with unaffected pleasure. 'How nice to see you again. I thought perhaps you had been in hiding, we have seen so little of you.'

'Alas, I have been kept busy with work,' Barrington said, conscious of Anna's eyes on him.

'Yes, so I understand.' Lady Lydia's eyes sparkled with mischief. 'I happened to bump into your sister at Hatchard's the other day. She said you haven't been round for a visit since the occasion of her last dinner party.'

Barrington's mouth twisted, remembering his less-than-memorable meeting with Lady Alice Stokes, a pleasant woman with whom he'd had absolutely nothing in common. 'I will go round and see Jenny this week. And apologise,' he added with a rueful smile. Then, bowing towards Anna, said, 'I trust all is well at home, Lady Annabelle?'

'Yes, thank you, Sir Barrington.' Her expression was tranquil, but Barrington thought he detected a quiver in her voice. Surely she wasn't nervous about seeing him again?

'And Mr Rand?' he asked.

'He is doing as well as can be expected, under the circumstances,' she said quietly. Her hair was drawn softly off her face and caught up with a cluster of deep pink roses. Barrington thought she had never looked lovelier. 'Are you acquainted with Baroness von Brohm?' she asked, adroitly changing the subject.

'I am not,' Barrington said, turning towards the third lady, who was watching him with undisguised interest. 'I was hoping I might prevail upon one of you to make the introduction?'

'With pleasure. Baroness, may I present Sir Barrington Parker,' Anna said smoothly. 'Sir Barrington—Baroness Julia von Brohm.'

The lady regally inclined her head. 'Sir Barrington.'

'Baroness.' Barrington bowed over her hand. 'I'm surprised it has taken this long for us to meet, given that word of your arrival has been swirling for weeks.'

'There has been a great deal to do and I have kept much to myself,' the baroness admitted. 'But Lady Annabelle felt it was time to make my appearance in society and I am grateful to her and Lady Bessmel for their kindness in making it happen.'

'We decided to take Julia under our wing,' Anna explained. 'I'm sure you won't find that surprising, given what you know of me.'

Barrington wasn't sure if she was taking him to task, but when he saw the twinkle in her eye, he allowed himself to hope that the remark intended nothing of the sort. 'Yet another convoluted life exercise?' he ventured.

He was relieved to see her smile, and for the first time since the arrival of her note, he felt himself breathe properly again.

'Ah, Parker, good evening,' Lord Cambermere said, joining them. 'Might have known I'd find you hoarding the three most beautiful women in the room.'

'On the contrary, having only just made the baroness's acquaintance, I cannot be accused of hoarding. Especially since the other two ladies are as well known to you as they are to me.'

'Julia, allow me to introduce my father, Lord Cambermere,' Anna said with a smile. 'Papa, Baroness von Brohm.'

The earl's gaze sharpened, a man appreciating the beauty of a woman. 'I had heard of your arrival, Baroness, and am compelled to say that Vienna's loss is our gain. I trust you are enjoying life in London?'

'To be honest, I have experienced very little of it, Lord Cambermere,' the baroness replied. 'As I told your daughter, I have been busy setting up my household. There has not been much time for sightseeing or socialising.'

'But now that Julia is finished with all that, I have assured her that we shall be seeing a great deal more of her in society,' Anna said. 'Tonight is her début, if you will.'

'And a splendid début it is,' the earl said quietly. 'Would you allow me to introduce you to a few of my friends, Baroness? Having seen me in conversation with you, they will not forgive me if I neglect to do so.'

Barrington saw the look of pleasure that warmed the baroness's face, but also noticed the look of startled surprise on Anna's. Obviously she wasn't used to her widowed father paying court to a beautiful woman, especially one who was also so recently widowed. But, true to form, she recovered with swiftness and grace. 'Yes, do go, Julia. Papa knows everyone and he is perfectly respectable. Just don't start him talking about horses.'

'Oh, but I love horses!' the Baroness was quick to say. 'My late husband's stable was one of the finest in Vienna.'

'Good Lord,' the earl said, leaning forwards. 'Never tell me that your late husband was Captain Baron Ulrich von Brohm?'

A soft gasp escaped the baroness. 'Yes. Did you know him?'

'I most certainly knew *of* him. I read several of his papers on early equine development and thought his ideas were nothing short of brilliant.' The earl offered the lady his arm. 'I would be honoured to have a chance to speak to you about him.'

As an opening gambit, it couldn't have been better. Barrington watched the baroness place her gloved hand on Cambermere's sleeve, aware that her eyes were bright with interest as they rested on his face. They were already talking about horses as he led her away, prompting Barrington to wonder how many of the earl's friends were likely to be introduced to the beautiful baroness that evening.

'I think you have a success on your hands, Anna,' Lady Lydia whispered. 'If everyone else is as taken with the baroness as your father, we will surely see her married before the end of the Season!'

Barrington tended to echo Lady Lydia's assessment, though he wondered how Anna felt at having her father's affection for the woman so bluntly stated. It wasn't always easy for daughters to accept a new woman into their father's life, especially daughters who still lived at home. The arrival of a stepmother could make their lives hellish. Still, given the friendship that seemed to exist between Anna and the baroness, Barrington doubted that would be the case here.

'Sir Barrington,' she said suddenly, breaking into his thoughts, 'I wonder if I might have a word with you? In private.'

He turned to find her sapphire gaze fixed on him. 'By all means.'

'Then I shall go and speak to Lady Bessmel,' Lady Lydia said promptly. 'She mentioned having received news of her son in Scotland and I have been longing to hear how Thomas goes on. I shall catch up with you later, Anna. Good evening, Sir Barrington.'

Barrington inclined his head, but he noticed that Anna waited until her friend was far enough away so as not to hear their conversation before turning to him and saying, 'I hoped I would have a chance to speak to you this evening, Sir Barrington. I'm sure we both recognise that I owe you an apology with regard to Peregrine.'

Barrington studied the face upturned to his, aware that it exposed far more than she realised. 'You owe me nothing, Lady Annabelle. I took no pleasure in being the bearer of bad news.'

'Nevertheless, I accused you of dealing in false information and that was a criticism of your professional conduct. For that, an apology must be offered.'

'*Must* be?' he repeated. 'Am I to conclude that you do not *wish* to apologise?'

Her gaze clouded over, a tiny frown appearing between her brows. 'Please don't misunderstand. If I appear reluctant to admit my error, it is only because it has caused me to question things about myself that I've not had reason to question before. I thought I knew Peregrine better than anyone. Certainly better than you. And I believed I was right in defending him when you first charged him with the affair. But, as it turns out, I really didn't know him at all. I was convinced he would never do something so foolish as to engage in an affair, yet that's exactly what he did.'

'But you and I both know that Mr Rand is not the first man to catch Lady Yew's eye, nor will he be the last,' Barrington said. 'She is the type of a woman who needs constant attention. Sadly, he is just the latest on a very long list of conquests.'

'I know, but that doesn't make it any better,' Anna said ruefully. 'And it certainly doesn't excuse what he did.'

'Love makes its own excuses. It has ever been thus.'

'Perhaps, but what disturbs me the most is that he truly *believed* she loved him.'

'He will get over it,' Barrington said with a smile. 'He is a young man and all young men must fall in love with at least one unsuitable woman in their life. It is a rite of passage. Useful in teaching us what to watch out for when we *do* finally go looking for a wife.'

Her smile was a reluctant twisting of her lips. 'I wish I could be as convinced of that as you, but when I see him suffering…'

'Women pine for love not found while men suffer from love already lost. It is our Achilles' heel, if you will. And for what it's worth, I suspect Rand was more in love with the idea of *being* in love than he was with the actual act of loving,' Barrington said, hoping to ease her guilt. 'By all accounts, he liked to read to her and she enjoyed listening to him.'

He saw a tiny smile lift the corners of her mouth. 'Peregrine has a lovely speaking voice. Not as mellifluous as yours, of course, but I expect he would have done well on the stage.'

She liked his voice. There was really no reason the compliment should have meant anything to him, but it did. Strange the things a man clung to. 'Regardless, I think it little more than a case of boyish infatuation. Lady Yew is a beautiful woman. She was probably flattered that a good-looking man so much younger than she would find her attractive and offered more encouragement than she should.'

'For all the good it did either of them,' Anna said with an edge to her voice. 'But I *am* sorry, Sir Barrington. You told me that collecting information was what you did and you obviously do it very well. I will not be so foolish as to doubt you again.'

Barrington inclined his head, wondering why he felt as though she was saying goodbye. 'With luck, there will be no occasion for us to find ourselves in a situation like this again.'

Then she smiled and, with her very next words, confirmed his suspicions. 'I suppose not. In fact, given what we know of each other, I doubt our paths will have any reason to cross again.'

As expected, the baroness's introduction to London society was a complete success and doors that had been closed to her in the past were suddenly thrown open with abandon. Society embraced her with the fervour of a shepherd welcoming home a long-lost lamb and gentlemen flocked to her side, eager to secure favour.

Because she was seen to be such good friends with Lady Bessmel and the daughters of the Earl of Cambermere and the Marquess of Bailley, her name constantly appeared high on the list of society events, both intimate and grand. Not surprisingly, Anna's brother and father were frequent visitors to Julia's afternoon salons, though the earl was very careful not to do anything that might result in scandal being attached to her name. He never stayed longer than was appropriate, or tried to take up too much of her time. But it was noted and remarked upon, after several society gatherings where both were in attendance, that the widowed Earl of Cambermere was evidencing a marked partiality for the company of the beautiful Baroness von Brohm.

Naturally, Julia was delighted with all the attention, but Anna noticed that she, too, was careful not to indicate a preference for any one gentleman over another, perhaps because she was still clinging to the memory of her late husband. But she was a gracious and entertaining guest, and though her list of contacts grew by the day, she never forgot that it was Anna's kindness that had originally launched her into society.

As such, she decided to hold a dinner party in Anna's honour, inviting, along with the rest of her family, twenty other guests including Lord and Lady Bessmel and Lady Lydia Winston. Knowing the company would be very smart, Anna decided to wear one of her newest gowns, an elegant creation in pale gold silk, a colour that was exceedingly flattering to her fair complexion. Her hair was arranged in a loose cluster of curls with a few wisps hanging free to frame her face. Elbow-length gloves, her mother's pearls and a light sweep of colour across her cheeks were all that were required to complete the ensemble.

Half an hour later, she stepped out of the carriage in front of Julia's house, with her father and Edward close behind. Both looked very elegant in their black-and-white evening attire, her father especially so. Peregrine, who was still reluctant to show his face in society, had decided to remain at home.

'Good thing, too,' Edward said in the disparaging tone he always used when Peregrine's name came up. 'No point the boy thinking he's entitled to move in good society when it's obvious he belongs in the country.' He plucked a strand of hair from the sleeve of his jacket. 'Besides, he'd likely just embarrass us in front of the baroness. He does, after all, have an eye for older women.'

'That was unkind,' Anna said flatly. 'You are as much to blame for Peregrine's fall from grace as he is.'

'I don't see how. I wasn't the one who jumped into bed with Lady Yew.'

'Don't be coarse, Edward, and please keep your voice down,' Anna said in a fierce whisper. 'You shouldn't have told him about the state of their marriage.'

'My dear Anna, there isn't a soul in London who doesn't know the state of the Yews' marriage,' Edward said blandly. 'Why should I have left Rand in ignorance? He would have found out sooner or later. And just because I told him Lady Yew was open to lovers didn't mean he had to go sniffing after her as though she were a bitch in season. And you needn't look at me like that,' he said when she turned a chilling glance on him. 'You're too old to pretend an ignorance of what goes on between a man and a woman. I know how besotted you were over Anthony Colder.'

Anna winced, the mere sound of the man's name causing her pain. 'I would thank you not to mention him in my presence again.'

'Why not? Surely you're not still pining over the fellow. He wasn't worth it, you know. The stories I could tell—'

'This conversation is over,' Anna said coldly. 'Please keep your opinions to yourself and refrain from making damaging comments about Peregrine in public, lest you find yourself defending rumours about your own less than sterling behaviour.'

'*My* behaviour?' Her brother's eyes widened in a credible imitation of innocence. 'What possible concern could you have about that?'

'I see no need to explain myself. We are both aware of your reputation with women.'

He slowly began to smile, clearly enjoying himself. 'And what have you heard about my reputation, pray tell?'

'Amongst other things, that you are fickle and heartless,' Anna said, boldly meeting his gaze. 'We've gone through three maids in the last year and I suspect your unwelcome attentions towards them had much to do with the reasons they all left. If you must indulge yourself, kindly do so in a manner that does not disrupt the household or result in frightened young girls being sent back to the country in tears.'

His eyes narrowed and for a long moment he stared at her in silence. 'Well, well, so the pretty bird has sharp talons,' he murmured finally. 'Who would have guessed?'

'Guessed what?' their father asked, joining them.

'Nothing.' Anna turned her back on Edward, shutting out his obnoxious comments and his condescending gaze. She knew he enjoyed goading her and most of the time she was able to rise above his petty teasing, to treat his remarks with the chilly disdain they deserved. But tonight he'd touched a nerve and, despite her best intentions, she had lashed out at him, a reaction she would no doubt come to regret. 'We should go in. I have no desire to keep the Baroness waiting.'

They were escorted by the butler into an elegant drawing room where most of the guests had already assembled. Anna saw Lydia talking to Lord and Lady Bessmel and smiled in acknowledgement of her friend's wave. She left her father and brother and went to join them.

'Good evening, Lord Bessmel, Lady Bessmel,' she greeted the older couple. 'And, Lydia, I'm so pleased to see you. How is your mother this evening?'

'Much better, thank heavens,' the girl said, clearly relieved. 'This last megrim has been very difficult for her, but the doctor gave her something that seems to be helping. But what an exquisite gown, Anna. Surely one of Madame Delors's?'

'I thought the occasion demanded something suitably festive.' Anna took a deep breath and glanced around the room. She had no idea if Sir Barrington had been invited, but she found herself looking for him regardless. 'Have you seen our hostess yet?'

'No, but I expect she will be down shortly.'

'Not the thing for a lady to be late for her own dinner party,' Lord Bessmel remarked.

'Patience, Harry,' Lady Bessmel said, patting her husband's arm. 'I'm sure the baroness is simply waiting for the right moment to make her appearance. Most Europeans have a flair for the dramatic. But what lovely pearls, Annabelle. Your mother's, if I'm not mistaken.'

'Yes,' Anna said, surprised that the countess would recognise them. 'How did you know?'

'I remember her wearing them. White or pink pearls are relatively common, but that shade of gold is quite rare.'

'They were a gift to her from Papa,' Anna said fondly. 'He always said Mama had the perfect complexion for them.'

'She did. Fortunately, so do you and they go perfectly with your gown, which I must tell you is absolutely exquisite. But look, I do believe the baroness comes.'

As expected, all eyes turned towards the door where the baroness, resplendent in sapphire satin, stood for a moment framed in the doorway. Her lovely face was wreathed in smiles, but Anna was quite sure it wasn't her smile or her gown that caused the collective gasp of astonishment that echoed around the room, but the magnificent diamond-and-sapphire necklace that was draped around her throat.

'Forgive me, dear friends, but a minor crisis upstairs

delayed my arrival,' she announced to her assembled guests. 'I trust you have been attended to in my absence.'

'We have been very well treated,' Lord Bessmel said as the baroness joined them. 'The important thing is that you are here now and looking quite spectacular, if you don't mind my saying so.'

'I don't mind you saying so at all, Lord Bessmel,' Julia said with a soft gurgle of laughter. 'In fact, I am convinced it is the one thing a lady *never* tires of hearing. Anna, my dear,' she said, pressing her cheek to Anna's. 'How beautiful you look tonight. You will most certainly rob the gentlemen of their senses. And, Lady Lydia, how delightful to see you again. I trust your mother is feeling better?'

'She is, Julia, thank you; she is so sorry she couldn't be here this evening. Unfortunately, noise tends to aggravate her condition.'

'I understand,' Julia said with a sympathetic nod. 'Megrims are such tiresome things. You are lucky not to be afflicted.'

'Good evening, Baroness.'

Julia turned and her smile brightened. 'Lord Cambermere, Lord Hayle, I am so pleased you were both able to attend.'

'An opportunity to spend time in the company of a beautiful woman should never be missed,' Cambermere said as he brushed his lips over her hand in a courtly, old-world gesture. 'And may I say you look magnificent this evening.'

A becoming flush rose in her cheeks. 'You are very kind to say so.'

'Kindness has nothing to do with it,' the earl assured her. 'I'm sure there isn't a gentleman in the room who doesn't agree with me.'

'Fortunately, most of them come with wives,' Edward cut in smoothly. 'Those of us who are single definitely have the advantage this evening.'

His smile was charismatic and his words flattering. Anna

saw her father's expression falter as Edward neatly inserted himself between them, but Julia's attention was already diverted, her head turned towards the door. 'And here is yet another handsome gentleman come to join our group. Good evening, Sir Barrington.'

Anna hadn't needed to hear Barrington's name to know that he was in the room. She'd felt the atmosphere change, a subtle quickening of interest as he crossed the floor like a sleek black panther moving through the forest. She saw heads turn, watched eyes widen and flirtatious smiles disappear behind discreetly raised fans. Obviously she wasn't the only one impressed by the width of his shoulders and the unfathomable depths of those cool grey eyes—

'Anna!'

Hearing Lydia's voice, Anna turned, but it wasn't until she saw the slight widening of her friend's eyes that she realised she had been staring. Botheration! The last thing she needed was Sir Barrington Parker mistakenly thinking she was interested in him. Or worse, infatuated by him.

Fortunately, the gentleman seemed completely unaware of her preoccupation, his attention now focused solely on his hostess. 'Good evening, Baroness,' he greeted her in that distinctively low, seductive voice. 'Forgive my late arrival. I was unavoidably detained.'

'You owe us no apologies, Sir Barrington,' Julia said easily. 'You are here now and that is all that matters. I believe you know everyone?'

Sir Barrington nodded, his gaze touching briefly on each of them as he paid his respects. Finally, he turned to Anna, his mouth curving in that maddeningly provocative smile. 'Lady Annabelle.'

'Sir Barrington,' she said, wishing she possessed even a fraction of his composure. 'We have not seen much of you this past while.'

'I was out of London for a few days on business, but made sure to return in time for this evening's gathering.'

'And for the fencing demonstration,' Lord Bessmel said with a wink.

Sir Barrington turned to stare at him. 'I beg your pardon?'

'The fencing demonstration. The one Lord Yew asked you to put on.'

'Forgive me, Lord Bessmel, but I am not aware I was giving a fencing demonstration. Where did you hear news of it?'

'From Lord Hadley,' the older man replied. 'He said he'd heard you speaking to Lord Yew, and that you had agreed to a series of open engagements at Angelo's.'

'Open engagements?' Anna repeated. 'What does that mean?'

'It means that every red-blooded male capable of lifting a sword will be there looking to take Parker on,' Bessmel explained with a smile. 'Should make for a damn good show!'

Anna glanced at Sir Barrington in bewilderment. Surely Lord Bessmel was mistaken. Sir Barrington Parker didn't give demonstrations. Everyone knew that. And if he did choose to spar, it would be with someone of his own choosing.

Could this be the Marquess of Yew's doing? she wondered. Had he demanded this of Sir Barrington as well as everything he had already asked of Peregrine? 'Is this true, Sir Barrington?' she asked in a low voice. 'Is this what you agreed to do?'

'Not exactly,' he murmured. 'What I agreed to was a private lesson with Yew's son, pointing out areas where he might improve. I certainly said nothing about a series of engagements with anyone who felt up to sparring with me.'

'But I fear that is what everyone is expecting,' Bessmel said, adding hesitantly, 'are you going to back out?'

'Surely it cannot be called backing out when one never agreed to it in the first place,' Lydia objected.

'I wouldn't have thought so,' Sir Barrington agreed, 'but I shall speak to Lord Yew about it when next I see him.' Then, seemingly unconcerned, he turned his attention to their hostess again. 'Baroness, that is an exceptionally beautiful necklace.'

'Why, thank you, Sir Barrington.' Julia caressed the deep blue stones with loving fingers. 'My late husband bought it for me. He knew my partiality for sapphires.'

'It is a remarkable piece of workmanship,' Cambermere agreed. 'I hope you keep it safely locked away.'

'I haven't thus far.' Julia's eyes widened. 'Is London such a dangerous place that one need fear being robbed in one's own home?'

'Not as a rule, but I regret to say there have been a series of jewel thefts in London of late,' Sir Barrington informed her. 'I understand Lord Houghton's home was broken into two nights ago and a number of valuable items taken.'

'You should be on guard yourself, Cambermere,' Bessmel said. 'I dare say your daughter's pearls are worth a pretty penny.'

'They are, but I suspect to Anna, like myself, their value is far more sentimental.' The earl turned to smile at her. 'My wife loved pearls. She always said they drew their warmth from the one who wore them. I gave her that necklace on our wedding day.'

'Was your wife born in June, my lord?' Julia enquired.

Cambermere looked surprised by the question. 'She was.'

'Then she was fortunate to be able to wear them without

tears. It is considered bad luck to give a bride pearls unless they are her birthstone.'

'Then you must also have been born in June, Lady Annabelle,' Sir Barrington said quietly, 'for the pearls to glow so richly against your skin.'

Anna felt her cheeks grow warm at the subtle caress in his voice. 'On the contrary, my birthday is in September.'

'Then, like the baroness, you should be wearing sapphires.'

'I say, Cambermere, these women could bankrupt us if they were of a mind to!' Lord Bessmel said with a hearty laugh. 'Now you will have to go out and buy your daughter a string of sapphires, just to appease the superstitious amongst us.'

'I think not,' Anna said quickly. 'Sapphires are beautiful stones, but, like Mama, I prefer the warmth of pearls.'

'I can understand why,' Sir Barrington said as the others turned away to chat amongst themselves. 'They are exceptional, as is the lady wearing them.'

Anna slowly raised her eyes to his face, aware of the fire in his eyes as his gaze lingered on her necklace. The low *décolleté* of the gown exposed far more skin than she was used to and she could almost feel the heat of his eyes burning her. When he finally raised his eyes to meet hers, the desire in them was plain. Was it any wonder her heart was beating double time?

Thankfully, Julia, catching the eye of her butler, said, 'Dear guests, shall we proceed to the dining room? I do believe dinner is served.'

Chapter Six

At the conclusion of an exceptional meal, the baroness led the ladies into the drawing room, leaving the gentlemen to enjoy masculine conversation, good cigars and several fine bottles of port. Barrington, who enjoyed these sessions more for the information they provided than for the chance to socialise, accepted the offer of a light from Viscount Hayle, who settled into the chair next to his. Noticing the man's obvious boredom, Barrington said, 'Is the evening not to your liking, Hayle?'

Hayle slanted him a mocking glance. 'I get tired of listening to men like Bessmel and Richards bickering over political situations about which they know nothing. It's a waste of everyone's time and, frankly, I'd rather spend the night gambling or in the arms of a mistress.'

Barrington drew on his cigar, taking a moment to study the other man through the rising curl of smoke. 'I'm surprised Mr Rand didn't come with you tonight. I thought he usually accompanied your sister to these kinds of events.'

'He was invited but, thankfully, he declined,' Hayle said

tersely. 'It's bad enough having him around the house all the time, let alone being forced into society with him.'

'You do not care for Mr Rand?'

'Would you?' Hayle fired back.

Barrington was startled by the flash of raw emotion he saw in the other man's eyes and wondered if Hayle knew how much of himself he had given away. 'I'm not sure I know what you mean.'

'Then you're the only one who doesn't,' Hayle muttered. 'All you have to do is *look* at Rand to know he's no more my father's *godson* than he is the bloody Prince of Wales's.'

So, that was it. The son suspected the connection and wasn't in the least happy about it. Barrington tapped ash from the end of his cigar. 'I'd be lying if I said I hadn't heard rumours, but I don't believe anything's been substantiated.'

'Of course not. My father's the only one who can substantiate rumours like that and you can be damn sure he's not going to. Not now that he's met the baroness.' Hayle's eyes narrowed as he glared at his father sitting farther up the table. 'It's embarrassing the way he carries on with her. God knows, he's old enough to be her father.'

'I take it you do not care for the fact that the earl and the baroness seem to like one another?'

'I do not. It's unseemly the way he follows her around, hanging on every word she says. He might just as well come out and ask her to go to bed with him.'

Barrington reached for his glass of port, intrigued by the depth of vitriol pouring from the other man. 'I think you judge them too harshly. Your father is an amiable gentleman and the baroness is an exceedingly gracious woman. And as they are both widowed, why should they not enjoy one another's company?'

'There *is* a considerable difference in their ages.'

Barrington shrugged. 'The baroness can't be any more

than twenty-nine or thirty, and your father is, what…in his late forties? There are far wider gaps in age between husbands and wives in society.'

Hayle slowly began to smile. 'Yes. Like Lord Yew and his wife. But then, I suspect you already know all about that.'

Barrington inhaled deeply on his cigar. Hayle was bound to know about Peregrine's folly, but he was damned if he'd be the one to shed any light on the matter. When it came to secrets, he was as adept at keeping them as he was at prying them out of others.

Fortunately, Hayle didn't appear to be in need of an answer. 'How much do you think that sapphire necklace is worth?' he asked instead.

Barrington's shrug was carefully non-committal. 'I'm no expert, but, given the size and quality of the stones, I should think it considerable.'

'Enough to keep a man in brandy and cigars for the rest of his life, I'll wager.'

'Probably. How fortunate that you and I need not worry about such things.'

Hayle snorted. 'Speak for yourself.'

Barrington's gaze sharpened. 'You are your father's heir.'

'Oh, yes. But as he's still in his forties and hale and hearty, I'm not likely to inherit any time soon,' Hayle said sourly. 'So, what's your connection with the baroness?'

'We have no connection, *per se*,' Barrington said, aware that the man changed subjects more often than a lady changed her mind. 'We were introduced by your sister at Lady Bessmel's reception and have seen each other at a few society gatherings since, but nothing beyond that.' He gazed at the earl's son through a fine wisp of smoke. 'I understand it was your sister's idea to launch the baroness into society.'

'Of course it was. Anna loves to manage other people's lives. Personally, I think her time would be better spent smoothing her way into some man's bed,' Hayle said in a disagreeable tone, adding when he saw Barrington's stern look, '*After* she marries him, of course. Anna would never do anything as irresponsible as compromise herself. But it's long past time she was wed. Father's too soft. He won't force her into an arranged marriage, even though he knows it would be best for all concerned.'

'I'm sure your sister would have no problem finding a husband if that was something she truly wanted,' Barrington said, careful to keep the annoyance from his voice. 'She is an exceedingly beautiful woman.'

'But meddlesome and outspoken,' Hayle remarked. 'Men don't like that in a wife. They want quiet, biddable women who know their place. Anna is neither biddable nor accommodating, as I'm sure you know from the brief time you've spent with her. Mind, I've heard her mention *your* name more than once and that's saying something. Better watch yourself, Parker, or she'll have you in the parson's mousetrap before you can turn around.' He drained the contents of his glass, then signalled the waiter for a refill. 'So, I hear you're giving a fencing demonstration at Angelo's this week.'

Barrington's hand tightened on his glass. 'No. I am giving Lord Yew's son a lesson. In private.'

'I heard you were going to fight.'

'You heard wrong.'

'But why wouldn't you fight?' Hayle asked. 'You're reputed to be the finest swordsman in London. Why not show everyone that you are?'

'Because that's not what I do.'

'Then why are you giving Yew's boy a lesson?'

'I agreed to it as a favour to the marquess. I also happen to like Lord Gerald. He shows a great deal of promise with the foil and he is anxious to better himself.'

'Maybe, but you'll never make a fighter of him. He's too

soft,' Hayle said. 'He hasn't the heart for it. You'd do far better sparring with me. At least I'd give you a run for your money. So what do you say? Are you up for it?'

Barrington's expression was deceptively benign. He was used to cocky young men challenging him. At one time, he'd encouraged it, fond of pitting his skills against all comers. But that game had lost its appeal years ago.

He was about to say as much when the door to the dining room opened and one of the younger maids walked in. He hadn't noticed her earlier in the evening, which meant she likely hadn't been in the room. He would certainly have remembered her if she had. She was somewhere in her early twenties, with dark brown hair and rather startling green eyes—

Barrington stiffened. Green eyes and dark brown hair. Was it possible he'd found Colonel Tanner's elusive Miss Paisley? If so, he wasn't surprised that the Colonel had asked him to look for her. Though petite, she had a lush, curving figure that was nicely displayed in the black gown and white apron. Her face was heart shaped and delicate and she had a truly lovely smile. But equally aware of having drawn the attention of nearly every man in the room, her cheeks turned bright pink as she made her way towards the butler, who was standing in the corner overseeing the proceedings.

A whispered conversation followed, during which the butler's heavy eyebrows drew together in annoyance. Then, with a flick of his hand, he dismissed her.

As she headed back in their direction, Barrington noticed Hayle doing a leisurely appraisal of her charms. Then, slowly raising his glass, he watched her over the rim and when she was no more than five feet away, coughed. Not discreetly, as a gentleman might, but in a manner that was guaranteed to draw attention.

The girl glanced in their direction—and her step faltered.

Barrington heard her breath catch and saw her eyes widen as they met those of the man sitting next to him. Beside him, Hayle just smiled. Coldly. Like a spider watching a fly, knowing it was doomed.

The butler, noticing her standing in the middle of the room, said sharply, 'Be off with you, girl!'

She went, all but running to the door. Hayle turned away, seemingly uninterested. 'Bloody endless evening,' he muttered into his glass.

But the girl didn't leave. Barrington saw her hesitate by the door, saw her turn around to take one last look at Hayle, and the expression in her eyes said it all.

'Oh, I don't know,' Barrington remarked, drawing deeply on his cigar. 'Seems to me it's all in how you look at it.'

Anna was seated at the pianoforte playing an air by Bach when the drawing-room door opened and the gentlemen filed in. She knew the piece well enough not to be flustered by their arrival and kept on playing, watching with interest as they took their various seats and settled into conversation with the ladies. Her father stopped to chat with Lady Bessmel, but eventually ended up at Julia's side. His face was flushed and he was smiling. No doubt the result of an extra glass of port after dinner.

Edward spoke briefly to Lady Lydia Winston, but, judging from the expression on her face, the conversation was not at all to her liking. She stiffly got up and walked away. Edward just laughed.

'I was going to ask if I might turn the pages for you,' Sir Barrington said, quietly appearing at her side. 'But since it's obvious you play from memory, I doubt you are in need of my help.'

The glow of his smile warmed her. 'Nevertheless, it is kind of you to offer, Sir Barrington.'

'Kindness had nothing to do with it. I was looking for an excuse to talk to you.'

Anna was tempted to ask why he felt the need of an excuse, but the teasing quip died on her lips when she saw the way he was looking down at her. 'About something in particular?'

'Of course.' He stared a moment longer, before turning his attention back to the room.

Anna kept her eyes on the keyboard, waiting for her breathing to settle. Would it always be like this? Was she destined to feel this trembling excitement every time Barrington drew near? She certainly hoped not. It wouldn't bode well for their friendship if she did.

She cast a sideways glance at him and knew he was taking it all in. Making mental lists about the people and situations that intrigued him. Watching. Always watching.

'It must get tiresome,' she said at length. 'Always having to watch the behaviour of others.'

He turned back to smile at her, one eyebrow raised in amusement. 'That depends on your point of view. Some people spend their entire lives studying the behaviour of others. Wanting to know what their friends and acquaintances are doing. It's called being nosy and society suffers from it excessively.'

Her lips twitched. 'That's quite true, but what you do is entirely different.'

'Why would you say so?'

'Because you don't watch people with the intention of catching them doing something wrong. You watch with a view to catalogue it all for future reference. You notice who they speak to and who they ignore, if they drink too much or not at all, and if they dance with that person and not this one.'

'You make me sound rather devious,' he observed.

'No. Just observant. Something that probably serves you well given the nature of your…occupation.'

The piece of music came to an end and Anna rose to the polite applause of the guests. Miss Constantine was to play next, and as that young lady moved forwards to take her place at the piano, Anna dropped back and fell in beside Barrington.

'Did I detect a note of censure in your voice just then?' he asked as they slowly walked away from the instrument.

Did he? Anna didn't like to think she was revealing too much of herself, but with him, it wasn't always easy to know. 'I have the feeling, Sir Barrington, that one is never entirely safe around you. You see a great deal without ever giving the appearance of actually looking. That makes you dangerous.'

'Only to those with something to hide. The innocent have no reason to fear me.' His eyes found hers and held them captive. 'I trust *you* do not find me dangerous, Lady Annabelle?'

'Danger comes in many forms. I suspect knowing a man like you does not come without risks.'

'*Life* does not come without risks,' he said softly. 'But you're right. A man like myself is always more of a target, as are the people who associate with me.'

Thinking he was being overly dramatic, Anna smiled and said, 'In that case, you'd best warn Miss Erickson to keep her distance.'

'Miss Erickson?'

'Miss Sofia Erickson. I happen to know she is very fond of you.'

Barrington said, 'I'm not sure I know her.'

'Of course you do. Eldest daughter of Viscount Oswell and recently returned from visiting her aunt in Edinburgh. She made her come out this Season and has already been acknowledged as one of its greatest successes. She speaks French and Italian fluently, is an accomplished rider, and an exceptional singer.'

A smile ruffled his mouth. 'And have you had occasion to save the young lady from herself?'

'Good Lord, no.' The sensual curve of his lips brought a series of highly inappropriate thoughts to mind, but Anna forced herself to ignore them. 'She is one of the most intelligent young women I've ever met. She is mindful of the proprieties and quite capable of telling a gentleman to watch his manners if she feels he is out of line.'

'Tell me, how do you come to be so involved in the lives of all these young women?' Barrington asked curiously as they sat down together on the velvet settee. 'Surely your father would wish you to pay more attention to your own future than chasing around after everyone else's?'

Anna felt the familiar warmth creep into her cheeks—an annoyingly common occurrence since meeting this man. 'One can do both at the same time. Helping someone else navigate the path towards marriage does not mean I cannot walk the path myself.'

'But if you are too busy looking out for the welfare of others, how can you see to your own?'

'I hardly think I am doing one to the exclusion of the other,' Anna said defensively. 'Besides, what I do for these girls is important. All too often they find themselves swept up in the emotion of the moment and don't stop to think about the repercussions.'

'And so you step in,' he said softly. 'Like you did with Mercy Banks and Fiona Whitfield, and God knows how many others, in an attempt to save them from themselves.'

'It is all very well for you to mock me, Sir Barrington, but you cannot deny that—' Anna broke off to stare at him. 'How did you know I was involved with Fiona Whitfield?'

'Do you really need ask?'

'Yes, I fear I must. Fiona's mother and father were adamant that word of what happened to Fiona not leak out. I gave them my word that I would say nothing and, since the young man was sent abroad, I don't see how you could possibly be aware of what took place.'

'As it happens, I was making enquiries into the activities of Miss Whitfield's uncle,' Barrington told her. 'I learned of your association with the family at that time. And though I did not delve into the particulars of Miss Whitfield's situation, I did learn of *your* involvement with her whilst speaking to another family member.'

Anna gasped. 'Someone else knew what happened to Fiona?'

'I'm afraid so. But, like you, they were sworn to secrecy. And it worked out well enough in the end. She married Lord Priestley's son earlier this year and I understand they are very happy together.'

'Yes, thank goodness. It could have turned out so badly for her, and all because of that despicable man.' Anna sighed. 'It really isn't fair, you know. A man may tempt a woman with honeyed words and longing looks, yet *she* is the one who must behave with propriety at all times. If he manages to steal a kiss, he is not thought of any the less, whereas she is deemed to have loose morals.'

'Sadly, it has always been thus,' Barrington remarked. 'Society makes the rules and we must obey.'

'No. *Men* make the rules and then demand that women follow them. It is no wonder we sometimes falter.'

She saw the surprise in his face. 'Am I to assume from your comment, Lady Annabelle, that you yourself have faltered in the past?'

'That is none of your business!' she exclaimed.

'No, I don't suppose it is.' He laughed softly, the sound

sending shivers up her spine. 'But your reputation doesn't suggest a woman who would be easily led astray. I find my curiosity piqued at the thought of you having ever done anything wrong.'

'Then you will just have to live with piqued curiosity,' Anna said, abruptly standing up.

'Anna, wait, I meant no offence,' he said, likewise getting to his feet. 'If I've inadvertently touched a nerve, I apologise. It was never my intention to hurt you.'

Anna shook her head, too distracted by unpleasant memories of the past to notice his lapse into familiarity. 'And I did not mean to be abrupt, Sir Barrington, but I have no wish to talk about what happened in my past.'

'I understand. We've all made mistakes, some worse than others. But given your untarnished reputation and excellent standing in society, it's obvious your mistake, if that's what it was, did not serve as your undoing.'

'It could have,' Anna whispered, 'had a friend not come along when she had.'

And that was the tragic truth of her brief flirtation with the Honourable Anthony Colder. As a naïve seventeen-year-old, Anna had all but thrown herself at the god-like creature, believing the smiles he had bestowed upon her were the result of a genuine and mutual affection. Little had she known that his interest had more to do with her father being the Earl of Cambermere than it did with any charms she might possess herself. Anthony had been an avid social climber, as well as the most handsome man she had ever met. With those laughing blue eyes and a smile that set butterflies dancing in her stomach, she would have given him anything he'd asked for. And if he'd had his chance, he would have taken it.

Mrs Mary Fielding had known that, too. A twice-married woman wise to the ways of men like Anthony Colder, Mrs Fielding had seen the growing infatuation between the two young people and had guessed at its source, being more familiar with Anthony's background than most. She had known of his gambling debts, his easy way with women, and his devil-may-care attitude. And on that evening when Anthony, having drunk too much brandy and feeling far too sure of himself, had caught Anna alone in the gazebo by the lake and torn her gown in a boorish attempt at seduction, Mrs Fielding had appeared and promptly sent him packing. She had stayed with Anna until the worst of her grief had passed, and then, after drying Anna's tears, she had lent her a shawl to cover the tear and had sent her regrets back to their hostess, explaining that Lady Annabelle was unwell and that she was seeing her home in her own carriage.

It had been a painful lesson, but one Anna had learned well. She had gone home that evening and made no mention of the event to anyone. She regretted having told her parents and her brother of her affection for Anthony, but after that night she never mentioned his name again. Nor, thankfully, did she see him. Mrs Fielding informed her not long after that he had left the country.

Anna had never been so glad to see the back of anyone in her life. And though she thought it was impossible for her to blush any deeper, she was wrong. Even after all this time, her face burned at the memory of her stupid, stupid mistake…

'Tell me what happened, Lady Annabelle,' Barrington said in a low voice. 'Your secrets are safe with me. I know, better than most, the value of discretion.'

'Yes, I'm sure you do,' Anna said quietly. 'But the only way to completely ensure one's secrets is by keeping them entirely to oneself.'

'I'm sorry you cannot bring yourself to trust me.'

She looked up at him, surprised that he would mention trust in such a situation. 'I do not know you, Sir Barrington.

And the trust of which you speak is generally reserved for relationships between husbands and wives.'

'I've always thought that bonds of trust can exist between friends as well as lovers.'

'Perhaps, but it takes time to establish that kind of bond,' she said, sounding flustered even to her own ears. 'You are a single gentleman and I a single lady. It isn't the thing for us to...share secrets of an intimate nature. But if you were looking for a wife, you would do well to consider Miss Erickson. Apart from her many other attributes, she is a genuinely nice young woman.'

'What makes you think I'm looking for a wife?' he asked.

'Why would you not be? You just told me that we must abide by society's rules, and society dictates that men and women should marry. Is that not the purpose of these gatherings? To place one in the path of the other?'

'I suppose it is.' He hesitated a moment before adding, 'But I think it only right to tell you that Miss Erickson would not be of interest to me, even if I were of a mind to marry.'

If he were of a *mind* to marry? 'Are you telling me you intend to remain single?' Anna asked, eyebrows lifting in shock.

'That was my plan, yes.'

'But what of your obligation to your family?'

'I fear the task of continuing the Parker name will fall to a distant cousin with whom I am not acquainted,' Barrington said blandly. 'As to the obligation owed, I am more concerned with the welfare of the lady with whom I might wish to spend my life than I am to the furthering of my ancestral line.'

'Then I would have to say you are unique in your thinking,' Anna said. 'Most society gentlemen are concerned with their family name and marry to beget an heir.'

'Yes, but you should know by now that my life is not that

of a typical society gentleman. My reputation is such that people come to me when they wish to learn things about others. And because I ask questions people have no wish to be asked, I continuously put myself at risk.'

'Surely you exaggerate the danger.'

'I do not.' His smile held secrets she could not begin to imagine. 'The people I usually investigate are not the honourable men you meet in society, Lady Annabelle. They are scoundrels and blackmailers, men who operate beyond the boundaries of the law and who are completely without conscience. When I get too close, they get nervous. And when I convict them, they look for retribution.'

'But surely not of a life-threatening kind!'

He shrugged, as though trying to make light of it. 'There have been attempts on my life in the past and I have no reason to believe there will not be attempts in the future. The easiest way to ensure my silence is to eliminate the possibility of my saying anything at all. That said, I will not knowingly put anyone else in danger.'

'But if these men have issues with you, why should you fear for the safety of those close to you?'

'Because there *is* no better way to strike back at me than to hurt someone I care about.' They had walked, by tacit agreement, onto the balcony. Barrington rested his arms against the stone balustrade and stared down into the garden. 'And who could be dearer to me than the woman to whom I would give my name…and my heart.'

Anna felt her mouth go dry. Strange that the breeze should suddenly feel so cool. Was her body overly warm? They were standing quite close; close enough that she could feel the heat radiating from his body. 'So you would choose to live… without a woman to share your life,' she whispered, 'rather than expose your wife to possible harm?'

'In a heartbeat.' He turned his head so that his eyes bored

into hers. 'How could I say I loved someone if I didn't care about their safety? If the thought of something happening to them didn't tear me apart?'

Anna shivered. 'You could give up what you're doing. You are a gentleman. You have no need to work.'

'And what would I do with myself then?' He reached out and took her hand in his. 'I have servants to run my estate and stewards and secretaries to see to my affairs. But a man must have something of his own or what reason has he for getting up each day?'

As he spoke, his fingers caressed the palm of her hand, smoothing the tender skin at the base of her wrist. His touch was light, non-threatening—and it turned Anna's world upside down.

She closed her eyes, the sounds of the room beyond fading into the distance. She knew she should pull her hand free, but she was neither willing nor anxious to do so. His thumb was painting circles on her skin, lulling her with a touch.

'We get up because…that is what the world expects of us,' she said huskily. Dear Lord, what was he doing? Not content with massaging her palm and wrist, his thumb was continuing its treacherous voyage along the inside of her arm, causing disturbing quakes in her sanity. 'Surely there is…a kind of security, perhaps even of comfort, in the carrying out of our daily task?'

'Ah, but there are far sweeter pleasures to be enjoyed than that, my lady,' Barrington murmured as he brushed the back of his free hand against her cheek. 'The smoothness of a woman's skin, the softness of her hair.' He gently twined a lock around his finger and held it to his face, inhaling the delicate fragrance. 'Finer than silk and more precious than gold.' Then, releasing it, he gently grasped her chin between thumb and forefinger and tilted her face up. 'Last but not least, the sweetness of her lips…'

Anna had been kissed before…but never like this. Never by a man whose touch was enough to make her long to release her tenuous hold on respectability. His mouth moved over hers slowly, thoughtfully, shattering her resolve and filling her with a desperate need to be loved. Surely she deserved this. Surely, after everything she'd been through, she was entitled to some small measure of love and affection for herself?

As he deepened the kiss, Anna raised her arms, twining them around his neck, wanting to be close and then closer still. His tongue teased her lips apart and heat poured through her body, flowing like molten fire through her veins. She moaned, feeling desire rise and want settle low in her belly. Ah, the sweet, sweet pleasure…

But the pleasure was bittersweet. Even as his arms tightened around her, Anna knew it could come to nothing. Barrington had no intention of marrying. He'd just told her as much. And if he wasn't willing to offer marriage, what they were doing now was not only wrong, it was self-destructive. She wanted more from him. Much more than he was willing to give. And in the end, she would be the one who walked away with her heart in ruins. And therein lay the true sadness of the situation. The one man with whom she could have foreseen a future was the one man with whom it would never be.

'Stupid, stupid, *stupid*!' she whispered, breaking free of his arms.

'Anna, what's wrong?' he asked huskily.

'What's wrong? *I'm* wrong,' she whispered. '*This* is wrong. Because right now, I'm no better than the foolish young women whose reputations I fight to protect.'

'That's ridiculous!'

'Is it? You just told me you have no intention of marrying, yet I allowed myself to be held in your arms and kissed like any cheap whore. What is that if not the height of stupidity?'

Anna flung at him. 'At least Mercy Banks was hopeful of a marriage resulting from her liaison with Lieutenant Blokker! You've made it clear there is no such happy ending in sight.'

His face darkened, his breathing heavy and uneven. 'I said that because I don't want you harbouring false hope. But it doesn't change the way I feel about you.'

'And is that supposed to make me feel *better*? Am I supposed to be comforted by the knowledge that you desire me, yet have no intention of offering marriage?' Anna shook her head. 'There is a word for that kind of relationship, Sir Barrington, and it is not flattering.'

'It was never my intention to compromise you, Anna,' he said quietly. 'I care too much for you.'

'My name is Lady Annabelle. And if you care so much for me, leave me alone!'

Without waiting for his answer, Anna picked up her skirts and fled. Angry tears blurred her vision as she ran down the length of the balcony. *Idiot!* She'd made a fool of herself again, allowing herself to be held and kissed as though she were a naïve young schoolgirl. She, who prided herself on knowing all the games and all the excuses, had let herself be taken in. And by doing so, Barrington had undermined everything she believed in. When she had allowed him to kiss her, she had wanted to believe that it meant something. But it was obvious to anyone with an iota of sense that it meant absolutely nothing. Sophisticated Barrington might be, but he was still a man, and when it came right down to it, he wanted the same thing as every other man. Pleasure without commitment. Love without obligation. The very things she kept warning her young ladies to avoid.

The breeze came up and, once again, Anna felt chilled. She hadn't stopped to fetch her wrap before venturing outside, but neither was she about to run back into the drawing room now.

Observant eyes would see the evidence of her tears, recognise the flush in her cheeks and put their own interpretation on the events—and nothing on earth was going to persuade her to tell anyone what had really happened.

She glanced back over her shoulder, wondering if Barrington had followed her. She didn't know whether to be relieved or disappointed when she saw that he hadn't. All right, so she'd made a mistake. It wasn't the first time she'd done so, but at least this time she was old enough to recognise it for herself. Barrington had made his feelings for her clear. The episode would not be repeated. From now on, she would treat him exactly the same way he treated everyone else. Coolly. Professionally. Without emotion. He would never make her cry again.

It was a good ten minutes before Anna felt calm enough to venture back into the house. Not by the drawing room through which she'd left. That would be far too embarrassing, especially knowing that Barrington had gone back in only a short time ago. Instead, she walked to the end of the balcony and, finding another set of glass doors, tried the handle. Thankfully, it was unlocked and pushing it open, she walked into a small study—only to stop and gasp in shock.

Her brother and Julia's maid were standing by the door, locked together in a passionate embrace. *'Edward!'*

At once, the pair sprang apart, but it was too late to disguise what they had been doing. The maid's dark hair had come down around her shoulders, her gown was in disarray and her lips were red and swollen.

Embarrassed, Anna looked away. Obviously, her brother wasn't above seducing pretty housemaids, whether they be his own or someone else's. Refusing to meet his eyes, she murmured, 'Excuse me', and then immediately made her way to the door. Edward said nothing, but she heard his mocking laughter following her through the door. She supposed she shouldn't have been surprised. Her brother had once again proven himself the immoral creature she believed him to be.

And what about you? the little voice nagged. *Are you so much better? So much more virtuous?*

Anna felt her face burn with humiliation. No, perhaps she wasn't. She kept remembering the passionate encounter she'd just shared with Barrington, the shameless manner in which she had allowed him to kiss her. Oh, yes, she'd *let* him kiss her. She wasn't about to lay the blame for what had happened entirely at his door. He was gentleman enough that if she had asked him to stop, he would have—but she hadn't done that. She'd wanted to know how it would feel to kiss him. To watch his head bend slowly towards her, and to feel his mouth close intimately over hers.

It had been everything she'd expected—and more.

But Barrington was no more likely to become her husband than Julia's maid was to become Edward's wife. They had both been indulging in impossible fantasies.

'Let he who is without sin cast the first stone…'

A sobering thought. As Anna made her way back to the drawing room, she realised that the proverbial stone would never find its way to her hand.

Chapter Seven

For the next few days, Barrington went around like a bear with a sore head. Unable to forget what had happened between Anna and himself at the baroness's dinner party, he was quick to anger and slow to unwind, because he knew he'd hurt her. And hurting her was the last thing he'd ever wanted to do.

He'd still been in the drawing room when Anna had finally returned, but she hadn't approached him again. She had remained coldly aloof, treating him as though he wasn't there. He wasn't surprised that she had left shortly after.

He'd left early as well, all pleasure in the evening gone. Upon returning home, he'd made for his study and downed a stiff glass of brandy, followed in quick succession by two more. But the potent liquor had done nothing to assuage his guilt, or to help him find escape in sleep. When the morning had come, he'd been as tired and as irritable as when he'd gone to bed.

Much as he was this morning, three days later, as he made his way to Angelo's Haymarket rooms for his ten o'clock appointment with the Marquess of Yew's son.

Barrington deeply regretted having made the appointment.

The last thing he felt like doing was teaching the finer points of fencing to the gangly nineteen-year-old son of a man he neither liked nor respected. However, he had given Yew his promise that he would show the boy a few things and he was a man who kept his word. All he could do now was hope the hour passed quickly and that he didn't do the boy an unintentional injury.

Unfortunately, Lord Bessmel was right when he'd said that word of the lesson—or demonstration—had spread. By the time Barrington arrived, the room was filled to overflowing with gentlemen of all ages, some carrying swords, some just there to observe. It was worse than he'd expected.

'Ah, Parker,' Lord Yew greeted him with a smile. 'Good to see you. Quite the turnout, eh? I vow you draw a larger crowd than Prinnie.'

'Perhaps because you put it about that this was to be a demonstration, rather than the private lesson we agreed to,' Barrington said.

'Really?' the marquess said lazily. 'I don't recall saying this was to be a lesson. But never mind, now you and Gerald have a suitable audience.'

'An audience that comes armed and ready to spar?'

The marquess smiled. 'You should be thanking me, Parker. You have your pick of opponents and since we both know there's not a man in the room who can best you, you're guaranteed to come out on top. Why not just have fun with it?'

'Because that's not what I do.' Barrington's jaw tightened. Unfortunately, they both knew this was something of a command performance. A 'small additional favour' in exchange for the marquess's silence over Peregrine Rand's affair with his wife. And while Barrington would normally have refused to play a part, all it took was the memory of the look on Anna's face when she had spoken of Rand's guilt to make him change his mind. He didn't particularly care about the other man's feelings, but he would have done almost anything to prevent hers being further injured.

'I've lived up to my side of the bargain, Yew. I trust you intend to do the same.'

'Are you questioning my integrity?' the marquess asked, peering down his long, patrician nose.

'No. But I know how angry you were with Rand and I don't want to think that all of this has been for naught.'

The marquess chuckled. 'I can assure you it has not. In point of fact, I wasn't really angry at all.'

Barrington's mouth tightened. 'I beg your pardon?'

The marquess's expression was remote as he gazed at the milling crowd. 'Rand is not the first man to make love to my wife, and, God knows, he won't be the last. Susan is voracious in that regard and while I enjoy sex as much as the next man, I am not inclined to engage in it as often as she might wish. So I turn a blind eye to her affairs. It flatters me to know that she is still beautiful enough to attract other men; it flatters her to know that she is desired by men younger than herself.'

No stranger to the unusual, Barrington was none the less bewildered by Yew's unexpected admission. 'Then why did you go to the trouble of persecuting him?'

The marquess's gaze narrowed. 'You really don't know?' When Barrington shook his head, Yew said in amusement, 'Because I was asked to.'

Having casually dropped his bomb, the marquess strolled away. Barrington, aware that the eyes of the room were on him, allowed nothing of his anger to show, knowing it would incite too many questions he wasn't prepared to answer. But he *was* angry. Furiously so. Someone had been playing with Peregrine Rand—and, by association, with him.

'Good m-morning, Sir B-Barrington,' Lord Gerald Fitzhenry said, coming up to him. 'It's v-very good of you to d-do this for me.'

Lord Yew's youngest son was a quiet, unassuming young man, who, though raised in an atmosphere of wealth and privilege, had managed to lose none of his good nature as a result. Perhaps the stutter kept him from becoming too arrogant, Barrington reflected. It wasn't a fashionable affectation, but a lifelong affliction, one the boy had desperately tried to overcome. But it was exacerbated by nerves and, given the unexpected turnout in the room, Barrington knew this morning's performance would be more difficult for Lord Gerald than usual. As such, he turned to face the lad with a reassuring smile. 'You show a great deal of promise, Lord Gerald. Perhaps I can point out a few things that will help you become an even better fencer.'

The boy's face shone. 'I would l-like that, very much.'

'Good. Then shall we take our positions?'

As Barrington led the way onto the floor, he was conscious of every eye in the room following him. He was acquainted with many of the gentlemen present and knew that some of them were decent fencers and were here for that reason alone. Having been taught by one of the finest swordsmen in France, Barrington possessed skills few others did and the chance to watch him spar today was an opportunity too good to miss.

But not all the gentlemen in the room had come simply to observe his technique. A movement at the far end of the room drew Barrington's attention. Looking up, he saw Hayle leaning against the wall, sword in hand. He had come to fight. He'd made that very clear.

Barrington had no intention of indulging him. Men like Hayle only wanted to prove their superiority over others. It was likely one of the reasons Hayle resented Rand's presence in the house. Though Rand offered no tangible threat, he was a competitor for the earl's attention, perhaps even for his affection. And if Hayle believed that Rand was his half-brother, he would naturally assume there was an affinity between his father and the other man he couldn't affect or control.

He wouldn't like that. Hayle needed to be seen as the only cock of the roost, and, so far, he had. Lord only knew what would happen if and when he found out otherwise.

An hour later, it was all over.

'You did well,' Barrington said, removing his mask and walking towards Lord Gerald. 'But you would do better if you kept your arm straight and the weight of your body on the front of your feet. You need to be able to move quickly around your opponent. Try to catch him off balance.'

'Yes, Sir B-Barrington,' said the grateful but sweating youth.

'And don't forget what I said about practising your double and triple feints. They'll stand you in good stead when you find yourself pushed to defend yourself. If you like, come round to the house and I'll lend you a couple of books that helped me when I was where you are.'

The boy's face shone as though he'd been given the keys to the kingdom. 'Thank you so much, Sir B-Barrington. I will t-try to d-do that.'

Barrington smiled and clapped the lad on the shoulder. He was glad now that he'd agreed to the lesson. Lord Gerald had turned out to be a surprisingly good swordsman and he was appreciative of the time he'd been given. He would benefit by what he'd learned today.

'Who's next then, Sir Barrington?' someone called out from the crowd.

Despite the cheers that greeted the man's words, Barrington shook his head. 'Sorry, gentlemen, the show's over. You can all go home now.'

Amidst the rumble of disappointment, another voice said,

'But this was to be a demonstration. Surely you wouldn't send everyone away without giving them what they really came here to see.'

Barrington's mouth compressed into a thin line. So, Hayle would challenge him publicly. A foolish thing to do. 'I'm sure there are others who would favour you with a match, Lord Hayle.'

'But it is with you I wish to engage, Sir Barrington,' Hayle said softly. 'Will you not stand and face me? I have been acknowledged a better than average fencer and would welcome an opportunity to go up against the best.'

Hearing the room suddenly fall silent, Barrington sighed. 'My purpose this morning was to instruct Lord Yew's son. It was not a general invitation to spar.'

'But surely there can be no harm in engaging in a friendly match,' Hayle said, advancing on to the floor. 'You are acknowledged the finest swordsman in England. Every one of us here could benefit by watching and learning, and I am willing to put myself forward as your student. If nothing else, I promise you a better match than the one you just concluded.'

'I was not engaged in a match,' Barrington reminded him. 'I was giving a lesson.'

'Then consider me your student and this an opportunity to improve *my* skills,' Hayle said with a grin.

Hearing murmurs in the crowd that were pushing for the match, Barrington sighed. Hayle obviously wasn't going to back down, especially if he felt he had the backing of his friends. And while he needed a lesson, Barrington knew it was in humility rather than sword play. 'Very well.' He walked back into the room and donned his mask. 'Prepare to engage.'

An excited murmur rolled through the crowd. Men who were halfway to the door quickly turned around and ran back into the room, aware that a far more entertaining show was about to get underway. Triumph and anticipation suffused Hayle's face as he stripped off his jacket and donned a mask.

In silence the two men made their way to the centre of the floor. After offering the traditional salute, they both took their opening stance.

It didn't take long for Barrington to assess his opponent's level of skill. Hayle was a showy fencer and quick on his feet, but there was no strategy to his play; at times, his technique was downright sloppy. Barrington easily scored five hits in a matter of minutes—and watched his opponent's face grow redder with each one.

'I think that's enough for one morning,' he said, starting to remove his mask.

'Stand your ground, sir!' Hayle shouted. '*I* will say when this is finished.' He took up his stance again. *'En guarde!'*

Barrington saw the anger in the other man's eyes and knew this could only end badly. He had no wish to humiliate Hayle in front of a room full of his friends and acquaintances, but neither was he about to throw the game in order to appease his vanity. 'Very well. We shall play one more bout and then call a halt. Does that meet with your approval?'

Hayle gave a terse nod and resumed his position.

The match recommenced. Barrington tried not to make the other man look bad, but the more desperate Hayle became, the more careless his play. He was caught flat footed several times and as the bout went on his moves became more and more erratic. After receiving his fourth hit, he shouted, 'Damn you, Parker!', then, abandoning sportsmanlike conduct altogether, he lunged, aiming the point of his sword directly at Barrington's throat.

Barrington heard the gasp from the crowd, but was already out of range. He stepped lithely to one side and quickly raised his own foil, deflecting the blow. Hayle spun around and was about to charge again when a voice rang out, 'Enough, Edward! Put down your sword! This engagement is at an end!'

The command vibrated with anger, but Hayle was oblivious, his attention riveted on his adversary. Barrington held his position, too, unwilling to trust his opponent. He risked a quick glance across the room and saw the Earl of Cambermere standing by the edge of the crowd. His face was red and he was shaking with barely suppressed fury. 'Did you not hear me, sir?' he called again. 'I said put down your sword!'

'I will not, sir!' His son's face was equally flushed. 'How dare you ask me to!'

'How dare *I*?' his father exploded, marching on to the floor. 'You impugn our family's honour by behaving in such a way and then have the audacity to question me? No, sir, I *will* not have it! If you cannot control your temper, find another sport in which to indulge.' He ripped the foil from his son's hand and threw it on the floor. 'This is a gentleman's game. You will apologise to Sir Barrington at once or I'll know the reason why!'

Barrington slowly lowered his sword, but remained in a ready position, prepared to fight if Hayle picked up his sword and re-engaged him. He had no idea what the man was going to do, but it was evident to everyone in the place that Hayle was beyond furious. In that moment, Barrington wasn't sure the man wouldn't turn on his own father and run him through.

Thankfully, the moment passed. As if realising he couldn't win and that his reputation would only suffer further by prolonging the encounter, Hayle took a step back, then bent to pick up his sword. 'I will not apologise to you this day or any other, Sir Barrington,' he said coldly. 'But I do regret that we were unable to finish our match. I look forward to the opportunity of doing so in the future.' Then, without so much as a second glance at his father, he snatched up his jacket and left.

Barely had the door closed before the level of conversation swelled to fill the silence. Barrington heard snippets of conversations, some questioning, many derogatory. Overall, none were particularly complimentary of Hayle's behaviour on the floor. Fencing was, after all, a gentleman's sport and what the audience had just witnessed was a display of anything but.

It was a few minutes before the earl was calm enough to speak. When he did, Barrington could see it was with considerable effort. 'Sir Barrington, pray accept my apologies on behalf of my son. His behaviour was unforgivable and I am truly sorry.'

'Apology accepted, but I suggest you do not take this too much to heart, Cambermere,' Barrington said. 'It is not uncommon for a young man to wish to win, especially in front of his peers.'

'If a man cannot win fairly or lose graciously, he should not play the game,' Cambermere snapped. 'I'm sorry you had to see that side of Edward's nature. He's always been a competitive lad, but of late, he has become even more so. I suspect it has much to do with Peregrine's arrival.' The earl sighed. 'They have not become the friends I'd hoped.'

'Was it realistic to believe they would?'

The earl glanced up, his sharp eyes meeting Barrington's. But Barrington's didn't waver, and, not surprisingly, the earl was the first to look away. 'Perhaps not. But they had to meet at some time.'

'Did they? I would have thought it possible for their paths never to have crossed. But it's a moot point now. You made the decision to invite Rand to London and must now deal with the consequences,' Barrington said.

'I know. But I was asked if I would have him,' the earl said quietly. 'And I wanted him to come.'

Used to gleaning meanings from things that were left unsaid, Barrington inclined his head. 'Then it really is none of anyone else's business.'

'Yet people choose to make it so,' Cambermere said fiercely.

Barrington's smile was tight. 'People like to pass judgement on matters that do not concern them. Some do it with the best of intentions, others do it without any care for the consequences at all. But as we said, the matter is private and one that concerns you and your family alone.'

Even has he said it, however, Barrington realised he had been given another glimpse into the complicated workings of Lord Cambermere's family, and it was evident from the morning's events that all was far from harmonious. There were simmering resentments, unsettled grievances, and barely restrained tempers. Instead of warming to the fact that his father had brought his godson to London, Hayle intended to do whatever he could to make Rand feel unwelcome—even to the point of humiliating him in front of his peers.

That much had become patently clear. As Barrington left the club and climbed into his carriage for the drive home, he *knew* who had asked the Marquess of Yew to make an example of Peregrine Rand. And, sadly, he also knew the reason why.

A full week passed during which Anna neither saw nor heard from Barrington. She told herself she didn't care, but as she lay awake in the dark hours of the night, she knew she was lying to herself. She *did* care. And it troubled her deeply that they had parted on such bad terms.

Try as she might, she couldn't forget the feeling of Barrington's arms closing warm and strong around her. She kept remembering the tenderness of his mouth as it moved with deliberate slowness over hers, sending shivers of delight up and down her spine.

It still made her quiver when she thought about it.

Still, longing for something you couldn't have was a complete waste of one's time, and there wasn't a doubt in Anna's mind that she would never have a life with Barrington. He'd made it perfectly clear that he had no intention of getting married, and it certainly wasn't her place to get him to change his mind. *She* was the foolish one if she thought there was any merit in that.

'Ah, Anna, there you are,' her father said, walking into the drawing room. 'Not going out this evening?'

'I'm not, but it would seem you are,' she said, rousing herself. 'Is that a new coat?'

To her amusement, her father's cheeks took on a ruddy hue. 'I decided it was time to spruce up my wardrobe. Doesn't do for a gentleman to let himself go and I haven't paid much attention to things like that since your mother died.' His voice softened. 'I had no reason to.'

'And have you a reason now?'

He glanced at her, suddenly looking boyish. 'Would it disturb you if I said I had?'

'Not at all. I like Julia very much.' Anna hesitated. 'I take it we are referring to Julia?'

'Of course!'

'Good. Then if she makes you happy, why should I object?'

'Oh, I don't know,' the earl grumbled. 'Some people say I'm past such things. That I'm too old for her. I am nearly twenty years her senior, after all.'

'If the lady does not mind, why should you? You don't

look your age, and she *is* past thirty, Papa. Old enough to make her own decisions.'

Her father glanced down at the floor. 'Your brother is not pleased by the association.'

Anna sighed. 'My brother is not pleased with anything at the moment so I shouldn't worry about it. Do what I do. Ignore him.'

'Can you not try to get along, Anna? He is your brother, after all.'

'Yes, he is, but I cannot bring myself to like the way he treats people; his attitude towards Peregrine is abysmal. He demonstrates a resentment that is neither warranted nor deserved. I've tried to tell him as much, but he refuses to listen.'

Her father looked as though he wanted to say something, but then he sighed, and shook his head. 'I blame myself for the distance between the two of you. Perhaps had I paid more attention to Edward when he was younger—'

'The fault is not yours, Papa,' Anna interrupted firmly. 'Edward has been given every opportunity to show himself the better man. He has wealth and position—there is absolutely no reason for him to be so harsh and judgemental towards others.'

'Perhaps he will change when he meets the right woman. It is my sincere wish that you both find suitable marriage partners and leave this house to start your own lives.' Her father regarded her hopefully. 'Is there no one for whom you feel even the slightest affection, my dear?'

Sadly, there was. But while Anna would have liked to give her father the reassurance he so desperately craved, there was no point in raising his hopes. Or hers. 'I fear not. But am I such a trouble to you that you would try to make me leave?'

'Far from it. You're a good girl, Anna. And though I don't

say it often, I am very proud of you. A week doesn't go by that some grateful mother doesn't tell me how helpful you've been in smoothing the troubled waters between her and her daughter. Most of them credit you with having saved their sanity!'

Surprised by the admission, Anna said, 'I can assure you they were exaggerating. None of the situations was that dire. It is simply easier for a stranger to see what needs to be done than someone who is intimately involved.'

'Nevertheless, they all told me how helpful you were and that I should be very proud to have such an admirable young woman for a daughter. And I told them all they were right.'

Her father was not normally an affectionate man, so when he suddenly bent down and pressed his lips to her forehead, Anna was deeply moved. 'Oh, Papa.' She got up and hugged him, aware that it had been a long time since she'd done so. If this was Julia's doing, she could only hope that the romance continued.

'Yes, well, I'd best be off,' the earl said gruffly. He stepped back and smoothed his jacket. 'Jul—that is, the baroness and I are having dinner together and then going on to the theatre.'

'Sounds lovely. Have a good time.'

'Yes, I expect we will.'

Anna smiled as she watched him go. It was strange to suddenly find herself in the role of the parent. She was well aware that she was the one who should have been going out for the evening and her father the one wishing her well. But there was only one man with whom Anna wished to spend time and the chances of that happening were getting slimmer all the time.

Troubled as he was by his feelings for Anna, Barrington knew he couldn't afford to ignore his other commissions. In particular, the locating of Miss Elizabeth Paisley. His belief that he'd found her at Baroness von Brohm's house had turned out to be false. He had gone back a few days later to question her, but the moment she'd walked into the drawing room, he'd known he was mistaken. The maid's name was Justine Smith, and though she was the right age, the right height, and had the right colour hair, her eyes were all wrong. Hers had actually been a pale misty blue where the Colonel had specifically told him that Elizabeth Paisley's were a deep, clear green. Barrington thought that in the candlelit room the night of the baroness's dinner party, he must have been mistaken when he'd thought the maid's eyes were green.

And so, at eleven o'clock that morning, Barrington resumed his investigation by visiting the premises of one Madame Delors, fashionable modiste. Dressmakers were privy to a great deal of gossip about wives and mistresses, and if someone had taken over the protection of Miss Elizabeth Paisley, there was a good chance Madame Delors would know about it.

Barrington stopped inside the door and glanced around the compact little shop. It was years since he'd had reason to frequent such an establishment, but it was evident they hadn't changed. Bolts of richly coloured fabric of every type and shade filled the shelves; dress patterns were tacked to the walls; and in the centre of the room stood a raised podium surrounded on three sides by mirrors.

'*Bonjour, monsieur,*' called a charmingly accented French voice. '*Puis-je vous aidez?*'

The owner of the establishment was small and compact, with dark inquisitive eyes and a head of flaming red hair that surely owed more to artifice than it did to nature. Still, it suited her well and Barrington doffed his hat. '*Bonjour, madame.* My name is Sir Barrington Parker. I would like to ask you a few questions, if you have a moment to spare.'

The woman's eyes narrowed, his comment obviously having put her on guard. 'What kind of questions, *monsieur*?'

'About a woman.' He purposely didn't use the term lady. 'One I believe you dressed in the not-too-distant past.'

'I dress many women, *monsieur*. You will 'ave to give me 'er name.'

'Miss Elizabeth Paisley. Petite, lovely, with dark brown hair and uncommonly pretty green eyes.'

The modiste evidenced neither surprise nor recognition. 'I do not think I know the lady.'

'Really? I was told you'd made clothes for her. Perhaps you dealt with the gentleman who bought them. A Colonel Tanner?'

Madame Delors obviously knew a thing or two about what one did and didn't say to gentlemen asking questions about other gentlemen's ladies. 'I 'ave many gentlemen coming to buy clothes for their ladies, *monsieur*. But they do not always give me the names of the ladies they are buying for.'

'No, I suppose not. And perhaps I should explain my interest in her.' Barrington walked farther into the store, cataloguing a thousand details in a single glance. 'Miss Paisley has recently come under my protection and it is my desire that she wear…a particular type of clothing when we are together. But because her taste and mine do not coincide, I am not willing to allow her to come in and order her own garments. Hence my reason for coming to see you today.'

'Ah, *je comprends*,' Madame Delors said. 'You would like me to make 'er a new wardrobe suitable only for you.'

'Precisely. Naturally, money is not a concern.'

'*D'accord*. What type of clothes do you wish to see 'er in, *monsieur*?'

'Intimate evening gowns, white and silver only, with simple but elegant lines. Semi-transparent. No heavy swatches of lace. No artificial birds or flowers. Nothing that will detract from the tantalising lines of her body.'

Madame Delors slowly began to smile. 'So the lady will not be wearing these gowns in public?'

'Definitely not,' Barrington said, resting both hands on the carved head of his ebony cane. 'They are for my eyes only. But I cannot tell you what size to make her garments because I do not have her measurements.'

Madame Delors smiled and nodded. 'I think I know the lady you speak of, *monsieur.*'

'Excellent. I trust it hasn't been too long since you last saw her? Women's figures do tend to change,' Barrington said, adding with a wink, 'a little more weight this week, a little less the following.'

Madame Delors's smile was reassuring. 'I saw 'er not all that long ago and 'er figure 'as not changed.'

'Good. Did she seem happy?'

The modiste gave a snort. 'The ladies come to me for clothes, *monsieur.* It is up to you gentlemen to make them 'appy!'

Barrington carefully hid a smile. Oh, yes, Madame Delors was definitely a shrewd business woman. He pulled three coins from his pocket. 'Do you happen to remember, on the occasion of her last visit,' he said, dropping one into her palm, 'if she collected the clothes herself or if you sent them somewhere else?'

The modiste's eyes locked on the shimmer of gold in her hand. 'I'm not sure…'

Barrington dropped another coin. 'Perhaps now?'

'The lady picked up the clothes,' the modiste said slowly, 'but I sent the bill to the gentleman.'

'To Colonel Tanner?'

When the modiste shook her head, Barrington dropped

the last of the coins into her palm. 'Then to whom did you send the bill?'

The modiste smiled and pocketed all three. 'Viscount Hayle.'

Anna was on her way to visit Julia when she remembered that Madame Delors had sent her a note asking her if she might be able to come in for a fitting. Anna had ordered two new morning dresses and a ball gown the previous week; although most fashionable modistes made house calls to their better clients, Madame Delors preferred to have her ladies come to her, saying it was easier to work in her showroom where she had everything necessary for making the required alternations.

Anna didn't mind. It was an excuse to get out of the house and it wasn't that much out of her way. But as she walked up to the front of the shop and went to open the door, it was suddenly opened from within and by none other than the man who had been uppermost in her mind for the last several days. 'Sir Barrington!'

'Good morning, Lady Annabelle. Lovely morning, isn't it?' He spoke without concern, as though it was the most natural thing in the world for her to find him coming out of a dressmaker's shop.

'Indeed. I feared it might come on to rain, but the skies have cleared up nicely.' Anna said, striving to match the casualness of his tone. There was only one reason a single gentleman frequented a shop like this, and it wasn't to keep abreast of the latest fashions. 'I've not seen much of you about town of late.'

'I have been otherwise occupied,' he said, drawing her aside as a mother and her three giggling daughters made to enter the shop. 'This is a very busy place.'

'Madame Delors is London's darling when it comes to

fashion,' Anna said. 'She boasts an illustrious clientele, most recently the Duchess of Briscombe.'

Barrington smiled. Given that Madame Delors also dressed the Duke of Briscombe's latest mistress, he knew better than to place too high a value on her level of exclusivity. 'Speaking of not being visible around town, how is Mr Rand going on?'

Anna sighed. 'Not at all well. He misses Lady Yew dreadfully; though I have told him she is not worthy of the heartache, I cannot dissuade him from his feelings.'

'Of course not. Love isn't logical,' Barrington said. 'It finds warmth in the most inhospitable of environments and draws comfort from the most uncomfortable of people. It demands neither explanation nor excuse. It is content merely to be.'

Anna stared at him in surprise. Such sentiments from a man like this? 'How is it you know so much about love, Sir Barrington, when, by your own admission, you have chosen to banish it from your life?'

'Who better than a man who has chosen to live without love when it comes to knowing how easily it takes root?' His grey eyes impaled her. 'I am not immune to the emotion, Lady Annabelle. I simply cannot give it a home. As I tried to explain to you the other night and failed so miserably.'

It was an olive branch, and Anna recognised it as such. But she knew she had to be cautious. The wounds from their last encounter were not yet healed. 'You didn't fail. It was simply not something I wished to hear. I do not believe any man or woman is truly happier spending their life alone.'

'It is not the natural order,' he agreed. 'God intended that man and woman should live together. It was the reason He gave them a home in Eden.'

'Until the serpent tempted Eve and they were cast out.'

Barrington smiled. 'As I recall, it was Adam's willingness

to eat the forbidden fruit that incurred God's wrath. Temptation has always been there. It is simply a man's ability to resist that sets him apart from others.'

'A philosopher,' Anna mused. 'I would not have thought it of you.'

'When you have learned as much about your fellow man as I have, you tend to become either jaded or philosophical. I choose the latter.'

Of course he would, Anna reflected, because he was that type of man. 'Well, I mustn't keep you here.' She gave him a falsely bright smile, aware that she was still no wiser as to why he was coming out of a busy modiste's shop now than she had been a few minutes earlier. 'I'm sure you have business elsewhere.'

'I do, my lady,' he murmured. 'But none, I can assure you, as pleasurable as this.'

As soon as she finished her business with Madame Delors, Anna headed for Julia's house and was pleasantly surprised to find Lady Lydia already there. She and Julia were partaking of tea and cakes and no doubt sharing the latest *on-dits* that were enlivening the drawing rooms of society. Her pleasure soon evaporated, however, when she discovered that it was not society's goings on that were keeping her two friends so occupied, but an unexpected crime.

'Your sapphire-and-diamond necklace has been *stolen*?' Anna said when Lydia informed her of it. 'But how? And when?'

'I have no idea how *or* when,' Julia admitted forlornly. 'I was dressing for the Buckerfields' reception last night and asked Smith to bring my jewellery case. When she did, I unlocked it to find the necklace gone.'

'But surely it has not been stolen,' Anna said. 'Perhaps just misplaced?'

Julia shook her head. 'I am very careful with my jewellery, Anna. I always take it off and put it immediately into the case. Then I lock it and put it away.'

'Is it possible someone took the key?'

'I keep the key on a ribbon around my neck. I only take it off to bathe and, sometimes, when I go to bed.'

'Have you questioned the servants about the matter?' Lydia asked. 'Your maid, for example. She would be in a perfect position to steal it.'

'I have spoken to all of them and to a person they denied knowing anything about it,' Julia said. 'And given how horrified they looked at the idea of something of mine being stolen, I can't imagine any of them actually *doing* it.'

'So what are you going to do?' Anna asked.

'I suppose I shall have to report it, but I don't like what I am going to have to tell whoever comes to take down the details.'

Lydia frowned. 'Why not?'

'Because the only people who knew about that necklace were the ones who came to my dinner party. I haven't worn it on any other occasion.' Julia bit her lip. 'What if one of my guests took it?'

'I don't believe that for a moment,' Anna said flatly. 'The people you invited were friends. They would never steal from you.'

'And if a thief did break into your house,' Lydia said, 'he would naturally go for the most valuable piece of jewellery he could find, don't you think?'

'So you believe this the work of a random criminal?' Julia asked doubtfully.

'I think it must have been,' Anna said. 'For one thing, what would any of your friends, or even other members of society, gain by taking the necklace? They would never be able to wear it in public.'

'But they could break it up and sell the stones individually,' Julia said. 'They might even be able to have some of the larger diamonds cut into smaller pieces.'

Anna didn't know what to say. It seemed impossible to imagine a thief breaking into Julia's house and stealing her favourite piece of jewellery, but it was even more incredible to think that someone she knew might have done it. 'I honestly don't know what to say, Julia,' she said at length. 'Other than that I am so very sorry this has happened.'

'Your father did warn me about keeping my jewels in a safe,' Julia said. 'But I truly did not think it would be necessary.'

'Have you hired any new servants?' Lydia asked. 'Or had people in the house who wouldn't normally be here. Chimney sweeps, for example, or trades people coming and going?'

'There have certainly been trades people in and out,' Julia admitted. 'The entire house is being redecorated and there has been a steady stream of paper hangers and plasterers coming through on a daily basis. But I instructed my maid to make sure they were never alone in my room and I have no reason to believe my orders were not followed. No, I shall have to hire a private investigator and ask him to look into it.'

'I say,' Lydia said, glancing at Anna. 'Why don't you get in touch with Sir Barrington Parker?'

'Sir Barrington?' Julia frowned. 'What would he know about matters like this?'

'You'd be surprised,' Anna murmured. 'However, he is very good at finding things out and I agree with Lydia that he is probably the best person to contact about this. He is nothing if not discreet.'

'Well, if you think that highly of him, I will certainly speak to him,' Julia said. 'I would very much like to have my necklace back. It has sentimental value far beyond any monetary value I could ever put upon it.'

'I don't think you will be disappointed with Sir Barrington's methods,' Lydia said, adding with a sly look at her friend, 'he has made quite an impression on Anna.'

'Lydia!'

But Julia was beaming. 'Has he really? How wonderful! I thought I detected something between the two of you at my dinner party, but when things became rather chilly later in the evening, I didn't want to appear rude by asking personal questions.'

'There is nothing between myself and Sir Barrington Parker,' Anna said quickly. 'I will not deny that he is…an attractive and engaging man—'

'Exceptionally so,' Lydia added.

'But we do not see eye to eye on several important matters and I doubt we will do so in the future,' Anna concluded. She reached for an iced *petit four*, hoping to distract the attention of the other two. 'However, I do stand by my assertion that he can be of help in this situation.'

Julia got up and crossed to the bell pull. 'Well, I am grateful for the recommendation, Anna, though I am sorry to hear there is nothing of a more romantic nature going on between the two of you. Sir Barrington really is such a handsome man. And that *voice*! I could listen to him all night. However, it is the heart that dictates these matters and, if you are not in love with him, there is nothing more to say. Ah, there you are, Smith. We'd like some fresh tea, please. This has gone cold.'

'Yes, ma'am.' The maid bobbed a curtsy, but something in the way she bent to pick up the tray drew Anna's attention. On her previous visits, the maid had served tea with both skill and efficiency. This time, however, she seemed slightly ill at ease. She also seemed thinner than she had on those earlier occasions, her black gown hanging loose around her shoulders. Anna thought it might have been a different girl, but upon closer inspection, she realised she was mistaken. The girl had the same heart-shaped face and the same dark brown hair pulled back in a tight chignon.

Perhaps she had things on her mind, Anna reflected as she reached for a macaroon. Servants had problems just like their employers. Maybe she'd recently fallen out with her gentleman friend, or a member of her family wasn't well. There were any number of reasons she might be looking poorly.

Still, it was none of her business, and as they waited for fresh tea to arrive, the conversation veered back to more congenial topics. Anna was simply thankful they had moved away from the subject of Sir Barrington Parker. His name was coming up far too often in conversation for her liking, and she wasn't at all happy at hearing that Julia thought there was something going on between them. She'd even been tempted to correct Julia's phrasing of her recommendation of Barrington, by saying it wasn't Sir Barrington of whom she thought so highly, but, rather, his skills as an investigator.

Unfortunately, that wasn't true either and when it came right down to it, Anna preferred not to lie to Julia. But she had to stand firm when it came to her feelings for him. She had to accept his reasons for keeping her at arm's length and move on. She had every intention of marrying one day; while she hoped it would be for love, she was intelligent enough to know that the luxury of feelings did not always accompany a proposal of marriage.

As to whether or not Sir Barrington Parker ever married, that was really no concern of hers.

Chapter Eight

Barrington received a visit from Baroness von Brohm at half past ten the following morning. She was shown into the gold salon, whereupon she briefly told him about the theft of her necklace and of her sincere hopes for its recovery. He then asked a series of pointed questions, which she answered to the best of her ability. An hour later, he stood by the window and reviewed everything she had told him. He didn't have a lot to go on, but he had already concluded that there were four possible answers to the question of who might have stolen her necklace.

The first was that the jewel thief who had been plaguing London for the past three months had returned and struck again. He would have had a relatively easy time getting into the baroness's house. During his questioning, Barrington discovered that she often slept with her window open and that her bedroom was located at the rear of the house on the second floor, close to a small clump of trees. It was possible that someone had climbed a tree to the second floor, gained access through the open window and, after taking the baroness's necklace, had managed to escape the same way.

The stumbling block was that in order to get into the baroness's jewellery box, the thief would have had to get at the key the baroness kept on a ribbon around her throat. Barrington doubted any thief would have been able to remove the ribbon, steal the necklace, and make his escape, all without disturbing the baroness's slumber.

The second option was that a servant had taken it. This was certainly the more logical answer. The baroness employed a butler, a housekeeper, three maids, and a parlour maid, all of whom would have had access to her room at times when she was not present. But again, they would have needed the key to open the locked box, and, according to the baroness, the box showed no signs of a forced entry. It had been neatly opened and closed.

The third possibility was that a visitor to the house had taken the necklace. Barrington thought this the least likely of the four, but experience had taught him that it was often the *least* likely suspect who actually committed the crime. In this case, it meant that one of the many people who had paid calls on the baroness had gone up to her room and taken the necklace. But again, there was the matter of the key.

Which left the fourth and most likely possibility—that the baroness had simply misplaced the necklace. That kind of thing happened all the time. It explained why the jewellery case hadn't been tampered with and why the key hadn't gone missing. It also cleared any visitors to the house of the theft.

Unfortunately, the baroness had stated most emphatically that she had *not* misplaced the necklace and that she was in the habit of locking her jewellery away immediately after taking it off. The practice had been instilled in her by her late husband.

So where did that leave him? What was he missing with regard to the stolen necklace?

'Excuse me, Sir Barrington,' Sam said from the doorway. 'Lord Richard Crew is here.'

'Thank you, Sam. Be so good as to show him in.'

Barrington was relieved to have caught Crew at home. He'd sent a note to him immediately following the baroness's departure, but given his friend's sexual proclivities, one never knew where he was or what state he might be in. A fact confirmed when Crew walked into the room, looking slightly dishevelled and none too bright-eyed.

'You'd better have a damned good excuse for this, Parker,' he said testily. 'I was enjoying a rather delicious breakfast in bed when your note arrived.'

'Forgive me,' Barrington said, grinning, 'but I'm sure the lady won't mind drinking champagne alone.'

'Probably not, but I'm not sure I *want* her drinking it alone. I was rather enjoying what she was doing *before* your letter arrived, demanding that I present myself at your door.'

'It was not a demand. And I did say at *your* convenience.'

'Hah!' Crew said, collapsing into a chair. 'We both know that at *my* convenience really means at *yours*. So what was so urgent that it couldn't wait until later in the day?'

'Two things. I need you to make some discreet inquiries on behalf of a lady.'

'A lady?' He brightened. 'Always ready to be of service. Do I know her?'

'Baroness Julia von Brohm.'

'Ah, the merry widow. Yes, we were introduced at some gathering, though the name of my host and hostess escapes me at the moment. What has happened to the poor lady that she requires your services?'

'A rather magnificent sapphire-and-diamond necklace was stolen from her home a few days ago. I want you to keep your ear to the ground for any information that might come to light about it.'

'Do you think it's our jewel thief again?' Crew asked.

'It's possible, but I need to check out all avenues. I'll be questioning the baroness's staff over the next few days, but if someone's stolen the necklace with a view to selling it, you might catch wind of it before I do.'

'Wouldn't be the first time,' Crew agreed, putting his hands behind his head. 'I'll drop in at a few of the clubs and see if anyone's suddenly turned up flush.'

'You might want to check the hells as well. A necklace like that would go a long way towards settling a man's debts,' Barrington suggested.

'No doubt. What's the second request?'

Barrington opened the top drawer of the desk and took out an envelope. 'I need you to do some digging into an old family tree. The specifics are in the letter. Read it at your leisure—'

'But report back to you as soon as possible,' Crew said in a dry voice.

'Expedience is always the order of the day. By the by, how did your meeting go with the lovely Rebecca?' Barrington enquired as his friend got up to leave. 'Has she agreed to marry you yet?'

'No, though I expect an acceptance very soon. As I was leaving, Lady Yew brushed her hand against a rather sensitive part of my anatomy—and I'm quite sure it wasn't by accident.'

Barrington burst out laughing. 'I *beg* your pardon?'

'You needn't sound so shocked; I am more or less the right age; given that she is looking for a replacement for Peregrine Rand, she obviously thought to see if I was interested.'

'Even though you have been paying court to her daughter?'

'Perhaps she wants to bed me before her daughter gets the chance.' Crew's eyes flashed wickedly. 'Make sure I have all the necessary equipment.'

'As if your reputation would leave anyone in doubt,' Barrington said cynically. 'How did Lady Rebecca take to her mother's interest in you?'

Crew slowly began to smile. 'If I don't miss my guess, the next time I call, the dear girl will be pushing the butler aside in her haste to throw open the front door and give me her answer—which I have every expectation of being yes. After all, if she doesn't, she knows damn well whose bedroom I *could* be spending my nights in!'

Anna trotted Ophelia through Hyde Park, alert for the gentleman to whom she had sent a hastily scrawled note, asking that he meet her. It had been a bold gesture, and secretly she feared Barrington might soon tire of these imperious messages. But she had to know if Julia had been to see him and, if so, what he thought the chances of recovering the stolen necklace were. While she might not approve of or agree with his marital aspirations or lack thereof, Anna did believe that if anyone could find the missing necklace it was he.

Thankfully, he appeared within moments, sitting tall and easy in the saddle, his coat as black as that of the spirited thoroughbred he so easily controlled. His hands were strong and steady on the reins; in spite of her best intentions, Anna felt a quiver of anticipation at the thought of being close to him again. She'd told herself over and over that there was no hope of anything developing between them, but that didn't take away from the strength of her attraction for him. The way he looked at her, without the lewdness or speculation she saw so often in other men's eyes, made her feel as though she mattered, both as a woman and as a person. And the memory of the one kiss they had shared still caused her heart to quicken…

She really had to get over this. It was bad enough that thoughts of him kept filling her mind, but this silly racing of her pulse every time she saw him was ridiculous! It was imperative that she appear as cool as he was. As impervious to his charm as he so obviously was to hers.

He raised his hand and then put his horse to a brisk trot in her direction. Anna used the time to bring her breathing under control.

'Lady Annabelle,' he greeted her, drawing to a halt.

'Good afternoon, Sir Barrington. Thank you for agreeing to meet with me.'

'To quote your father, the opportunity to spend time with a beautiful woman should never be missed.'

And now she was blushing again. *So much for being impervious.* 'Forgive me for being so inquisitive, but I was anxious to know if Julia had been to see you?'

'As a matter of fact, we spent time together this morning.'

'And? Do you think you will be able to help her?'

'I will do what I can, of course, but there are many questions that need to be asked and several possible leads to follow. It will take time.'

'But there may not *be* that much time!' Anna cried. 'Given the size of the stones, Julia said the thief might decide to take the necklace apart, or to have the gems cut smaller.'

'That possibility does exist,' Barrington acknowledged. 'The jewels are too large to sell as they are, unless whoever took the necklace intends to sell it outside London. If they have contacts on the Continent, it could easily be sold intact in Paris or Brussels.'

Anna bit her lip. 'Julia will be heartbroken. That necklace means the world to her.'

'I know and am making inquiries. But whoever took the necklace isn't going to make it easy for us to find him.'

Anna ran her gloved hand over the smoothness of the mare's neck. 'Nevertheless, I'm glad you're involved. I know you'll find who did this and bring him or her to justice.'

He raised an eyebrow. 'Her?'

'Why not? Desperation knows no gender. A woman who needs money to feed her family is just as likely to steal as a man.'

'But it is more often a man who will take that kind of risk. A woman on her own is more likely to avail herself of...other avenues.'

'Such as prostitution?' she said quietly.

He met her regard evenly. 'Yes. Or, if she is attractive enough, becoming the mistress of a wealthy man. However, I would caution you not to let your thoughts dwell on this, Lady Annabelle. It will not result in the culprit being brought to justice any faster and will only serve to cause you needless worry. I will advise you of whatever results I am able to find as soon as I have them.'

'Thank you.' Anna wished she could think of something else to say, but she didn't know how or where to start. She usually found conversation so easy, but with him it was always a challenge. 'Well, I suppose I had best be—'

'Lady Annabelle!'

Hearing the shrill feminine hail, Anna turned to see a carriage approaching and smiled when she recognised the mother and daughter sitting within. 'Mrs Banks, Miss Banks, good afternoon,' she said.

'Lady Annabelle, I thought it was you and I simply had to come and tell you the news,' Mercy Banks said, jumping up as the carriage drew to a halt.

'Mercy, for goodness' sake, sit down!' her mother admonished. 'A lady does not bounce up and down like a hoyden!

You must forgive my daughter, Lady Annabelle. She has become quite uncontrollable of late.'

'Because I am so happy, Mama,' Miss Banks said, and though she promptly sat down, her joy could not be contained. 'I am to be married, Lady Annabelle, and it is all thanks to *you*!'

Aware of Barrington's eyes on her, Anna laughed and said, 'On the contrary, I think you played a considerable part in the production. I take it your intended is Lieutenant Blokker?'

'Of course.' Mercy's face assumed that dreamy aspect Anna had come to associate with young men and women in love. 'There could never be anyone else. He proposed to me at home in the garden yesterday and naturally I said yes.'

'Then I am very happy for you. When is the wedding to be?'

'The date has not yet been set,' Mrs Banks said proudly. 'We have been invited to dine with the young man's parents in Hanover Square to go over the details.'

'Hanover Square,' Barrington murmured so that only Anna could hear. 'Very nice.'

Anna only just refrained from rolling her eyes. 'Mrs Banks, Miss Banks, may I introduce Sir Barrington Parker.'

The gentleman gallantly doffed his beaver. 'Ladies.'

'Sir Barrington,' Mrs Banks said graciously. 'I believe I saw you in conversation with Lady Annabelle at Lady Montby's reception.'

'You did, though it was only in passing since we had not been formally introduced at that time,' Sir Barrington said smoothly. 'Unlike your daughter, I was not fortunate enough to have someone make the introduction for me.'

'Happily, it seems to have been made in the interim. And we will, of course, be sending Lady Annabelle an invitation. We are happy to see her bring an escort,' Mrs Banks said. 'I expect the affair to be quite grand.'

This time, Anna knew better than to look at the man beside her. 'Thank you, Mrs Banks. That would be very nice.'

'Well, we must be off. There is so much to do between now and the wedding, whenever it turns out to be. Good afternoon, Lady Annabelle, Sir Barrington.'

'Goodbye, dear Lady Annabelle!' Mercy called as the carriage pulled away. 'And thank you again!'

In the silence that followed, Anna heard Barrington chuckle—and felt her cheeks burn. 'I would have preferred that you not be a witness to that.'

'Why not? I found it highly diverting,' the odious man said. 'And you should be proud. You managed to get Miss Mercy Banks engaged, though in truth I'm not sure who is the more pleased: the mother or the daughter.'

'I venture to say they are equally delighted for entirely different reasons.'

'True. Hanover Square does have a very nice ring,' Barrington murmured. 'But I've no doubt it *will* be a splendid affair.' He turned to her and smiled. 'The wedding breakfast alone will be reason enough to attend.'

'Good. Since you *will* be attending, at least you can be assured of a good meal.'

'I beg your pardon?'

'Well, you didn't think I was going to this on my own, did you?' Anna enquired innocently. 'You are as much to blame for their engagement as I, so it seems only fair that you should accompany me to the celebration.'

It was an audacious statement and Anna held her breath as she waited for him to answer. What had got into her? A lady *never* asked a gentleman—it simply wasn't done. Fortunately, Barrington didn't seem to mind. Ever so slowly, he began to smile. 'It would be my honour to escort you, Lady Annabelle. Assuming, of course, that I am not engaged in resolving the convoluted lives of others on that particular day.'

Suppressing a ridiculous desire to laugh, Anna gathered the reins in her hands and lightly flicked her crop against the mare's withers. 'I trust, Sir Barrington, that on this most auspicious occasion, the convoluted lives of others will just have to go on without you.'

As well as involving Lord Richard Crew in the investigation of the baroness's necklace, Barrington made his own enquiries in a part of town the gentry seldom frequented. He wore clothes specifically chosen for the occasion: a hacking jacket a few years out of date, an old pair of topboots, scuffed and in need of a polish, and a beaver, too wide at the brim and looking decidedly worn. The effect was the appearance of a man down on his luck. One who was right at home with the patrons of the Rose and Thistle. Only the elegance of the ebony cane hinted at the presence of wealth, but Barrington wasn't about to venture into London's seedier neighbourhoods without it. The specially constructed walking stick had saved his life on more than one occasion.

He strolled into the inn at a few minutes past midnight and caught the eye of the landlord standing behind the bar. Jack Drummond nodded, drew two shots of whisky and, after a brief whisper in the barmaid's ear, led the way into a quiet back room. Barrington kept a watchful eye on the bar's patrons, but no one paid any attention to them as they passed. When they reached the small room at the end of the hall, Jack closed and locked the door behind them.

'Been a while, Sir Barrington,' the burly man said. He set the glasses down on a table and pulled up a couple of chairs. 'Everything all right with you?'

'Can't complain, Jack, can't complain.' Barrington leaned his cane against the back of the chair and sat down. 'You?'

'Never been better. Had a baby since last I saw yer and a

right little beauty she is. Don't know how with an ugly mug like me for a father.'

Barrington grinned. 'I suspect Molly had a lot to do with it. Is she well?'

'Aye, sir, she's fit as a fiddle.' Jack's face lit up like a child's on Christmas morning. 'Still happy to put up with me and that's saying something. Best day's work I ever did marrying that woman and it was only thanks to you I got the chance.'

Barrington shook his head. 'If you hadn't knocked the knife out of that Irishman's hand, I wouldn't be sitting here tonight.'

'And if *you* hadn't come running round that corner, shouting to wake the dead, that knife would have been buried in my chest clear up to the hilt.' Jack glanced at the ebony cane and smiled. 'Still carrying it, I see.'

'Never go out without it.' Barrington smiled. 'Some things are best not left to chance.'

'Can't argue with that. But you didn't come all the way down here to reminisce about the old days. What can I do for you?'

'I need you to keep an eye out,' Barrington said without preamble. 'A rather spectacular necklace was recently stolen from a lady's house and it's possible that over the next while, whispers about the necklace, or the necklace itself, may make its way into your inn. I want to know who's doing the talking and what they're saying.'

'I can do that,' Jack said with a nod. 'What kind of jewels are we talking about?'

'Sapphires and diamonds. Fairly large stones, so the thief may try to sell it by the piece. Or, if he leaves it whole, he may try to smuggle it out of the country. I'd appreciate you letting me know if you hear anything.'

'You've got my word on that, Sir Barrington,' Jack assured him.

Barrington pulled an envelope from his pocket. 'Use this if you think it will help. Otherwise, spend it on Molly and that new baby.'

Jack took the envelope, but didn't open it. 'You're a good man, Sir Barrington. I'll let you know if I hear anything. Chances are, if something that valuable's making its way around London, I'll hear about it sooner or later. Shall I contact you in the usual way?'

Barrington nodded as he tossed back his brandy. 'It's worked well in the past.' He stood up and held out his hand. 'Thanks, Jack.'

'A pleasure doing business, Sir Barrington,' Jack said, likewise getting to his feet. 'You can be sure if that necklace or any of its parts makes it down this neck of the woods, you'll be the first to know.'

Anna had intended to tell her father about Julia's necklace as soon as she'd heard about its theft, but one thing led to another and the days passed without her having a chance. Consequently, when she and her father finally sat together in the breakfast parlour a few days later, Anna wasn't surprised to find out that he already knew.

'Julia informed me of it over supper at the Hastings' last night,' the earl said, cutting into a slice of ham. 'Shocking turn of events. I told her to contact the authorities, but she informed me she had already engaged Sir Barrington Parker to look into the matter and that she'd done so on your recommendation.' He sent Anna a speculative glance. 'I thought you didn't like the man.'

'I do not like or dislike him. In truth, it was Lady Lydia's suggestion that Julia get in touch with him,' Anna said. 'I merely agreed that he would be a good choice because he was bound to be more discreet than most. He also seems to be privy to a great deal of information not known to the general public.'

'And how have *you* come to know that?'

Aware that her father was watching her a little too intently, Anna said casually, 'During my dealings with one of the young ladies whose life I was endeavouring to fix, I met Sir Barrington and he was able to provide me with information that was extremely valuable in securing the lady's happiness.'

'I see. So you've spent considerable time talking with him, then?'

'Not considerable, no.' Anna set her knife down. 'We met at Lady Montby's, spoke briefly at Julia's dinner party, then chanced to encounter one another in the park the other day.' She decided not to tell her father about the visit she had paid to the baronet's house over Peregrine's affair with Lady Yew. That would spark far too many awkward questions. 'It was then he informed me of his meeting with Julia.'

'I see.'

Anna sighed. 'Why is it gentlemen say that all the time, when I am quite convinced none of you see anything at all!'

'Oh, I don't know.' She was annoyed to see her father smile in that knowing kind of way. 'I think I'm beginning to see *some* things very clearly indeed.'

Disappointingly, very little information surfaced about the stolen necklace. London's underworld kept to itself, and those who were foolish enough to divulge what they knew suffered a noticeably shortened life. Consequently, neither Jack Drummond nor Lord Richard Crew were able to provide Barrington with the information he needed.

Closer to home, he questioned each member of the

baroness's personal staff, but turned up nothing of use. They were all extremely upset by the nature of the theft, but none were able to offer anything that pointed him in the right direction.

It was discouraging to say the least, but he still had one more avenue to explore. Knowing that gentlemen who imbibed too freely often tended to say far more than was wise, Barrington paid a late-night visit to one of his old haunts. The hell was known for high stakes' play and the young bucks who flocked to it were willing to risk all on the turn of a card.

Barrington knew many of them personally. Heirs to great estates who frittered away the years engaged in various debaucheries while waiting for their fathers to die. Restless second sons with little expectation of inheriting anything, but with allowances generous enough to allow them to gamble or drink their way into serious trouble. And the inevitable hangers-on. Those who clung to the coat-tails of the wealthy with either enough money or enough charm to make them tolerable.

Barrington knew them all. He had watched both his father and his grandfather drink themselves into oblivion and had sworn as a young man that he would never follow in their footsteps. As a result, for the first time in over two hundred years, the Parker name bore not a trace of scandal. And while his own line of work had not made him the most popular man in London, at least he knew he was doing what he could to make life better for those who were deserving of it.

But at what cost to yourself?

The question was unsettling. As was the fact that of late, he'd been asking it of himself more and more often. At one time, he had been able to ignore it because he had honestly believed there was nothing he would rather be doing, that there was no cost to exposing the dregs of London society.

But that wasn't true any more. His happiness was the cost. The warmth of a woman's love was the cost.

Anna was the cost—and the realisation hit him hard. Until recently, he hadn't allowed himself to say it. Even to think it. But ever since that night on the balcony, he realised that his feelings had begun to change. The idea of spending his life alone wasn't so appealing any more—and it was all because of Anna. He wanted to go to sleep with her curled up next to him, then to wake up and see her smiling at him. He wanted to lose himself in the lush warmth of her body and to experience the passion he knew he would find in her arms. Passion a few short minutes on a balcony had given him a tantalising glimpse of.

But, out of habit, he had put her off, telling her that he had no intention of marrying and using what he did as an excuse to keep her at a distance.

For the first time in his life, he wished he hadn't needed to.

Around one o'clock in the morning, after three hours of hard play, Barrington was getting ready to call it a night when one of the doxies came over to him and sat down in his lap. Her faded gown left little to the imagination and, as she draped her arm around his neck, Barrington was treated to a glimpse of full, rounded breasts and a long, slim neck. 'Sir Barrington Parker?' she whispered.

He looked up into a face that was still pretty and nodded. 'Yes.'

'Then somebody wants to see you.'

Surprised at not being propositioned, he said, 'What makes you think I want to see him?'

'Beats me, love, but he said he'd wait for you in the garden and not to be long about it. Said he had something to tell you.'

As she slowly straightened, she ran her hand up his chest, her fingers lingering for a moment at his throat. His shirt was open, his cravat long since having been shed. As she stroked the warm bare skin, she watched his face for signs that her attempts at seduction were succeeding. When she saw none, she sighed and moved away, obviously on the prowl for more lucrative business.

Barrington collected his winnings, picked up his cane and slowly got to his feet. It never paid to appear anxious in a place like this. Though most of the patrons were either drunk or unconscious, one never knew when watchful eyes might be following one's movements. Instead, he sauntered past the other tables, stopping to pretend an interest in one of the games, before heading towards the door.

The light grew dim as the corridor narrowed and the sounds of conversation and laughter faded away. Barrington concentrated on moving carefully now, senses alert for danger. Someone had gone to the trouble of following him here and of trying to make contact. He had no idea whether it was friend or foe, but experience had taught him well. The last thing he needed was an ambush by someone hiding in a darkened doorway.

Fortunately, no such attack came to pass and when he finally reached the unlocked back door, he stepped out into a small patch of heavily overgrown garden and looked around. For a moment, he saw nothing. Then, as his eyes adjusted to the gloom, he saw the faint outline of a man standing against the stone wall at the far end of the garden.

'Sir Barrington Parker?' The man's voice was coarse, the accent more north country than London.

'Yes.' Barrington slowly walked forwards. 'Who are you and how did you know to find me here?'

'Who I am doesn't matter. What I've got to say does. I understand you're looking for a necklace.'

Barrington stopped dead. So, the rats were finally making their way to the surface. He wished the light was such that he could put a face to the voice, but the man had positioned himself in such a way that his features remained in complete obscurity. 'What do you know about that?'

'Just what I was told to pass along.'

Barrington raised one eyebrow in surprise. So, the man was merely a conduit, a lackey of the person in possession of the necessary information. 'Does your master require payment for his information?'

'No. Said it was enough that the guilty party be exposed for what he'd done. A settling of an old score, if you will.'

Barrington smiled. A vendetta. How Italian. 'Very well,' he said slowly. 'What can you tell me?'

It took three minutes. Three minutes and Barrington had his name. A name he would have spent an eternity looking for and never found. After that, his informant slipped quietly into the night, the creaking of the back gate the only indication he'd ever been there.

Barrington stood alone in the silence of the neglected garden. He was used to hearing lies and rumours. Used to sifting through mounds of trivial information until he stumbled upon that one piece that might be of value. And he could honestly say there were only a handful of times in his entire life when he had truly been surprised by the nature of a revelation. This was one of those times.

But as he turned and slowly headed back into the house, he realised he wasn't only surprised, he was deeply apprehensive. The line he walked now was one of the finest he ever would. More than the reputation of a gentleman was at stake. Personal boundaries were about to be crossed. Feelings would be trammelled into the dust, beliefs battered, and impressions irrevocably altered.

He had the name of his thief. And, if his identity proved true, Barrington knew he risked losing everything that had come to matter in his life.

Chapter Nine

Having just returned from a drive in the park, Anna was about to enter the house when she heard the clatter of carriage wheels in the street behind her. Aware that it was slowing down, she turned in time to see a matched pair of greys pulling an elegant black cabriolet draw to a halt in front of the house. Moments later, Sir Barrington stepped out, ebony cane in hand, his black beaver glistening in the afternoon sun.

'Sir Barrington,' Anna said, cursing the tiny catch in her voice. 'This is a surprise.'

He looked as startled as she, but there was something else in his expression she couldn't quite define. 'Lady Annabelle. I thought you would be out paying calls.'

'In fact, Lord Andrews has just returned me home from a drive in the park.'

'Andrews!' His countenance darkened. 'You allowed him to take you driving?'

'I did,' Anna said, caught off guard by the sudden intensity in his voice. 'He has been after me for weeks to allow him to show me his new pair of blacks, so when the weather turned fine this morning, I decided I would allow him to do so.'

'And did you enjoy your drive?'

Remembering several rather alarming moments when the horses had been going too fast for safety, Anna was tempted to tell him no, but pride demanded a different answer. 'It was…invigorating.'

He snorted. 'Invigorating. Andrews is a mediocre whip at best and notorious for buying troublesome animals. He has an inflated opinion of his ability to train them, so when a seller tells him a horse is bad tempered, Andrews tells them they're not using the right methods of control. But most of the time, he ends up selling the horses back to whoever he bought them from and always at a loss.'

'I admit, they were a touch wild,' Anna conceded, 'but for the most part, he seemed able to keep them under control.'

'Nevertheless, I would ask you not to drive out with him again. He is not a man I would encourage you or any other young woman to spend time with.'

Anna bristled. Having already made up her mind not to see Lord Andrews again, the warning was unnecessary, but she resented Barrington's belief that he had the right to tell her who she should and should not see. 'I think you are too hard on the gentleman, Sir Barrington. He was very pleasant to me. Attentive to my wishes and interested in what I had to say.'

'What do you know about the viscount, Lady Annabelle?' Barrington asked softly.

'Not a great deal,' she was forced to confess. 'He told me his wife died two years ago and that he has three married sisters he seldom sees.'

'He also has four children ranging in ages from six to thirteen and he is looking for a new wife to take care of them.'

'He cannot be looking very hard,' Anna said. 'I've spoken to several young ladies who told me of their desire to become the next Lady Andrews, but apparently, he offered them no encouragement whatsoever.'

'Yet he seemed interested in you?'

'Actually, no. During the course of our drive, he asked me a great many questions about Miss Dora Preston.'

'Miss Preston?' Barrington said quietly. 'Of course. A painfully shy young woman of nine and twenty, who now finds herself in a precarious financial situation as a result of her parents' death. She is neither pretty nor accomplished and has received no offers of marriage. Furthermore, as an only child, she has no brothers or sisters to whom she can apply for help.'

'Then why, given all that, should you not be pleased to hear that Lord Andrews is interested in her?' Anna asked, thinking it a logical question—until she saw the look on his face. 'Don't tell me you know something about him as well?'

'I'm afraid I do. And it is not the kind of information that recommends him to *any* woman, let alone one who is alone in the world and so terribly naïve.'

'Dare I ask why not?'

'Because Lord Andrews can be…unstable.'

'Unstable.'

'He has been known to suffer from hallucinations and bouts of paranoia.'

'The poor man. Is he not well?'

'Not when under the influence of opium, no.'

'Opium! *Lord Andrews?*'

'For obvious reasons, it is not something the man publicises,' Barrington said. 'It started out as a medical treatment for some unspecified condition several years ago, but over time, he grew addicted to its more…pleasurable aspects. It is the reason he has no communication with his sisters. They are afraid for the welfare of his children when he is under the influence. I know for a fact that the eldest sister has tried to remove the children from his care, but has been unsuccessful in her attempts. Marrying someone like Miss Preston leads me to believe he is looking for the kind of wife who will not ask questions. One who will be grateful just to have been asked and who has no family to worry about her. With such a wife in place, Andrews's sisters won't have a hope of taking the children away from him.'

Dear Lord, it was enough to make her feel ill. Anna couldn't believe that the man with whom she had just parted company would be the type to take opium, but neither could she dismiss it out of hand. Not when it was Barrington who had made her aware of it.

'If what you say is true, I must warn Miss Preston not to entertain his suit,' Anna said quickly. 'Though for the life of me, I cannot imagine what reason I am going to give her. She knows what her chances of marrying are. She'll never have another opportunity like this.'

'I have every confidence you will find a convincing explanation. If not, you can always tell her the truth. For her sake, she must not consider his offer. Nor must any other young lady for that matter.'

'I cannot protect them all!'

'I know. Fortunately, Andrews will likely retire to the country before the end of the Season, especially if he meets with no success in London. He will probably marry a woman from the local village. He does not look to marry well, only quickly.'

Anna nodded, aware that once again she was in his debt. 'Thank you for the information, Sir Barrington. Though I do not feel better for having learned of it, I know it will help Miss Preston in the long run.'

'There are, unfortunately, many men like Andrews in

society. Hallucinatory drugs will always hold an appeal for that sort of man.'

Aware that they were still standing on her front step, Anna said, 'Forgive me, I have rudely kept you out here talking. Would you like to come in?'

'Only if your father is at home.'

'I don't believe he is,' Anna said, wondering at the nature of his call. Surely the Marquess of Yew hadn't some further issue with Peregrine. 'He informed me when I left with Lord Andrews that he would be out until later this evening.'

'Then perhaps I will try again later.' He touched the brim of his beaver, then turned to go.

'Sir Barrington?' When he stopped and turned back, Anna said, 'Have you had any luck finding Julia's necklace?'

His expression didn't change, but something in his eyes hardened. 'No, though I have recently been made aware of information pertaining to the theft. But it is nothing I am at liberty to share at this time. Good afternoon, Lady Annabelle.'

With that he walked back down the path and climbed into his waiting carriage. The driver flicked the whip and the horses set off.

Anna walked into the house, unable to shake a feeling of gloom. Finding out the truth about Lord Andrews had not been pleasant and she made a promise to herself to send a note to Miss Preston that very afternoon. But it wasn't only that. Barrington had called to see her father and in finding him absent had made it perfectly clear that he had no desire to spend time in *her* company. Contrary to what she'd believed, it was obvious that the breach between them wasn't healed at all.

The rest of the day passed uneventfully, though Anna was aware of feeling strangely on edge. Even in the carriage en route to an evening engagement, the conversation she'd had with Barrington lingered in her mind. Was there anything the man *didn't* know? He seemed to be in possession of the most disturbing information about almost everyone she knew. Even unassuming Lord Andrews, whom she found herself observing during the course of the evening, harboured secrets that were both dark and disturbing. Watching him speak quietly to an elderly lady, Anna found it difficult to equate the seemingly upright gentleman with a man who indulged in a substance whose prolonged use was known to affect the mind and body in terrible ways.

'Are you sure you did not misunderstand Sir Barrington?' Lydia asked after Anna had acquainted her with Lord Andrew's unsavoury pastime.

'I can assure you I did not,' Anna said, keeping her voice down. 'Sir Barrington was very convincing in his description of the man's activities; given that I've no reason to doubt him, I took the liberty of writing to Miss Preston and advising her not to encourage Lord Andrews's suit. I told her Mr. Atlander would be a far better choice.'

'Until you speak to Sir Barrington about *him*,' Lydia murmured. 'And find out that *he* is not all he seems to be either. Faith, it must be disturbing to know so much about so many people. Only think of the kind of secrets Sir Barrington is forced to keep. He could utterly destroy people if he was of a mind to.'

'Only if they did something foolish. If one is innocent of all crimes, people have nothing to fear from him.'

'And what about you, Anna?' Lydia asked quietly. 'Have you anything to fear from Sir Barrington Parker?'

Anna took a sip of champagne. That was the problem with close friends. They saw far too much. 'I have no idea what you mean.'

'I think you do. You speak of him quite often, you know,' Lydia said, 'and in a tone of voice that leads me to believe you are not entirely indifferent to him.'

'Be that as it may, we both know exactly where we stand.'

'You may know where you stand, Anna, but are you happy about it?'

Anna raised her glass to her lips instead of replying. *That* was a different question altogether.

The house was quiet when Anna got home. Milford met her at the door and took her evening cape. 'Thank you, Milford. Is my father still up?'

'He is, my lady, but he went to his room and said he was not to be disturbed.'

Anna paused in the act of removing her gloves. 'Did Sir Barrington Parker call this evening?'

'He most certainly did,' Edward said, coming down the stairs. 'That will be all, Milford.'

Anna wasn't surprised by her brother's curt dismissal of the servant, but she was surprised to find him still at home. 'You're not usually here this time of evening,' she said as the butler withdrew.

'I had planned on going out, but when Parker arrived, I decided to stay. I'm glad I did, though you won't be.'

Anna flinched at his tone of voice. 'I assume he came to speak to Papa about Peregrine?'

'On the contrary, he came to speak to Father about the baroness's necklace. It seems the thief has been found.'

Something in his face set Anna's heart racing. 'Who is it?' she whispered.

'Can you not guess?'

Dear God, it was someone she knew? 'Stop playing games, Edward. Just *tell* me and be done with it!'

'Oh, I'll tell you, but you won't so easily be done with it. Because the thief is someone you know. A man you were raised to love and respect.' Her brother donned his hat and started for the door. 'A man who has lied and deceived us all. Our much loved and revered father!'

Her father had stolen the baroness's necklace?

Impossible! In fact, it was more than impossible. It was ludicrous! Her father was a wealthy man. He had no reason to steal anything—and he certainly wouldn't have stolen something from Julia. So why on earth had Barrington come here and accused him of having done so?

Woodenly, Anna made her way to the drawing room. There had to be a mistake. Barrington had been given the wrong information. One of his informants had followed the wrong lead. Tracked down the wrong man. Her father was *not* a thief. She was willing to stake her life on that.

She closed the door behind her and walked on unwilling feet towards the fireplace. She was cold, chilled from the inside out, her mind struggling to come to grips with what she had just learned. What kind of man was Barrington that he could do this to her family? He had *spoken* to her father. Socialised with him. Yet he had still come here and accused him of this heinous crime.

'How could you, Barrington?' she whispered. 'How *could* you do this unspeakable thing to my father?' She bit her lip, fighting back tears. 'To *me*.'

Barrington stood in his study, gazing into the fire, his conscience burning as hot as the flames in the grate. How long would it be? How long before she arrived on his doorstep demanding an explanation to the accusations he had laid at her father's feet?

It couldn't be long. She might even come tonight…straight from having spoken to her father. Unless she didn't get a chance to speak to him. The earl might well have gone out, or refused to speak to her. No doubt he needed time to come to grips with the fact that someone had supposedly seen him stealing the baroness's necklace while she lay sleeping in her bed.

Certainly Barrington had needed time. When the shadowy figure had first mentioned the earl's name, Barrington was sure he must have heard wrong. The Earl of Cambermere a thief? It was laughable! The man was a peer of the realm. An aristocrat. Such conduct would be anathema to him.

Yet, the man had repeated the earl's name several times over the course of the next few minutes, though never once had he vouchsafed the name of the person who was the apparent source of the information.

Not that it mattered, Barrington reflected grimly. He had been given the Earl of Cambermere's name as the person who had committed the crime. And, as his first and only suspect, he was obliged to follow it through. For Anna's sake, he prayed God it wasn't the only name he received.

Anna had no idea how she had passed the hours of that terrible night. It certainly wasn't in sleep. She had lain awake through the long midnight hours, getting up several times to pace the length of the room. At one point, she had opened the curtains and stared at the moon, but it gave her no comfort and eventually she had staggered back to bed. But she hadn't been able to sleep and still lay awake when the first fingers of light began to creep into her room. She watched the blackness of the night sky give way to a dark indigo hue, then to lighter blue as the sun climbed higher in the sky. She heard the sounds of the servants moving about in the house below. Laying fires. Dusting furniture. Setting out breakfast. And still she thought about Edward's words.

A man you were raised to love and respect…a man who has lied and deceived us all…

No, she *wouldn't* believe it. Nor would she wait any longer to have it shown up as the lie she knew it to be. She got up and dressed even before her maid arrived to help her, then went down to the library where she knew her father spent most of his early morning hours. He would be off to his club for lunch, but Anna had no intention of seeing him leave *before* she'd had a chance to speak with him. Not today.

She knocked on the library door, but waited until she heard his voice before pushing it open. 'May I come in, Papa?'

'Anna.' He rose as she entered, surprise and uncertainty reflected in his eyes. His complexion was grey and he looked as though he hadn't slept. 'What are you doing here?'

'I came to see you.' Swallowing hard, Anna closed the door and took a step towards him. 'I needed to hear it from your lips that this is all an abominable lie.'

He knew what she was talking about. Anna saw it in the way his eyes closed ever so briefly. The way his shoulders sagged. 'Did Parker tell you?'

'No. Edward did.'

'Ah.' Making no move to deny it, the earl sighed and sank back into his chair.

'I don't believe it, Papa,' Anna said. 'Someone has told a hurtful and outrageous lie!'

'Yes, they have,' he agreed. 'But they have also offered damning evidence to back up their claim.'

'What kind of evidence?'

'Someone told Parker that I was seen taking Julia's necklace.'

'*Seen...?*' Anna gasped. 'But...by whom?'

'He wouldn't tell me.'

'Why not?'

'He said it was an anonymous source.'

'Then how do you know he's telling the truth?'

Her father looked up. 'Because we're talking about Sir Barrington Parker and he doesn't lie.'

'I wasn't referring to Sir Barrington telling a lie,' Anna said tersely. 'I was talking about his anonymous source. How do we know *he* is telling the truth?'

'We don't. Right now, it's my word against his, whoever he is.'

'Then there can be no contest. You are the Earl of Cambermere!' she exclaimed.

'Which means nothing since the person who saw me was apparently *in* the house the night it happened,' her father said wearily.

'But that doesn't make sense. You've never been alone with Julia in her house,' Anna said. 'And how could you steal the necklace if she was there with you?'

She was surprised to see her father's cheeks darken as he turned away. 'Suffice it to say, that *is* what I stand accused of.'

'Well, it's ridiculous and I don't care what the gossip mill is saying. You are innocent and we are going to make sure everyone knows it!'

'Ah, Anna, have you forgotten how society works? It doesn't matter what people believe. It is enough that someone put it about that I stole the necklace for society to cry scandal.'

'But they have no proof!' Anna cried. 'So far, it is one

man's word against another's—and we don't even know who the other man is! Surely people are intelligent enough to know that, without proof, it is only lies and speculation.'

'One would hope so.'

Anna began to pace. 'Why would Sir Barrington not tell you the name of the person who claims to have seen you take it?'

'He told me he couldn't until further investigation was carried out.'

'Then for all we know, it could be someone deliberately making mischief,' Anna said, grasping at straws. Grasping at anything that might banish the wretchedness from her father's eyes. 'Someone who wishes to hurt you for some unknown reason.'

'I did think of that,' her father said. 'But who have I slighted to such an extent that they would wish to destroy my reputation like this?'

Anna bit her lip. 'You don't think Peregrine…?'

'Peregrine?' Anna was relieved to see a look of genuine shock appear on her father's face. 'Why on earth would he turn on me in such a manner?'

'Perhaps because of the situation with Lady Yew. He was angry and hurt that you didn't believe him when Sir Barrington accused him of having an affair.'

'Rightly so, given that it turned out Parker was correct.'

Reminded of the man who had brought this terrible news into the house, Anna felt a red-hot wave of anger. How dare he disrupt her family's life like this? She had been willing to believe him up until now, but not this time. He and he alone was the cause of her father's humiliation and unhappiness.

'Then I shall go to Sir Barrington myself. I will *demand* that he tell me who his source is and have him explain why he would believe such a ridiculous lie.'

'You're bringing emotion into it,' her father warned. 'Parker doesn't deal in emotion. He deals in facts.'

'Not any more,' Anna said tersely. 'This time, he is dealing with emotions. Yours and mine and Julia's. And by the time I'm through with him, he is going to know *exactly* how challenging dealing with an emotional woman can be!'

Barrington was in the long gallery sparring with his brother-in-law when his secretary arrived to tell him that Lady Annabelle Durst had called and was waiting below.

'Shall I inform her that you are engaged, Sir Barrington?' Sam asked.

'No.' Barrington slowly lowered his foil. 'Ask her to wait in the salon. I shall be there directly.'

'Lady Annabelle Durst,' Tom repeated after the secretary left. 'The Earl of Cambermere's daughter?'

'Yes.'

'Interesting. Is she calling on a business matter or may I have the pleasure of telling your sister that a lady has finally caught her brother's eye?'

'You may definitely *not* tell her that because this is not a social call,' Barrington muttered. 'Lady Annabelle is here with regards to an investigation.'

'Pity. A liaison with Cambermere's daughter would do much to lessen Jenny's disappointment over what happened with Lady Alice,' Tom remarked.

'Duly noted,' Barrington said, ushering his brother-in-law towards the door. He wasn't about to tell Tom that appeasing his sister was the least of his worries right now. 'I trust you can see yourself out.'

Without waiting for an answer, Barrington hurried to his bedroom to change into more appropriate attire. The coming confrontation was not going to be easy and he needed to be prepared. A fact proven true when he opened the door to the salon five minutes later and Anna flew at him like a tigress on the attack. 'How could you do this?' she demanded.

'Do what?'

'Accuse my father of stealing the baroness's necklace. You know he would never do such a thing!'

Barrington slowly closed the door behind him. 'I did what I had to after receiving information from a credible source—'

'Damn your credible sources!' Anna cried. 'We're talking about *my father*. And you know as well as I do that he would never steal anything from anyone! *Especially* Julia!'

'Calm yourself, Anna. I didn't say that I *believed* what I had been told, nor did I charge your father with any crime. But I was given a piece of information and it was my duty to follow it up. So I asked him a few questions.'

'What kind of questions?'

'That is between your father and myself,' he replied evasively.

'But I don't understand. If you don't believe him guilty, why are you putting him through all this?'

'Because there are procedures that must be followed.' Barrington linked his hands behind his back and slowly walked towards the window. 'When did he tell you of my visit?'

'He didn't,' Anna said tightly. 'Edward did.'

'Edward?' Barrington's head came up. 'When?'

'Last night. He waited until I arrived home to tell me that you had called to see Father. I assumed it had something to do with Peregrine, but Edward said you had come to see Papa about the theft of Julia's necklace.'

Barrington didn't trouble to hide his surprise. 'I wonder

how he knew? Your brother wasn't in the room when I spoke to your father.'

'He must have been standing outside in the corridor listening to your conversation,' Anna said. 'Edward is not above doing such things, especially if he thought you'd come to see my father about Peregrine.'

'I see,' Barrington said quietly. He was beginning to have his own suspicions about Viscount Hayle, but knew it was best he keep them to himself for the time being. 'What did your father say when you spoke to him?'

'He told me what *you* had accused him of, but said that you would not name the person who had made this foul accusation against him,' Anna said in a low voice. 'How could you not tell him, Barrington? Surely my father has a right to know who is bringing these charges against him.'

'He will. But for now, I thought it best not to reveal too much. To say something out of turn won't do anyone any good,' he advised.

'But you must know what this will do to his reputation,' she said, 'whether it turns out to be true or not. Why can't you just *say* that the other person is lying and proclaim my father innocent?'

'Because until I am convinced of the part that *everyone* has played in this, I'm not willing to say who is guilty and who is not.'

'But you just said my father didn't do it—and why would he? He likes Julia,' Anna said. 'Why on earth would he jeopardise a possible future with her by stealing something so precious to her?'

'Trust me when I tell you that thought has already occurred to me.' Barrington hesitated a moment before saying, 'You said Edward spoke to you about your father?'

'Yes.'

'It hasn't escaped my notice that there is a certain amount of tension between your father and your brother at the moment,' he said.

'It's hardly surprising,' Anna said in a voice of resignation. 'Papa is pressuring Edward to marry Lady Harriet Green and Edward wants nothing to do with it.'

'Why? Is he opposed to the idea of marriage or just the lady your father wishes him to wed?'

'A bit of both, I think,' Anna admitted. 'Papa thinks very highly of Lady Harriet and he's told Edward so any number of times. He says she possesses all the qualities necessary to be the next Countess of Cambermere.'

'And your brother doesn't share his opinion.'

'Edward says that who he marries is no one's business but his own. I suppose he's right, but Papa is concerned about the future of the family. He says Edward has lived the life of the gentleman about town long enough and that it's time he settled down to his obligations.'

'Which means marrying and producing an heir,' Barrington said.

'Precisely.'

'Are there no other members of the family capable of doing so?' Barrington asked. 'I believe your father has several brothers and sisters?'

'Two brothers, one sister,' Anna said. 'Aunt Hestia is married to a Scottish laird and lives in Edinburgh. I remember meeting her when I was about six and not liking her very much. She has two girls. Father's youngest brother, Cyril, went away to France and was eventually killed in battle, and his next eldest brother sailed off to China and never came back. I suspect he knew he wouldn't have much of a life, given that Papa was heir.'

'So it *is* up to Edward to continue the family name,' Barrington said thoughtfully.

'Yes, and given that he is showing absolutely no inclination to do so, it is only to be expected that relations between him and my father are strained,' Anna sighed.

'Yes, I can see why they would be,' Barrington said. 'Anna, I cannot share with you what I was told, but I promise I will do everything I can to get to the truth of the matter.'

'There is only one truth: that is that my father is innocent of this vile charge,' Anna said, raising her chin in defiance. 'I don't care what manner of evidence has been brought against him. He is a good man. An honourable man. And if you don't believe that, we have absolutely nothing more to say to one another.'

Chapter Ten

The evidence against her father *was* damning, Barrington reflected in the silence after Anna left. It was part of the reason he hadn't been willing to share it with her. He was loathe to provide her with details of a circumstance that would put the blame for the theft squarely on her father's shoulders *and* give her undeniable proof that the earl and the baroness were engaged in an intimate relationship. But that was what the messenger had told him and what he was obligated to follow up on.

A servant in the baroness's household had seen Lord Cambermere take the necklace after leaving the baroness sleeping peacefully in her bed. Apparently, the maid had gone into her mistress's bedroom, expecting her lady to be alone, and had discovered the earl in the act of taking the necklace from the jewellery case. She claimed that Lord Cambermere hadn't seen her, but that from where she had been standing, she'd had a clear view of the proceedings. After locking the jewellery box, the earl had slipped the necklace into the pocket of his coat, and then returned to the baroness's bed.

The baroness had not woken and, shocked beyond words, the maid had backed quietly out of the room.

Barrington sighed. It might be only the word of a servant against that of an earl, but the messenger had provided details too specific to be dismissed as fabrication or hoax. Details of the room's interior. A description of the jewellery box. Even where the dressing table was located in relation to the bed, what colour the curtains were, and what manner of knick-knacks had adorned the top of the bedside table. Only a maid, with unrestricted access to the baroness's bedroom, would have been able to provide details like that.

Besides, what reason had she to lie? She claimed to have no prior knowledge of the earl. She hadn't worked in his household and had no reason to hold a grudge against him. All she cared about was her mistress and how upset she had been when she'd found out the necklace was missing. It was that grief, combined with a sense of loyalty, that had prompted Miss Smith to tell *someone* what she had seen that night. And, in turn, for that person to tell the man who'd met with Barrington in the darkened garden.

If it *was* true, it meant Cambermere had certainly had the opportunity to commit the crime. But he still lacked a motive and Barrington didn't believe anything was done without motive. Dogs barked because they were frightened. Beggars stole because they were starving. Prostitutes sold their bodies because they needed a roof over their heads.

What reason had Cambermere for stealing?

Barrington idly picked up a piece of Venetian glass, turning it over in his fingers as his mind went back over his various encounters with the earl. Was it possible the man had serious debts? His home was quite grand, but there had been an air of genteel shabbiness about the place. Small signs of neglect a less observant person might have overlooked. Worn patches on the arms of the chairs. The burgundy velvet curtains faded, their bottom edges frayed. Even the mahogany desk had been in need of a good polish.

Barrington had originally put it down to a lack of interest on the earl's part, a sad consequence of Lady Cambermere's death. But now he wondered if it might be an indication of something more. Even the earl's appearance had been wanting, now that Barrington thought about it. Signs of wear at the man's cuffs. The style of the coat slightly out of date. Boots that had seen better days.

Still, if the earl was having financial difficulties, he wouldn't be the first peer to fall on hard times. Cambermere owned a house in town and several smaller estates in the English countryside. The upkeep of such establishments commanded a huge outlay of money. It was the reason many cash-strapped peers resorted to marrying heiresses. It was either that or risk sacrificing their family's land and holdings. But was the earl really in such dire financial straits?

Surprisingly, it was Lady Bessmel who provided some insight into the situation as the two of them stood chatting over lobster pâté the following evening.

'Yes, Cambermere has a lovely estate in Kent,' she told him. 'I used to visit him and Isabel there quite often.'

'What was Lady Cambermere like?' Barrington enquired.

'Quiet. And thoughtful. She enjoyed London, but she was far happier in the country. She loved her garden and her horses. And her books, of course. She would read for hours on end, saying she found precious little time for it in London.' Lady Bessmel sighed. 'I was very sorry when Isabel died. She was…a gentle person. The kind who gave of herself. I believe her death hit Peter quite hard.'

'Were they in love?'

The countess smiled. 'As much as anyone in our circle can be, I suppose. It was an arranged marriage, but it turned out quite well. Peter was a good husband. I never heard stories about him keeping a mistress or visiting the brothels. He seemed content with his life, at least until Isabel died. Then he seemed to lose focus. He couldn't settle to anything. That's why it's so nice to see him finally making an effort again.'

'Making an effort?' Barrington asked.

'With the baroness. It can't have escaped your notice that he is very much taken with her.'

'Yes, I had noticed.' Barrington smiled. 'Can you tell me anything more about the earl? Has he vices?'

'What man doesn't? He gambles at cards, but not a great deal, and he drinks no more or less than anyone else. I suppose his greatest weakness is horses.'

'Horses,' Barrington repeated. 'Is he a frequent visitor to the track?'

'More now than he used to be. I never remember him gambling while Isabel was alive, but a woman's death can change a man. In the beginning, I think it was simply a diversion,' Lady Bessmel said. 'Something to think about other than the fact that his wife wasn't there any more. But over time it gets into a man's blood.'

'Does he win more than he loses?' he asked idly.

'Who knows? Dame Fortune can turn either way. One day she smiles on you, the next she spits in your face. I'm sure Peter's had his share of both, but he's a private man so I doubt anyone knows the true extent of his winnings. Or of his losses.'

It was a conversation that stayed with Barrington the rest of the night—because if the earl *was* in serious debt, Barrington had his motive. The baroness's necklace was worth a small fortune, enough to cover most any man's debts. And given Cambermere's position in society, it was unlikely he would have to take the necklace apart. Connections here and abroad would allow him to dispose of the piece without the sale being traced back to him.

But if the earl was hopeful of marrying the baroness, why bother to steal her jewellery? Julia von Brohm was an exceedingly wealthy young woman with more than enough money for the two of them to live on. Of course, being a widow, her money was her own, and, if she chose, she could have a lawyer draw up papers to ensure it stayed that way. If Cambermere needed funds to pay off his gambling debts, he could apply to her, but given that his debts *were* the result of gambling, she might not wish to put any of her money to them. Barrington remembered a remark she'd once made about gentlemen foolish enough to squander their money on the roll of a dice not being worth the time or the trouble to know. That being the case, he doubted she would willingly give any of her money to a man who had bankrupted himself at the tables or the track.

However, if it was Cambermere's intention to pay off his debts *before* he married her so that he could go into the marriage free and clear, he would then be able to use her money to look after the maintenance of his estates. And surely she wouldn't object to that, given that she would be mistress of them all. So it really came down to two questions.

How deeply in debt had Cambermere landed himself? And how far was he willing to go to dig himself out?

The next morning Anna called for her horse to be saddled and went for a much-needed ride. She feared she might explode if she stayed at home any longer. Trying to read, or doing any one of a hundred and one other things that would normally have distracted her, would be of no use today. She needed to get out of the house and away from her thoughts.

Her father had already done so. Having been offered an invitation to a shooting party, he had left for the weekend gathering at a house about ten miles outside London. It was only to be a small gathering of gentlemen, but Anna knew her father would find comfort in their company. But it did leave her at loose ends. Peregrine was still quiet and withdrawn as he struggled through his own emotional healing and Edward was scarcely at home.

And Barrington didn't call.

Anna told herself she was glad of that. After all, they had nothing to say to one another. She'd made it quite plain that to take a stand against her father was to take a stand against her, and Barrington had made his own position perfectly clear. He intended to pursue the investigation against her father; in the absence of any other, her father was still the main suspect.

Well, loyalty and emotion might mean nothing to him, but they meant everything to Anna. She believed unequivocally that her father was innocent. Barrington was trying to prove him not guilty. There was a subtle but distinct difference.

Unfortunately, as much as Anna had hoped that fresh air and brisk exercise might distract her, neither served to ease her mind. She felt no more relaxed when she arrived home than when she'd left. And when Peregrine emerged from the drawing room, white-faced and shaken, her spirits plummeted even further. 'Goodness, Peregrine, what's wrong? You look positively ill.'

'Thank God you're back! Come in here!' he said urgently. 'And close the door.'

Anna did, wearily hoping his agitation had nothing to do with Lady Yew. She wasn't sure she could cope with one more piece of bad news—or with the mention of that woman's name again. 'What's this all about? If you tell me you've seen the marchioness—'

'This has nothing to do with her,' Peregrine assured her quickly. 'This is worse. Much worse!'

Worse? Anna didn't like the sound of that. And when

Peregrine began to pace up and down the length of the room, looking as though he might burst into tears at any time, she knew there was trouble in earnest. 'What's going on, Per? If it's bad news, just tell me and get it over with.'

He stopped pacing, but didn't look at her. 'I don't know *how* to tell you. I'm hardly able to believe it myself!'

'Believe what?'

He looked ready to say something, then squeezed his eyes shut and took a deep breath. 'No. It's best I show you. You won't believe me otherwise.' With that, he took her hand and led her out of the room and towards the staircase.

'Where are we going?'

'You'll see,' was all he would say. At the top of the stairs, he stopped and cocked his head, listening. Then, with a brief nod, he carried on until they were standing outside the last door in the hall.

'This is Papa's room,' Anna said unnecessarily.

'I know.' Peregrine took another quick glance in either direction, then, to Anna's astonishment, opened the door and dragged her in.

'Peregrine, what on earth are you doing?'

'I have to show you something.' Closing the door, he turned the key in the lock. Then, walking over to the door that connected the earl's room to his valet's, he locked that one as well.

'Peregrine, you're beginning to make me very nervous,' Anna said, unconsciously lowering her voice.

'I'm sorry, but I found something in your father's things that you really must see.'

'You were going through his things?' Anna said, shocked.

'I was looking for his watch.'

'His watch?' The story was getting more bizarre by the minute. 'Why?'

'Because Edward asked me to,' Peregrine admitted.

'I don't understand.'

'Edward was supposed to take your father's watch to Mr Munts for repair,' Peregrine explained, 'but he told me he was late for an appointment and asked me if I would take it instead. I said I would and asked him where the watch was. He told me the earl usually kept it in one of two places. I checked the first place and it wasn't there. But when I looked in the second...'

He stopped, prompting Anna to say, 'You found it?'

Peregrine nodded. 'But I found something else as well.' He led her to the large corner wardrobe and, pulling open the doors, pointed to a small drawer. 'Open it.'

Not sure why, Anna did—and saw a leather bag with a drawstring opening lying on a pile of neatly folded handkerchiefs. 'Is that what you want me to see?'

He nodded. 'Take it out.'

The bag was heavier than expected, and Anna felt the contents shift as she picked it up.

'Open it,' he whispered.

'We really shouldn't be going through Papa's things,' Anna whispered. 'This could be something personal.'

'Open it, Anna.'

There was an edge of fatalism in his voice, and reluctantly, she loosened the drawstring and tipped the contents of the bag into the palm of her hand.

The baroness's diamond-and-sapphire necklace twinkled up at her.

'Oh, dear God!' Anna said—and promptly dropped it. 'What on earth is *that* doing here?'

'I have no idea.' Peregrine reached down and plucked the necklace from the depths of the boot into which it had fallen. 'But we both know it's not supposed to be here.'

The discovery left Anna speechless. How could the necklace be here—in her father's room? In his wardrobe? He had professed his innocence and she had believed him. Then she had gone to Barrington and told him that her father was innocent of the charge and that if he didn't believe her, they had nothing further to say to one another. Yet now she found the baroness's necklace nestled amongst her father's things.

'It's impossible,' she whispered. 'Why would he do this?'

'I've been asking myself that all afternoon,' Peregrine said miserably. 'And coming up with nothing.'

Anna stared at the necklace. It didn't make sense. The necklace shouldn't be here. In fact, this was the last place in the world it should be…

'All right, let's not jump to conclusions,' she said, knowing there had to be a logical explanation. 'Just because we found the necklace here, doesn't mean Papa took it.'

'Then how did it come to be in his things?' Peregrine asked.

'Obviously, someone *put* it here.'

'Who? No one else comes into his room,' he said.

'*You* did!' she reminded him.

'Only because Edward asked me to. And I certainly didn't put *this* here.' He was silent for a moment. 'What about the servants? They come and go all the time.'

'But none of them would have an opportunity to steal a diamond necklace from the baroness,' Anna pointed out.

'And we *did*?' Peregrine demanded.

'Of course not! But at least we move in the same circles. We have access to her house.'

'But none of us would have taken it.'

Yet, the necklace was here. In her father's wardrobe. Peregrine was holding it in his hands.

'It really is fabulous, isn't it?' he said, staring down at it in fascination.

Anna didn't want to look, but it was almost impossible not to. She had never seen such amazing stones. Even in the dim light, the sapphires seemed to glow with brilliant blue fire and the diamonds were as white as any she'd ever seen. Truly, it was a necklace fit for a queen.

'A man would never have to work again if he owned something like that,' Peregrine whispered. 'He could buy anything he wanted. Go wherever he wanted. He'd never have to worry about money—'

'Stop talking like that!' Anna admonished, finally taking the necklace away from him. 'This is going back to the baroness where it belongs.'

'*Back* to the baroness? But…aren't you going to tell anyone you found it?'

She stared at him as though he'd suddenly sprouted a second head. 'Are you *mad*? And have Papa implicated in a crime he didn't commit? Not on your life! Whoever put this necklace here clearly intended to make trouble for Papa and I'm not about to see that happen,' Anna said. 'We have been unbelievably fortunate in finding the necklace before he got home. And I am going to return it to Julia at the first opportunity.'

'I see.' Peregrine crossed his arms in front of his chest. 'And where, pray tell, are you going to tell her you *found* it?'

The question stopped Anna in her tracks. 'Oh.'

'Exactly. If you can't come up with a logical explanation, you're better off not giving it back to her at all. It will just make her suspicious.'

'But the longer the necklace is missing, the more time someone has to spread lies about Papa's having taken it,' Anna said.

Peregrine glanced at the necklace and shook his head. 'I

think you should tell Sir Barrington Parker. Isn't he the one the baroness asked to look into the matter?'

'Yes, and I'll tell you right now, he is the very *last* person I intend to tell about this!' Anna said fiercely. 'Can you imagine what he would say if he were to learn that we found it here? He would think Papa took it.'

'I hate to say this, but...' Peregrine looked distinctly uncomfortable. 'Are you absolutely sure your father *didn't* take it?'

Anna's mouth fell open in disbelief. 'Peregrine, how *could* you?'

'I'm not saying he did! It's just that—'

'I don't want to hear it,' Anna said, cutting him off. 'There isn't a doubt in my mind that my father is innocent. He would never do something like this. *Never!*'

'Then what are you going to do?'

'I'll tell you.' Anna slipped the necklace into the pocket of her riding skirt, a plan already forming in her mind. 'First off, *you* are going to take Papa's watch to Mr Munts and make sure you get a receipt for it.'

'A receipt,' Peregrine repeated in bewilderment.

'Yes. Then, upon returning home, you will give the receipt to Milford and make sure you tell him that Edward instructed you to take Papa's watch in for repair, and that either Milford or James can pick it up when it's ready.'

Peregrine's heavy brows drew together. 'Why am I doing all that?'

'Because I want the reasons for your *being* in Papa's wardrobe to be very clear. It's possible that whoever put the necklace here intended that someone other than Papa should find it. Most likely a servant. And knowing how servants gossip, the culprit hoped news of the necklace's discovery *in* Papa's wardrobe would start making its way through society.

Fortunately, *we* found it and can make sure no such rumours leak out,' Anna said.

Peregrine frowned. 'I don't understand the reason for all the secrecy. We certainly aren't going to say we saw the necklace.'

'Of course not. And before this day is out, the necklace will be safely back in Julia's hands. But if, for some bizarre reason, this does fall back on us, I want it made very clear that you went into the wardrobe looking for Papa's watch because it needed to go to Mr Munts for repair, and that you did *not* see anything untoward while you were there.'

'So if anyone asks, we're going to lie,' Peregrine said simply.

'Precisely. It's the *only* way we can protect Papa. Now if you'll excuse me, I have to get dressed. I have a very important call to make!'

There was only one thought on Anna's mind as she turned her phaeton into Mayfair a short time later. She *had* to get the necklace back into Julia's house—and she had to do it without anyone seeing her!

It should be relatively simple. Once in Julia's parlour, she would pass some pleasant time with tea and conversation before making an excuse to leave the room. A visit to the convenience would probably be the best. That would give her time to slip upstairs and make her way to Julia's bedchamber.

Once inside, she would place the necklace on the floor beneath Julia's bedside table, or better yet, under her dressing table, and then return to the drawing room to resume her visit. In the next few minutes, she would bring the conversation round to the necklace and casually ask if Julia had looked *under* the furniture in her room since jewellery could so easily slip off a night table or a dresser and become lost. If

Julia replied that she or the servants had already looked in such places, Anna would simply advise her to look again and casually change the subject; then, after a suitable amount of time, she would bid Julia a good day and leave.

Really, it was so simple. Julia would find the necklace exactly where Anna said it might be, laugh at herself for not having been more careful—and that would be an end of it. There would be no more stories about the necklace having been stolen. No more rumours about her father's possible involvement. And no need to involve Sir Barrington Parker at all.

Anna almost felt like laughing as she walked up to Julia's front door.

Unfortunately, her neatly laid plans began to fall apart the moment she walked into the house. As the butler opened the drawing room door and announced her, Anna was horrified to see Sir Barrington Parker sitting comfortably at Julia's side.

'Sir Barrington!' she gasped, completely ignoring her hostess.

'Lady Annabelle.' He rose to greet her, his voice decidedly amused. 'You look as though you've seen a ghost.'

'Do I?' *Calm.* Above all, she had to remain calm. No one must know this was anything but a routine visit in the course of her social day. Easier said than done given the weight in the bottom of her reticule. 'Perhaps just my…surprise at finding you here. I didn't see your carriage in the street.'

'It being such a lovely day, I decided to walk,' Barrington told her. 'A brisk walk is always good for clearing the mind.'

'So I've heard,' Anna murmured, wishing desperately for something that might clear hers. 'Julia, how rude you must think me. I greeted Sir Barrington without even acknowledging you.'

'No apologies are necessary, my dear,' Julia assured her with a smile. 'You probably came, hoping to have a cosy chat, and were surprised at encountering our mutual friend. I would have been similarly nonplussed.'

'You are too kind in your forgiveness. But how well you look today.' Anna flicked a cautious glance in Barrington's direction. 'Am I to hope you've had news concerning your necklace?'

'In fact, Sir Barrington and I were just talking about it.'

'Really?' Anna felt her heart skip a beat. 'What did he say?'

'I was about to inform the baroness,' Barrington said smoothly, 'that I am following up on several leads and hope to have an answer for her very soon.'

Anna pasted a smile on her lips. 'How encouraging.'

'Yes, isn't it?' Julia said happily. 'At this point, the only thing that matters is recovering the necklace. I really don't care who took it—'

'You don't? I mean…it's important that we know who *did* take it, of course,' Anna said as two pairs of eyes turned to stare at her. 'But surely its safe return is the more important issue.'

'It is to me,' Julia said. 'I was going to tell Sir Barrington that I won't press charges if he feels that might encourage the thief to return the necklace to me intact.'

'Oh, but that is exceedingly generous of you,' Anna said, aware that matters were improving by the minute.

Or were until Barrington said, 'It *is* generous of you, Baroness, but I doubt the authorities will agree. A law has been broken. Someone must be made to pay.'

'But surely if Julia does not wish to press charges, there is no need for the authorities to be involved,' Anna said, annoyed at his interference.

'As I said, a crime has been committed and retribution must

be made. I suspect the baroness's wishes will be taken into account, but I cannot guarantee they will be honoured.'

Anna abruptly stood up, her stomach twisting. 'Julia, will you excuse me for a moment?'

'Of course, Anna, but are you feeling all right? You've gone dreadfully pale.'

'Have I?' Anna clutched at her reticule. 'Perhaps it's the heat. I am feeling a bit faint.'

'Then you must lie down.' Julia immediately got to her feet. 'I would suggest my room—'

'Oh, yes, that would be perfect!'

'Except that I have workmen repapering all the bedrooms,' Julia finished. 'I fear you would have no solitude at all.'

'No, really, that would be fine,' Anna assured her. 'I just need to lie down for a moment—'

'Then you must lie here on the sofa,' Barrington interrupted, getting to his feet. 'And I shall leave the two of you to some quiet conversation.'

'No, please, that isn't necessary,' Anna said, seeing her carefully thought-out plan disintegrating. With workmen in the bedrooms and people coming and going, she wouldn't have a hope of secreting the necklace in Julia's bedroom without being seen. 'I hate to see you leave on my account.'

'Rest assured, I was preparing to depart when you arrived,' Barrington said with a smile. 'I only dropped by to apprise the baroness of my progress. But I do hope the next time we meet you are feeling more like your old self.'

Wondering if she would ever feel like her old self again, Anna murmured, 'Yes, I'm quite sure I shall be fully recovered by then.'

'If you will wait for me at the front door, Sir Barrington,' Julia said, 'I'll fetch that list of names you asked for. Anna, will you be all right on your own for a few minutes?'

'Yes, of course,' Anna said, fighting back disappointment

as she sank down on the sofa. 'I shall just…lie here and wait for you.'

She was aware of Barrington lingering in the doorway, but didn't have the courage to look back at him. The man was too observant by half. Anna was terrified of what he might read in her eyes. As it was, she felt the necklace glowing like a beacon in her hands. But what was she to do with it now? She couldn't take it away again. Not with the clock ticking on her father's exposure. She had to make sure Julia found the necklace today. And if she couldn't safely get upstairs, she would just have to leave the necklace somewhere in here. But where?

The moment the door closed, Anna sprang to her feet and started searching for a likely place. It couldn't be somewhere immediately visible or Julia would wonder why she hadn't seen it before. But if it was too well hidden, she wouldn't find the necklace at all and the point of the exercise was to put it somewhere that it *would* be found.

Then, Anna spotted it—a large palm standing by the half-open French door. If the necklace was found in the branches, it could be suggested that during his escape, the thief had clumsily dropped it and it had landed in the tree. It was feeble, Anna admitted, but at the moment she had nothing better. And she was fast running out of time. She *had* to make sure the necklace was found in Julia's house *today*.

With that in mind she moved towards the palm, scanning for a likely branch. The necklace was too heavy to be supported by the uppermost branches, but it would be obscured if it was dropped directly into the base. She could, of course, put the bulk of it in the base and leave part of it trailing out…

Risking another glance at the door, Anna unfastened her reticule and reached in for the necklace. She would try it in several places and leave it in the one that looked best. Unfortunately, one of the claws holding the centre diamond was tangled in the fabric, causing her to waste precious seconds extricating it. Finally, it came free and, with infinite care, Anna leaned forwards to place it amongst the thicker branches lower down on the trunk. She tried to arrange it in a manner that made it look as though it had fallen, but the dashed thing kept bending the branches and falling into the base.

And then, the unthinkable happened. Hearing a movement behind her, Anna turned—and blanched.

Sir Barrington Parker was standing by the door, watching her.

Chapter Eleven

Damnation! Caught red-handed—and by the last person on earth she could afford to be caught by!

Seconds dragged by like treacle in winter. Barrington didn't say a word, but she could tell from the look on his face that this wasn't going to be good.

Then Julia's voice, saying, 'Sir Barrington, where are you?'

Anna gasped—and in that split second, Barrington moved. Launching himself across the room, he pushed her aside and scooped the necklace out of the palm, dropping it into an inside pocket of his coat. Barely had it disappeared than the drawing-room door opened and Julia walked in. 'Ah, there you are, Sir Barrington,' she said in surprise. 'I thought you were going to wait for me by the front door.'

'I was until I suddenly remembered there was something I wished to ask Lady Annabelle,' Barrington said, as calmly as though he had been sitting in one of the chairs reading a magazine. 'So I came back and found her up and moving around.'

Julia glanced at her friend. 'Are you feeling better, Anna? Your colour certainly seems to have returned.'

In point of fact, Anna's face felt like it was on fire. 'I am, thank you, Julia. It must have been...the tea.'

'I'm so glad. I've always sworn by it as a restorative. Here is the information you wanted, Sir Barrington,' Julia said, handing him a folded piece of parchment. 'I hope it helps.'

'I have a feeling it will go a long way towards solving the case,' Barrington said, remarkably composed in light of what had just happened. He turned and gave Anna a bow, nothing on his face to indicate that he had just found her depositing a stolen necklace into the heart of an ornamental palm. 'I'm quite sure I will be seeing you again very soon, Lady Annabelle.'

Far too soon, Anna reflected after he left. She had botched the job as badly as it was possible to botch it. She could only imagine what was going through Sir Barrington's head at that moment.

In point of fact, Barrington had so many thoughts running through his head he hardly knew where to begin. Lady Annabelle Durst had come into the baroness's house in possession of the missing sapphire-and-diamond necklace. She had been attempting to hide it in the base of the palm tree when he had unexpectedly walked back into the room and caught her.

Who was she trying to protect? An unusual question given what he had just seen, but in truth, the possibility of *her* having stolen the necklace had never crossed his mind. She had absolutely no motive and likewise no opportunity. It was also highly unlikely that she had simply stumbled upon the necklace and gone to the baroness's house intending to return it to its rightful owner. If that had been the case, she would have given it to the baroness the moment she'd walked into the room.

But she hadn't. She had held on to the necklace; upon finding herself alone, she had taken it out of her reticule and tried to conceal it in the base of the palm. A place the baroness *would* eventually have found it, though not, perhaps, today.

Obviously Anna hadn't wanted the baroness to discover that *she* was the one returning it. That would have necessitated a series of explanations that would have been awkward to say the least. But having been caught red-handed, what kind of explanation would she offer *him*?

Barrington found himself looking forward to that discussion.

The next question was where to conduct the interrogation? He couldn't do it at her home. Her brother or Peregrine Rand might be present, and possibly her father as well. Nor could he do it at his own house. If he invited her to call on a matter of business, it might raise questions in other people's minds. But if she wasn't calling on business, it was morally inappropriate for her to be there at all.

For that reason, as soon as Barrington got home, he wrote Anna a note, asking if he might take her for a drive in the park that afternoon. Being a lovely day, he suggested using the open carriage and assured her that, if she wished, his secretary could come along as chaperon. He doubted she would elect to speak in front of her maid, given the delicate nature of what they would be discussing.

Her response came back with equal promptness. Yes, she was available for a drive, and, no, she would not bring her maid. If chaperonage was required, she was happy to have it provided by his secretary, who had been very pleasant to her on the occasion of their last meeting.

Barrington smiled. Obviously the lady had already considered her options. If she was going to speak in front of anyone, she clearly preferred that it be his servant rather than hers.

He called for her at half past four and was not at all surprised to find her waiting for him. She had changed into a carriage gown of rose-coloured silk, the lace bodice threaded with deeper pink ribbons. Her hair was tucked up under another of her wide-brimmed bonnets and she carried a white parasol trimmed with deep pink ribbons. She looked absolutely enchanting—and completely innocent.

Surprising for a woman who had stepped so easily into the role of accomplice to a thief.

'Good afternoon, Sir Barrington,' she said as she walked down the steps to meet him.

'Lady Annabelle.' He smiled as he handed her into the barouche, 'Thank you for agreeing to meet with me.'

'I assumed there was no point in putting it off.'

'None whatsoever.' Barrington climbed in and sat down in the seat opposite. She waited until Sam flicked the whip and set the horses moving, the clatter of their hooves making it difficult for the conversation to be overheard, before she began to speak.

'I suspect you wish to ask me about what happened at Julia's this morning without my family being present for the interrogation. Just as well, since I suspect you intend to ask some rather problematic questions,' she said.

Problematic. An understatement to say the least. 'Shall we start with how you came to be in possession of the baroness's necklace?' he suggested.

'Ah, but I was not in possession of it,' she told him. 'I was walking by the French doors and chanced to look down and there it was! Lodged in the base of the palm.'

'Really. And how do you suppose it came to be there?'

The look she gave him was comprised of equal parts

surprise and disappointment. 'Really, Sir Barrington, is the answer to that not obvious?'

'Not to me.'

'Clearly, the thief dropped it as he was attempting to make his getaway.'

'His…getaway,' he repeated blankly.

'Yes. After he took the necklace from Julia's bedroom,' she said helpfully.

'So he did not make his escape through her bedroom window, but came downstairs to the drawing room and slipped out through the French doors.'

'Precisely.'

'An interesting theory,' Barrington said slowly. 'And plausible, I suppose, had my timing not been such that I opened the door in time to see *you* removing the necklace from your reticule and carefully inserting it *into* the palm.'

'Ah,' Anna said, sitting back. 'How unfortunate. Then it would probably be safe to say that you would find any attempt on my part to make you believe that I found the necklace quite by chance equally unbelievable.'

'No. I believe you *did* find the necklace and probably by chance, but the question of import now is *where* did you find it?' He sat forwards. 'In your brother's room—or your father's?'

He watched her cheeks turn bright red as her mouth dropped open in an exclamation of surprise. 'I cannot imagine why you would say such a thing—'

'For what it's worth,' he interrupted, '*I* think you found it in your father's room.'

She went rigid. 'Why would you say that?'

'Because Rand is still getting over his affair with Lady Yew and hasn't the clarity of mind to plan something like this. Likewise, if your brother had taken the necklace, I suspect he would either have held on to it until things cooled down, or he would have arranged to have it cut into smaller pieces that he could sell more easily. That leaves your father. Who, as it turns out, had both the motive and the opportunity to take it.'

'Motive?' Anna snorted. 'What possible motive could my father have had for stealing Julia's necklace?'

'The same as claimed by so many gentlemen of the *ton*,' Barrington said softly. 'Debt. In your father's case, through losses incurred at the racetrack.'

'How dare you! My father does not bet on horses!'

'Ah, but he does, dear lady. And though he wins more than he loses, he did suffer an unfortunate streak of bad luck last year from which he has been struggling to recover. A necklace like the baroness's would go a long way towards taking him—indeed, your entire family—out of dun territory.'

He knew immediately that what he'd told her had come as a complete shock. She'd obviously had no idea that her father had amassed such staggering debts, so the thought of him stealing a priceless necklace in an effort to clear himself had never occurred to her.

'If what you say is true—and I am not saying for a moment that I believe it is,' Anna said, 'my father would surely have had other ways of raising the money necessary to cover his obligations.'

'If he has, he has not availed himself of them. But let us not deviate from what we are here to discuss,' Barrington said firmly. 'The fact is, *you* came into the baroness's house with her necklace in your reticule, therefore, I have no choice but to ask you *where* you found it and *how* it came to be there. Unless you also wish to be viewed as a suspect.'

He saw the indecision on her face and knew she was debating as to how much to reveal. To say too much was to condemn someone else. To say too little was to condemn herself.

'Sir Barrington, if I tell you where I found the necklace, would you be willing to let it go?'

'In all honesty, I don't see how I can.'

'But you heard what Julia said. She is willing to drop all charges as long as the necklace is returned.'

'I understand that. But without a logical explanation as to *why* it was taken, we cannot know what the thief had in mind. At the very least, someone is getting away with a crime.' Barrington leaned forwards so that his face was close to hers. 'Someone took that necklace out of the baroness's house, Anna. I need to know who it was and why they did it. Because if their intent was to incriminate the person in whose room it was found, it's possible they may try again when they realise their first attempt has failed.'

'Incriminate!' Barrington saw the brief but unmistakable flash of hope in her eyes. 'Then you're open to the possibility that the person who *took* the necklace may not be the same person in whose room the necklace ended up.'

'I am open to the possibility, yes,' he admitted.

'And to the idea that…foul play may have been involved.'

'Oh, foul play has most definitely been involved, but who was the target? The baroness—or your father?'

His words fell into a strained silence. Barrington didn't have to be a mind reader to know that Anna was waging a silent battle with herself, struggling with how much she should say. Once she told him where the necklace had been found, there was no going back. The guilty party would be exposed and she would have been the one to expose them.

But did she trust him enough to know that he was only interested in finding out the truth? Or would her natural inclination to protect the people she loved stop her from giving him the answers he needed?

'Anna, I'm not out to condemn anyone,' he said softly.

'And what you tell me today will stay between you and me. No one else need know.'

'But you told Julia you would have to contact the authorities—'

'I said that because I couldn't allow her to believe that the perpetrator of the crime would be allowed to go free. Not until I have more information. But if you know something that can put me on the right path, I beg you to make it known.'

He held his breath while she made her decision. It was within her power to compromise the entire investigation. If she refused to tell him where she'd found the necklace, he would have no choice but to make accusations that would ultimately force her hand. And in doing so, he risked sacrificing any chance of ever gaining her good opinion.

Fortunately, something in what he'd said must have got through to her. With a heavy sigh, she said, 'The necklace was in Papa's room. Peregrine found it when he went to retrieve one of my father's watches. The necklace was lying next to it.'

Barrington wasn't sure whether to feel relief or remorse. 'Was it hidden away?'

'No. It was inside a small leather bag, but the bag was in plain sight.'

'So the thief intended that it be found easily,' Barrington said, his mind working. 'Does your father know you found it?'

Anna shook her head. 'Papa went to the country three days ago. He knows nothing about any of this.'

'Then we have no choice but to wait for his return to ask him about it. Either way, you must prepare yourself for the fact that word may leak out about the necklace having been found in his possession.'

'But it can't!' Anna said urgently. 'Papa would be disgraced!'

'I will do whatever I can to keep this quiet, Anna, but other people are involved and we have no control over what they might say. If the necklace was planted in your father's things, someone obviously wished to make trouble for him. The only way they can do that is by spreading rumours about where it was found. All *we* can do is work at uncovering the truth as quickly as possible,' Barrington said.

'But if you *believe* him innocent—'

'What *I* believe has nothing to do with it. Opinions are just that. To unerringly affix blame, I must have proof.'

'Then *find* the proof, Barrington,' Anna urged. 'Do whatever you have to, but find it. There is no question that my father is innocent.'

'May I point out that you were equally convinced of Mr Rand's innocence when it came to the charges levelled against him?' he said gently.

Anna sucked in her breath. 'That was unfair! Peregrine lied to me because he believed himself in love with that wretched woman. The situation with my father is entirely different. He has no reason to lie.'

'From my perspective, no one ever does,' Barrington said softly. 'However, I shall call upon your father when he returns and ask him what he knows about the necklace. His answers will go a long way towards determining where we go from here.'

She was silent for a moment, considering, perhaps, what he had said. 'I want to be there,' she said unexpectedly.

'I beg your pardon?'

'I want to be there when you interview my father. I want to hear what he has to say.'

Foreseeing difficulties she couldn't imagine, he said, 'I strongly advise against it.'

'Why?'

'Because questions will be asked that will be…uncomfortable.'

'For whom?'

'For both of you.'

Anna's face twisted. 'But if they help to uncover the truth, they must be asked. And I wish to be there to bear witness to my father's innocence.'

'Anna—'

'It's settled,' she said. 'I shall send you a note upon his return. And when you reply to it, I want you to make it known that I am to be included. Will you do that for me, Barrington?'

He knew from the stubborn set of her mouth that she wasn't going to back down. She intended to be there to witness her father's absolution. Well, he'd warned her. He could do no more than that. 'I will do this, as long as you know that I do it under duress.'

She smiled, confident of having won the argument. 'I don't need your approval, Barrington. Only your agreement. Besides, I doubt there's anything you can say to my father in my presence that will embarrass me any more than you finding me secreting a stolen necklace in the base of Julia's palm.'

Barrington sat back and sighed. 'I wouldn't be so sure about that.'

Anna was as good as her word. The day after her father's return, she sent Barrington a note advising him that her father was home, and of his agreement to the interview regarding the baroness's necklace. As such, when Barrington called at the house the following evening, Anna met him at the door, saying she had already advised her father of her intention to be present at the interview, given that she was as much involved in the matter as anyone else.

Thankfully, both Hayle and Peregrine were out, though Barrington thought he saw Hayle's carriage pull away just as he arrived. What he might make of it, Barrington didn't know or care. He was far more concerned with what he was about to find out from the earl.

In the drawing room, Anna sat down in the chair by the fireplace and clasped her hands together in her lap. Her expression was composed, but her eyes betrayed the nervousness she was feeling over what was to come.

By comparison, her father's face was untroubled, the result of his being completely unaware of what had transpired in his absence. 'Evening, Parker,' he said as Barrington walked into the room. 'May I offer you something in the way of refreshment?'

'Thank you. I'll have a brandy.'

'I'll join you. Sherry, Anna?'

'Thank you, Papa.'

As Cambermere crossed to the credenza to pour the drinks, Barrington moved closer to where Anna sat. 'This is your last chance,' he said, leaning down to speak quietly in her ear. 'Things are going to be said that *will* be difficult for you to hear. Are you quite sure you wish to stay?'

'Quite sure,' she said, though the slight quiver of her bottom lip told a different story.

Unaccountably annoyed, Barrington turned away. He hated seeing her like this. Hated knowing that the next few minutes were going to be even more difficult than what she had already endured. But there was no easy way of asking the earl what he must; while he wished there was some way of comforting Anna, he realised it was neither his place nor his right to do so. A fiancé or a husband could offer comfort. Not a man charged with finding out the truth about a crime in which her father might or might not be implicated.

'So, Anna tells me you've news about the baroness's

necklace,' the earl said, handing Barrington his brandy. 'Is it good news or bad?'

'A bit of both, I'm afraid. Your good health, my Lord,' Barrington said, raising his glass. 'Lady Annabelle.'

He saw the delicate colour in her cheeks as she tipped back her glass and wondered if it was the potency of the sherry or the unwitting caress in his voice when he'd spoken her name. He'd have to be more careful about that in the future.

Thankfully, the earl seemed oblivious. 'Well, what have you to tell us?'

'The good news,' Barrington began, 'is that the necklace has been found.'

'Has it, by Jove! Excellent!' There was no mistaking the relief in the earl's voice. 'Jul—that is, the baroness will be very pleased. Where did you find it?'

'That, I'm afraid, is the bad news.' Barrington felt Anna's eyes on him, but purposely kept his gaze on her father. 'The necklace was found in your bedroom.'

'My *bedroom*?' There was a moment of stunned silence as Cambermere's smile gave way to a look of utter confusion. 'You found Julia's necklace in this house…in *my* room?'

'Actually, Peregrine found it,' Anna said unhappily.

Her father turned to stare at her in bewilderment. 'And would you care to tell me what Peregrine was doing in my room?'

'He was looking for your watch.'

'My watch.'

'Yes. Edward said you had asked him to take it in for repair.'

'Yes, I did. But I asked Edward, not Peregrine.'

'But Edward had to go out, so he asked Peregrine to take it instead,' Anna said quickly. 'Edward told him where the watch was and when Peregrine went to get it, he found…the necklace.'

'The necklace was in my *wardrobe*?'

Unhappily, Anna nodded. 'In a leather bag next to your watch.'

'But that's impossible!' Cambermere said. 'The last time I saw that necklace, it was around Julia's throat. You were both there, at the dinner party.'

'Then you have no idea how the necklace came to be in your room?' Barrington asked slowly.

'I no more know how it came to be in *my* house than how it came to be taken from the baroness's.' The earl's expression hardened. 'I understood that was *your* job, Parker.'

The note of accusation was unmistakable, but Barrington merely inclined his head. Now came the hard part. 'It was reported to me that someone saw you take the necklace from the baroness's bedroom while she lay sleeping.'

Anna's complexion paled. *'Wh-what?'*

The earl was furious. 'How dare you, sir!'

'Sorry, Cambermere. I'm only repeating what I was told,' Barrington said calmly.

'I don't care what you were told! It's a damned lie!'

'Do you deny being alone with the baroness in her bedroom?' Barrington pressed.

Upon hearing Anna's muffled exclamation, the earl hissed, 'Damn it, man! *Must* we talk about this in front of my daughter?'

Barrington glanced at Anna, aware that her face had gone as red as the glass globes over the lamps. He'd known it would, but it was too late to do anything about it now. 'She asked to be present for the interview and since this is a critical point in the investigation, discussion of it cannot be avoided. If you wish to leave, Lady Annabelle, you are welcome to do so. I will call you back at a more appropriate time.'

'Can't imagine there *being* a more appropriate time

for something like this,' Cambermere muttered under his breath.

But Anna shook her head, struggling to overcome her embarrassment. 'No, I'll stay. And I am sorry, Papa. It isn't Sir Barrington's fault that I'm here. I insisted on being present during his questioning and I am truly sorry if my being here causes you embarrassment. But it is necessary that we get to the truth of the matter.'

'Lady Annabelle isn't mistaken, my Lord,' Barrington said. 'And I regret that the nature of the question had to be so indelicate. But while what you and Baroness von Brohm do behind closed doors is your own business, you would do well to remember that servants talk.'

'Servants!' Cambermere barked. 'Are you telling me it was a servant who claimed to have seen me take the necklace?' At Barrington's brief nod, the earl's face darkened ominously. 'Give me his name, Parker. Give me his name and I'll get to the bottom of this myself. I'm damned if I'll have my name dragged through the mud like some three-legged dog dragging a stick. Whoever told you they saw me take Julia's necklace was telling a lie. An out-and-out lie!'

'Be that as it may, it isn't a lie that you've spent time alone with the baroness.'

The earl coloured. 'No.'

'Then it's possible a servant may have seen you in her bedroom—'

'Perhaps it *is* best I leave.' Anna abruptly stood up, glancing apologetically at Barrington. 'I'm sure it would be easier for my father to talk about this if I weren't here—'

'No, wait,' the earl said. 'Wait.' He cleared his throat, then reached for his glass. After downing the contents, he set the empty glass on the table. 'This isn't the kind of thing one normally discusses in front of…one's children. Especially one's unmarried daughter. But it would be naïve of me to think that…word of this might not leak out and that you wouldn't eventually come to hear of it.' He glanced at his daughter and sighed. 'Yes, I've spent time alone with Julia. We've come to care for one another. I haven't tried to hide that from you, Anna. And given that we are both widowed, we felt there was no harm in…moving forward with our relationship. Can you understand that, my dear?'

Anna nodded, and though Barrington could see that she was still having a hard time meeting her father's eyes, her voice was steady when she said, 'I understand. And I don't blame you, Papa. But it doesn't make things any easier.'

'No, it doesn't,' Barrington agreed. 'Because the question remains, why would a servant make up a story about having seen you take the necklace if there was no truth to it? What would they stand to gain by such a lie? And how do you explain the necklace turning up in your room?'

'I can't explain it.' The earl shook his head, his anger spent. 'I have no answer for any of your questions, Parker. I sincerely wish I did.'

'I think it's someone trying to stir up mischief,' Anna said. 'Someone who holds a grudge against you. The maid, perhaps?'

'I questioned the young lady at length,' Barrington said. 'But she said she doesn't know you and I believe that she's telling the truth, so I doubt a grudge enters into it. Might it be someone to whom you owe money wanting to make things… unpleasant for you?'

The earl's head snapped up. 'What do you know about that?'

'Only that you had a run of bad luck at the track last year,' Barrington said quietly, 'and that you have vowels outstanding to Lords Greening, Featherstone and Blakeley. Your son has also amassed rather staggering debts thanks to losses incurred at the faro table. Debts you have also been endeavouring to pay off.'

He heard Anna's sharp intake of breath. 'Is this true, Papa? Do you and Edward truly owe so much?' When he reluctantly nodded, Anna said, 'Why didn't you tell me?'

'Because it doesn't concern you,' Cambermere growled, though not unkindly. He glanced at Barrington and sighed. 'I can't deny that there are those to whom I owe money, but the debts are not so large that someone need go to these lengths. I assured Greening and Featherstone they would have their money by the end of the month, and Blakely a month or two after.'

'And your son's debts?'

'With luck, they'll be paid off by the end of the year.'

'But what have debts to do with the baroness's necklace being found in Papa's room?' Anna asked.

'They provide a reasonable motive for theft,' Barrington explained. 'A gentleman's debts are seldom a well-kept secret. One has only to read the morning papers. I found out without any difficulty that your father's and brother's combined debts tally to well over sixty thousand pounds.'

Anna blanched. 'Dear God, so *much*!'

'You needn't sound so horrified, it isn't as large as that,' her father muttered. 'I've managed to pay off thirty thousand of it already.'

'Unfortunately, your son accumulated another twenty this past week,' Barrington said quietly.

The earl was aghast. 'Twenty thousand pounds—in *five days*?'

'I'm sorry to be the one to break the bad news to you, Cambermere, but you would have found out soon enough. And I suspect that whoever took the necklace knew of those debts and planned on using them as the justification behind your stealing the necklace.'

The earl seemed to age ten years as he stood there. 'I can't believe that someone would go to these lengths to incriminate me. But I stand by what I said. I did *not* steal Julia's necklace. I wouldn't dream of doing such a cowardly, selfish thing. To think how it would hurt her...' He transferred his gaze to Barrington. 'I don't suppose you have any idea who *is* behind this?'

'Not yet,' Barrington said, 'but I will find out.'

'And until you do, I'm the guilty party,' the earl said heavily.

'You are *not*, Papa!' Anna cried. 'We all know you didn't take the necklace.'

'You and I know that, my dear, but I'll wager Parker has his doubts. And so he should. Right now, the finger of blame is pointing squarely at me.'

'Only as a result of circumstantial evidence.'

'No. As a result of the fact that I was supposedly seen taking the necklace by a member of Julia's staff, and that the said necklace was found in my room by a member of my own family,' her father said bluntly. 'The proof could hardly be less circumstantial.' He clasped his hands behind his back and glanced at the man standing opposite. 'Well, what do you intend to do?'

'For now, I shall tell the baroness that I know where the necklace is, but that I am not at liberty to say where, or to reveal the identity of the person who took it.'

'She's bound to ask,' Anna said.

'Yes, but I am not required to give her an answer. I'll tell her it may compromise the integrity of the investigation.'

'Decent of you, Parker,' the earl said gruffly. 'I'd hate having Julia think she couldn't trust me.'

It was that more than anything else that convinced Barrington of Cambermere's innocence. If a man was that worried about what a woman thought of him, he wouldn't knowingly do something that would destroy his chances of having a relationship with her.

And yet, as he walked home after the interview, Barrington thought about his feelings for Anna and realised he was guilty of doing just that. He was conducting an investigation into the theft of an extremely valuable necklace and, given the lack of any other viable culprit, was still holding her father up as the leading suspect—and earning Anna's resentment as a result.

But *was* Cambermere guilty? Barrington's gut told him no, but he'd met skilful liars before. Men who swore on their children's heads that they were good family men who never lied, cheated, or stole so much as a crust of bread. All the while they were beating their wives half-senseless and mugging old men for brass buttons.

Oh, yes, he knew all about the complexities of deceit. Lies rolled off the tongues of the rich as easily as they did off the tongues of the poor. He'd even come across men he'd *wanted* to believe. Upright, likeable men whom he had respected until he'd found out what they were beneath the polished manners and charming smiles.

Good men turned bad, Barrington called them. Whether by chance or inclination, somewhere along the line they'd made the wrong choices. Some were driven by greed, others by desperation. And once a man faltered, it was only a matter of time until he did so again; the crime becoming a little darker, the stakes a little higher.

Had the earl faltered? Or was it all a carefully constructed plot to make it look as though he had? That was the ultimate question. And until Barrington ascertained who stood to gain by the earl's downfall, the final answer would remain just beyond his grasp. Tantalisingly close, yet agonisingly far.

Chapter Twelve

Anna had no particular desire to pay a call on Julia the following day. Given what she knew about the necklace—*and* about her father's relationship with Julia—she feared it would be both embarrassing and awkward. But when she received Julia's beautifully written note asking her to visit, Anna knew it would be churlish to refuse. The woman's spirits were desperately low as it was. How could she possibly be so cruel as to avoid her now, simply because she had no idea how to act?

And so she went, determined to appear as positive as possible. After all, there was really no reason for Julia to talk about the necklace. She knew the investigation was ongoing and that Barrington would inform her of any new leads the moment they became available. And she certainly wouldn't bring up her relationship with Anna's father. Married or widowed ladies did not talk to single ladies about matters pertaining to the bedroom, so there was no reason to think she would bring that up.

No, Anna was quite sure she was making a mountain out of a molehill. She and Julia would pass their time talking about the new books they were reading, or the poetry recital at Mrs McInley's, or what they planned to wear to Lady Schuster's masquerade a week from Friday. Safe, comfortable topics all.

Unfortunately, all thoughts of comfort fled when Anna walked into the drawing room and found, not just Julia seated on the blue velvet settee, but her brother, Edward, as well.

'Edward! What are you doing here?' Anna exclaimed.

'Am I not allowed to pay morning calls the same as everyone else?'

'I thought you did not care for the custom,' she said bluntly.

Her brother's handsome face curved into an angelic smile. 'A man's likes and dislikes can change given the right motivation.'

'Pray do not take him to task him, Anna,' Julia said quickly. 'He has been most diverting company. He bade me speak about Vienna and I was amazed at how homesick I became. Then, we started talking about you—'

'Me?' Anna levelled a sardonic glance at her brother. 'I can't imagine what the two of you would have to say about me.'

'Can you not?' Edward said innocently. 'I would have thought the possibilities endless. However, in this instance, we were talking about Sir Barrington Parker and the fact that he seems rather taken with you. He calls frequently at the house and I understand you have driven with him in the park. Although,' Edward added with a smile, 'I think he calls as much to see Father and Peregrine as he does Anna, so I suppose I could be mistaken as to which member of the family he is the most interested in.'

'Perhaps it would be safe to say that Sir Barrington has become a good friend of the family,' Julia said, obviously sensing an edge of conflict in the air.

'You could say that.' Edward turned to smile at his sister. 'As you already know, Parker is something of an expert when it comes to investigating the dark doings of others. And unfortunately, my family is no stranger to infamy. Peregrine, for example, was foolish enough to involve himself in a sordid affair with the Marchioness of Yew—'

'I'm sure the baroness has no desire to hear about that, Edward,' Anna said coldly.

'Why not? I found it extremely amusing,' her brother replied unrepentantly. 'Can you imagine, Baroness, an unsophisticated country boy coming to London for the first time and believing himself of interest to the beautiful Lady Yew? In fact, he even went so far as to claim that she was in love with him and that she had every intention of leaving her husband to be with him.'

'Really?' Julia flicked an uncertain glance in Anna's direction. 'I had not heard.'

'It happened before you arrived in London,' Anna said tightly. 'And my brother has no business speaking of it. Apologies have been offered and given that the marquess is agreeable to putting the matter behind him, I see no reason why my brother should not do the same.'

It was an awkward moment and Anna could practically feel the tension vibrating in the air. But she was damned if she was going to let Edward embarrass her in front of Julia with sly remarks about Barrington or inflammatory ones about Peregrine.

Unfortunately, her brother was a master at turning the other cheek. 'How unfortunate it is that social calls must be of such limited duration, Baroness. I fear my time is up. But I did enjoy talking to you about Vienna. As you say, it is a beautiful city and I look forward to seeing it again, now that travel around Europe is so much easier.'

'You must be sure to visit Schonbrunn Palace,' Julia said,

happy for the change of subject. 'It is one of the loveliest places on earth.'

'If you recommend it, I will be sure to include it in my travels. Perhaps we might even visit it together one day.' Edward rose and bowed over her hand. 'Until tomorrow.' Then, straightening, he nodded at his sister. 'Anna.'

Anna inclined her head, not quite in dismissal, but not far off—and Edward knew it. His eyes cooled as he smiled down at her. 'You may be interested in knowing that just before you arrived, I was telling the baroness that I had stumbled upon some information with regards to her necklace. I expect to have more news very soon.'

He left the room with an elegant bow, but in the silence that followed, Anna felt as though a hand was closing around her throat. *He knew about the necklace. And he was going to tell Julia her father was the one who'd taken it.* There could be no other explanation for what he'd just said. And in exposing their father as the thief, Anna knew it would destroy any chance he might have had for a future with Julia. Worse, it would go a long way towards establishing Edward in a more favourable position with her—which meant she had to convince Barrington not only to tell Julia about the necklace, but to return it to her as soon as possible. Before any more harm could be done…

'Anna, are you all right?' Julia enquired softly.

Anna looked up, aware that her worries must have been reflected on her face. 'Fine. It's just that Edward and I are not on the best of terms these days.'

'No, I thought not. Never mind, I'm told it often happens between siblings,' Julia said, making an attempt at light-heartedness. 'But I am surprised Lord Hayle and Mr Rand are not on better terms. I would have thought they'd be good company for one another, being so close in age.'

'I believe that was my father's hope as well, but it is not to be,' Anna admitted with a sigh. 'They are two very different men and they do not see eye to eye on anything.'

'How unfortunate,' Julia murmured. 'Your brother has been so kind to me. He's called several times this week to see how I was faring and to ask if there was anything I needed. When I enquired as to how your father went on, he said it was unlikely he would call, given the nature of the investigation surrounding my necklace. I didn't know what he meant by that.' Julia chewed thoughtfully on her lower lip. 'Or what he meant when he said he was following up on some leads of his own.'

'I don't know either,' Anna said, hoping she sounded convincing. So, Edward was paying regular calls on Julia and dropping hints as to his father's involvement in the theft. What a dutiful son, she thought cynically.

She *had* to talk to Barrington. If Julia was to hear from Edward that their father had taken the necklace—

'Ah, Jones, there you are,' Julia said as a maid came in with the tea tray. 'I was just about to ring.'

'Beg pardon for the delay, ma'am,' the girl said. 'Cook wasn't able to find the right jam.' She put the tray down hard and one of the sandwiches fell to the floor. 'Oh, I'm ever so sorry.'

'That's all right,' Julia said as the girl bent to retrieve it. 'That will be all.'

The girl's cheeks went as bright as cherries, and hastily stuffing the fallen sandwich into her apron pocket, she bobbed a curtsy and left.

'My apologies, Anna,' Julia said. 'The girl is new and sadly in need of training.'

'What happened to your other maid?'

'Unfortunately, Miss Smith left to attend to her sick mother. At least, that's what she told me, though I wonder if there might not be a man involved,' Julia confided. 'I noticed a definite change in her over the last little while, both in manner and in appearance. She lost weight and didn't seem as competent at her job. When I asked her if she was all right, she assured me she was, but given that I wasn't about to pry into her personal life, I left it at that. But I was sorry to lose her. It's not easy finding good staff.'

No, it wasn't, Anna reflected, but neither was finding a good position. Were Miss Smith's reasons for leaving as simple as Julia made them out to be? Anna hadn't forgotten the sight of her brother and the maid locked in a passionate embrace. Had Miss Smith been caught in the arms of another guest and the discovery forced Julia's hand? If the maid had allowed Edward to kiss her, who was to say that she hadn't allowed other men to do the same—or worse?

Still, Anna knew it was none of her concern. Servants no more appreciated their affairs being discussed by their betters, than those above stairs liked thinking their problems were being discussed by those below. As such, she wasn't at all sorry when the conversation veered back to the upcoming masquerade and to the elaborate costume Julia was planning to wear. They spent the next half-hour happily discussing hairstyles, with neither Edward nor the missing necklace being mentioned again.

It wasn't often that Barrington found himself in a quandary. His nature was such that when he was given a task, he set about resolving it as efficiently as possible. That was the manner in which he had approached the Marquess of Yew's request that he find his wife's latest lover, and the manner in which he had expected to solve the case of the baroness's missing necklace.

But when faced with the daughter of the prime suspect *insisting* that he return the necklace *before* the identity of the thief could be confirmed, Barrington realised that resolution was going to be neither quick nor easy.

That was his dilemma as he stood beside her at the Billinghams' soirée two nights later and the reason for his preoccupation. Because by doing what Anna asked, he risked compromising the entire investigation. There were always a series of steps that needed to be followed. Questions that had to be asked. Leads that had to be investigated. Following the steps in order helped ensure that he didn't miss a vital piece of information.

Doing what Anna suggested threatened to throw everything off. It was like closing the barn door after the horse had bolted. Granted, he was relieved to have the necklace back in one piece, but it wasn't just a simple matter of handing it back to the baroness now and calling the case closed. He had to find out what had prompted the theft in the first place. He'd meant what he'd said when he'd told Anna that if the thief found out his first attempt to discredit the earl had failed, he might well try again.

But how could he not try to accommodate her when doing so would make her so happy—

'Barrington?'

Her voice, gently insistent, recalled him to the moment. Guiltily, he looked down to find her watching him. 'Forgive me, Anna, I was following a train of thought.' They had slipped into the comfortable habit of calling each other by their first names when they were alone and Barrington was glad of it. Somehow, it lessened the distance between them. Now, as he gazed down at her, he tried not to notice how glorious she looked in the beautiful cream-coloured gown, the soft swell of her breasts rising provocatively above the edging of fine lace. 'You were saying something about your brother?'

'I was saying that I'm afraid he's going to expose my father in front of Julia,' Anna whispered. 'Why else would he have said what he did?'

'I don't know.' Barrington tried focusing his attention on her face, but that didn't work either. Her smile captivated him, her mouth entranced him. And her lips…her lips were an invitation to seduction—

'Barrington, are you even listening to me?' she accused.

'Yes, of course.' He dragged his mind back with considerable effort. 'What makes you think your brother would turn on your father in such a way?'

'I'm not saying he would. But you said yourself, there's been tension between them of late and that's why I need you to return the necklace to Julia as soon as possible. If she has it in her hands, she won't believe that my father had anything to do with its theft, no matter what kind of rumours she hears.'

'Why would she believe your father guilty of having taken the necklace if she *didn't* have it in her hands?' Barrington asked logically. 'Has she any reason to doubt your father's integrity?'

'No, but Edward can be very persuasive when he wants to be. If he wished to put my father in a bad light with Julia, he is entirely capable of doing so. And I didn't like the way he was looking at her. It was far too…familiar. And Julia admitted that he had been to see her several times since the theft of the necklace.'

Barrington let his gaze travel around the room, his thoughts occupied with what she had just said. So, the son was paying court to the woman his father was in love with and making no attempt to hide it. It wasn't a pleasant situation for anyone and it had the potential to cause considerable harm. 'Anna, I understand your concern—'

'No, I don't think you do. You don't know my brother the way I do. You don't how vindictive he can be.'

Having born witness to Hayle's temper during the fencing match, Barrington was strongly tempted to disagree, but, equally aware that voicing an opinion would only stir up another hornet's nest, he said, 'Very well. If it means that much to you, I will return the necklace to the baroness tomorrow.'

'You will?'

'Yes, but you are to tell no one that I've done so, and I shall counsel the baroness to do the same. The integrity of the investigation *must* be maintained—as much as it is now possible to do so.'

Anna glanced down at the floor, but when she raised her head and smiled at him, Barrington caught his breath. He had been the recipient of a thousand smiles, but none had ever affected him to the degree hers did. 'Thank you, Barrington. I am now and for ever in your debt.'

And you are now and for ever in my heart.

The sentiment came unbidden, and Barrington stood motionless, the realisation having caught him totally unawares. *He was in love with her.* He had no idea when it had happened. All he knew was that he wanted to pull her into his arms and whisper a thousand secret longings in her ear. To take her to his bed and make love to her until they were both weak and trembling. To obliterate every thought from her mind that didn't involve him.

But he couldn't do any of those things because nothing had really changed. Anna was still who she was and he was still who he was. Their situations hadn't altered. Only the way he thought of her...

'Parker! A word in private, if you don't mind.'

The crisp, imperious voice had Barrington turning around in surprise. 'Good evening, Colonel.' Curious. Tanner never spoke to him when other people were around. He wondered what could have prompted the change. 'I was just finishing speaking to Lady Annabelle.' He turned back and bowed over her hand. 'Would you excuse me?'

'Of course. But we will speak again soon?'

He saw the glimmer of hope in her eyes and felt it echoed within his heart, though for entirely different reasons. 'You may be sure of it.'

She departed in a whisper of silk, the sweet scent of gardenias lingering in the air. Barrington didn't follow her progress across the room because he knew better than to display an interest in her here, where all the world could see. But he felt her absence keenly. 'You wished to speak to me, Colonel?'

'Damn right I wished to speak to you. I want to know if you've found Elizabeth!'

'I have, but I fear you will not be happy with what I am about to tell you.'

'Why not?'

'Because it turns out that Miss Paisley has come under someone else's protection.'

'The devil you say!' The Colonel's bushy white eyebrows drew together. 'You mean…she's left me?'

'I'm afraid so,' Barrington replied gently.

'But why? I gave her everything she asked for: gowns, trinkets, pretty ribbons for her hair.'

'Can you think of any other reason she might have left?'

The Colonel's cheeks coloured. 'I never asked her to do anything disrespectful, if that's what you're suggesting. Wouldn't consider such a thing.'

Barrington studied the face of the man before him and felt a genuine stab of pity. Tanner obviously had feelings of affection for Miss Paisley, but if *she* didn't care about him in return…

'I have no answers as to why she left, Colonel,' he said quietly. 'I can only tell you that she did.'

'Who is he?'

'I'd rather not say.'

'Why not? That's why I engaged you, isn't it?' Tanner said gruffly.

'No, you engaged me to find out where Miss Paisley was and if she was safe. That's what I've done. There's really no value in my telling you anything more than that.' Besides, he would no doubt find out soon enough on his own, Barrington reflected. The movement of mistresses between society gentlemen was not a closely guarded secret.

The Colonel knew it, too. He gazed across the room, disappointment evident on his face. 'So you don't think she will come back?'

'I have no reason to believe she will, no.'

The older man nodded. 'Right. Well then, I suppose that's an end to it. At least I know she's all right.' He cleared his throat, rocked back and forth on the balls of his feet. 'Appreciate you taking it on, Parker.'

'I'm sorry the news wasn't better, Colonel.'

Tanner nodded, but walked away before Barrington had a chance to say anything more. It was clear that Miss Paisley's defection had hurt him and Barrington was again moved to wonder what had prompted her to leave. The Colonel had taken her off the streets and given her a place to live, paid for the clothes on her back and made sure there was food on her table—yet she had still walked away.

Why? What prompted a woman like that to leave a man who had been so good to her? The arrival of a wealthier lover? One with a loftier title? Surely that could be of no consequence to a woman like Elizabeth Paisley. She was a lady's maid turned prostitute, not a blushing débutante looking for a husband. And while Hayle was certainly the younger man, Barrington doubted he would have given her more in the way of jewels or clothes than the Colonel. It was quite possible he'd given her less, believing that mistresses were twenty to the dozen. Tanner, being older and wiser, knew more about life and love…

Love. Oh, dear God, surely that wasn't what had lured Elizabeth Paisley away? The misplaced belief that Hayle might offer her more than just a bed? That he had genuine feelings for her?

As unlikely as it seemed, Barrington knew it wasn't an impossibility. If Miss Paisley had any degree of education, she would know more of the world than the hardened doxies who made their livings on the streets and might well believe that such things happened. According to Tanner, she *had* come from a decent family, only to fall on hard times when her parents had died. She had tried making a living as a lady's maid, but had fallen victim, as so many women did, to the wandering hands of the master and, without the references necessary to obtain another post, had ended up on the streets.

Yes, it was entirely possible that Eliza's move had been prompted by unattainable dreams, Barrington reflected sadly. He'd rather think it was that than something more disturbing. Something that bordered on the devious. Something that was in all ways far less admirable…

Anna stood by the edge of the dance floor and listened to the lilting strains of a waltz. The dance was far less scandalous than when it had first made its appearance in the ballrooms of society, but it was still one of the few that could raise eyebrows. Gentlemen sometimes moved a little too close and, if a mother's watchful eye was turned, a hand might draw a slender waist nearer or hold a lady's hand tighter than was acceptable.

Anna had spent a good deal of time watching the actions of couples on the floor. While it was not advisable for single girls to dance the waltz, there were always those who did and who had required Anna's services not long after. Tonight, however, her thoughts were not on the dancers, but on the situation with her father and her brother, and even more so with the uncomfortable predicament in which she found herself with Barrington.

She knew that by asking him to give the necklace back to Julia, she was asking him to do something that went against his principles, but she was so afraid for her father's reputation that it was more than she could do to withdraw the request. But what damage had it done to her relationship with Barrington? It felt as though they had not been easy with one another for an age. And though she knew they would not have a future together, why, oh, why couldn't she just put him from her mind altogether? This constant thinking about him was wearing her down. Why couldn't she just accept that he was beyond her reach and move on?

Because you want to be the one, whispered the voice inside her head. *The woman he turns to in the darkness of the night. The one who smoothes the lines of worry from his brow, and who makes him forget everything but the sweetness of the moment...*

'Anna, where have you been?' Lydia said, coming up to her. 'I've been looking for you all evening!'

'Why?' Anna said, lingering in dreams. 'Is something wrong?'

'I've just heard the most dreadful thing.' Lydia glanced around, lowered her voice. 'About your father.'

The dreams vanished, destroyed in the rush of returning reality. 'Tell me!'

'Not here.' Taking her arm, Lydia led Anna to a far corner of the room. When she was sure they were beyond anyone's hearing, she said, 'There's a rumour going around that—' she broke off, blushing furiously. 'Oh dear, this isn't at all easy.'

'Please, Lydia. I must know!'

'Yes, of course you must. It's just that…I can't believe he would do something like this.'

'He?'

'Mr Rand.'

'Peregrine?' Anna frowned in confusion. 'I thought you said you'd heard something about my father?'

'I have.' Lydia took a deep breath and said, 'Apparently, someone overheard Mr Rand say that…he'd found the baroness's necklace amongst your father's things.'

'What?' Anna didn't realise how loud she'd spoken until she saw heads begin to turn in their direction. Quickly forcing a smile, she waited for them to look away again before leaning in closer to Lydia. 'There must be some mistake. Peregrine thinks the world of my father. He would *never* do something like this.'

'That's what I thought, too, but I'm just repeating what I heard. And there's more,' Lydia said unhappily. 'Rumour has it that your brother's debts have been paid off and people are wondering where the money came from.'

Anna's first thought was that they had not acted quickly enough. Her second was to wonder how to stem the damage before matters got any worse. 'Who started the rumour?'

'No one seems to know. But it isn't a secret that your father and brother were having trouble meeting their debts. So when word leaked out that the baroness's necklace had been stolen and that she and your father were…well, involved, it was suggested that your father might have seen an easy way out of his financial difficulties. Then when Mr Rand said he'd found the necklace in your father's things, followed by word of your brother's debts being cleared, it only added fuel to the fire.' She broke off, sick at heart. 'I'm so sorry, Anna, but I thought you should know.'

Anna muttered something unrepeatable, apologised to

Lydia, then quickly left the room. She was seldom moved to profanity, but what else could she say when matters kept going so terribly wrong? Peregrine had been discovered in an illicit affair with Lady Yew. Everyone seemed to know that her father and brother were mired in debt. And now rumours were flying that her father was a thief and that a member of his own family had given him up.

It was enough to make a saint turn to the devil!

But even as anger and disbelief swelled at the thought of Peregrine having betrayed her father's secret, common sense told her it couldn't be true. Peregrine would *never* reveal what he had seen. She had been there with him the day he'd found the necklace. She had seen the anguish on his face and known that he'd suffered over that discovery as much as she had.

No, Peregrine wasn't the one who'd started the rumour. Barrington was right; the person who wished her father harm was definitely the one behind all this. The lie was just one more piece in a carefully devised plot to incriminate her father, and whoever had laid the groundwork for this unspeakable crime had done their job well. Her father's reputation couldn't *hope* to survive a constant barrage of rumours and innuendos. He would be destroyed, given the cut direct by those who mattered in society. Even those who might have the courage to defend him risked being cut, and those who believed him guilty would never speak to him again. But there had to be a way of finding out who it was and of exposing him for what he'd done.

Anna thought back over everything Barrington had said. *…a maid in the baroness's house…gone in to check on her mistress…saw him take the necklace…*

So, a maid had seen her father take the necklace. Which maid? The same one Anna had seen kissing her brother in the darkness of the deserted study? A very pretty maid who'd left the baroness's employ shortly after the necklace disappeared—

Anna gasped. Was it possible? She'd seen Edward and the maid together *before* the necklace had disappeared. Then the maid had left and a few days later Anna had discovered that Edward had acquired a new mistress. She'd overheard him talking to one of his friends about a girl named Eliza.

Coincidence—or something more calculated?

Unlike many of his friends, Edward didn't keep his mistresses close at hand. He preferred to put them up in a house on a quiet street south of Regent's Park. Fortunately, Anna had stumbled upon the address one day whilst cleaning out a desk drawer and committed it to memory.

Now, as she stepped out of the carriage onto what was a clearly less than affluent street, she was glad she'd thought to do so. She scanned the row of plates and found Number Nineteen second to last in the row—an unprepossessing brick townhouse with dark shutters and blackened chimney pots.

Paying the driver a guinea to wait, Anna took a deep breath and started towards the door. Her heart was pounding and though part of her wanted to turn around and get back in the cab, curiosity and a need to discover the truth drove her forwards. She raised her hand to the knocker and brought it down sharply, three times.

An older woman wearing a white apron over a stiff black gown opened the door. Her face was hard and unforgiving as she stared down at her caller. 'Yes?'

'Is Miss Smith in?' Anna enquired.

Watching the woman run a critical eye over her appearance, Anna was glad she'd thought to wear the clothes she had. Dressed in a plain gown and pelisse in a nondescript shade of brown, a straw bonnet the style of which was a few years out of date, and leather gloves that were far from new, she resembled nothing so much as a governess or a servant, an assessment clearly shared by the housekeeper. 'What would you be wanting with Eliza?'

'I'd like to talk to her, if I may. We used to work together at Baroness von Brohm's and I was wondering—'

'Justine, is that you?' a voice floated down from the landing. 'How did you get—oh!'

Eliza Smith was halfway down the stairs before she realised that her visitor wasn't who she thought. Her pretty face fell and her smile disappeared. But when she looked at Anna again and recognition dawned, her expression of disappointment changed to one of fear. With a muffled cry, she bolted back up the stairs.

'Miss Smith, wait!' Anna cried. 'I need to talk to you!' She went to move past the housekeeper, but found her way blocked. 'Kindly step aside.'

'I don't think the girl wants to see you,' the woman said.

'Well, I'd like to see her,' Anna said. 'If you'll just let me through…'

It was like trying to move a mountain. The woman wouldn't budge and, given that the doorway wasn't wide enough for Anna to go around her, she was stuck. 'Why won't you let me see her?'

'Because the master said I wasn't to let anyone in and I know better than to disobey,' the woman said. 'He'd have my job, and I've six mouths at home to feed.'

Recognising desperation, Anna stepped back, her eyes narrowing even as her stance straightened. 'How much does your master pay you?'

The woman's cheeks flushed, both as a result of the autocratic tone and by Anna's sudden change in stature. 'That's none of your business.'

'It could be.' Anna opened her reticule and taking out a

coin, held it in front of the woman's face. 'This would feed your family for a month.'

'That's a guinea!'

'It is. And if you let me pass, it's yours.'

'Who are you?' the housekeeper asked, staring at the coin like a hungry dog eyeing a bone. 'Maids and governesses don't carry that kind of blunt.'

'I am neither a lady's maid nor a governess. And I have plenty more of these.'

It was shameless blackmail, but Anna suspected it was the only way she was going to get what she wanted. She needed the woman's co-operation and, if necessary, she was prepared to buy her way into the house. Fortunately, she didn't have long to wait. The housekeeper grabbed the coin and jerked her head in the direction of the stairs.

'Go on then, but be quick about it. Gold won't keep me safe if he comes round and finds I've let you in. Five minutes is all you get!'

Deciding it would have to be enough, Anna ran up the darkened stairway, her soft-soled boots making no sound on the threadbare carpet. Turning right at the landing, she found herself standing in front of a closed door. 'Miss Smith?' she called, trying the handle and finding it locked.

'Go away!'

'Eliza, please! I need to talk to you!'

'I've got nothing to say!'

'That's not true. You can help a lot of people by talking to me,' Anna insisted.

'I don't care about other people,' came the girl's muffled reply. 'Nobody cares about *me*.'

'*I* care,' Anna said. 'And if you'll let me, I'll get you out of here.'

Silence followed her rashly offered promise, leaving Anna to wonder if she'd said the right thing. If this was the girl's only home, she might not be all that anxious to leave. But looking at the water stains in the ceiling, the faded and peeling wallpaper, and the warped floorboards beneath her feet, Anna couldn't help thinking how lowering it must be to come home to this every night.

'Eliza, please!' Seconds were ticking by. Any minute, the housekeeper would appear at the bottom of the stairs, demanding that she leave, and Anna wasn't so naïve as to think she would get a second chance at getting back inside. 'I promise you won't come to any harm. Just open the door.'

Out on the street, Anna heard a vendor raucously hawking his wares. She heard the sounds of children laughing and the clatter of carriage wheels as they rattled past the front door. Normal, everyday sounds—and still the door remained closed. Which meant Anna had no choice. She only had time for one last desperate attempt.

'You won't get away with it, Eliza,' she said quietly against the door. 'I know you took the necklace. And I *will* go to the authorities if you refuse to talk to me.'

Chapter Thirteen

That was all she said. Fear or anger would compel the girl to open the door now because it didn't matter whether the accusations were true or not. A servant accused of stealing from her employer couldn't hope to win her case.

Eliza Smith was obviously smart enough to know that. Moments later, the door opened and she stood silently in the doorway.

Anna caught her breath. The girl facing her now wasn't the same pretty maid who had served her tea at Julia's house. Her once-shining hair hung lank around her small face, her complexion was ashen and there were faint purple shadows on her cheeks and around her beautiful green eyes. Dear God, what had Edward done to her? 'Are you all right?'

'Fine.' The girl lifted her chin, but Anna saw the way her lips trembled. 'What do you want?'

'To ask you a few questions.' Anna made no attempt to move forwards. 'I think you know about what.'

The girl didn't say a word. She simply turned and walked back into the room, every step a reflection of her state of mind. Anna followed, mutely taking in the details of her surroundings. The walls were papered in the same faded maroon silk as in the hallway, the curtains were pale grey and frayed at the edges, and the bed and dressing table… well, she'd seen better furnishings in a boarding school. Her brother obviously hadn't expended any time or money on the upkeep of this house.

'How did you get past Betty?' Eliza asked in a flat voice. 'She was told not to let anyone in.'

'I bribed her,' Anna said, closing the door. 'I wasn't going to leave without seeing you.' She took a few steps into the room, and then stopped. 'What happened to you, Eliza? Those bruises on your face—'

'I fell,' the girl said, abruptly turning away. 'And hit my head on the door.'

'Eliza—'

'It was foolish you coming here,' Eliza said, an element of fear in her voice. 'My gentleman could be back at any time.'

'I know who owns this house, Eliza,' Anna said gently. 'And judging from those bruises, you would do well to get away from him as soon as possible.'

'I can't,' Eliza said, shaking her head. 'He'll kill me.'

'No, he won't,' Anna said. Her brother might be many things, but a murderer wasn't one of them. 'But I need you to tell me the truth about your relationship with Edward and about the baroness's necklace.'

The girl collapsed on to the bed, her dark hair falling forwards. 'I can't!'

'Yes, you can,' Anna sat down beside her. 'If you did nothing wrong, you have nothing to be afraid of.'

'But I *did* do something wrong.' The girl looked up and Anna saw tears forming in the huge green eyes. 'I didn't want to, but he told me it would be all right. That I wouldn't get caught.'

'He being my brother,' Anna clarified.

The girl nodded. 'He told me the baroness had so many other lovely bits of jewellery that she'd never miss that one piece. And he told me he'd protect me if anyone came along asking questions.'

'But if you knew that what you were doing was wrong, why did you do it?'

Eliza stared at the dirty bedcover. 'Because he asked me to. He said that…if he had the necklace, he could sell it and then we'd have the money we needed to run away together.'

The cruelty of the lie stabbed at Anna's heart. 'And you believed him.'

'I loved him,' Eliza said, dragging the back of her hand across her eyes. 'I did from the very first time I saw him. I would have done anything to make him happy. *Anything.*'

'But you must have known it couldn't work between you. What about the difference in your situations?'

'Edward assured me that it didn't matter.' Eliza looked at her and Anna saw the naked hope shining in her eyes even now. 'He said that because I spoke properly and carried myself well, no one would know I wasn't a lady. Especially when I was all dressed up. And I did have nice clothes when I met him.'

Suspecting that the clothes were cast-offs from a previous employer, Anna said, 'You were lucky that your former mistress was so generous.'

Eliza bit her lip, guilt adding to the misery on her face. 'They weren't from an employer, my lady. They were from a gentleman. I did work as a lady's maid, but when the mistress found her son trying to break into my room, she said I'd have to leave and that she wouldn't provide me with references. So I left, and when I couldn't find decent work, I ended up in a brothel.'

Anna sighed. It wasn't an unusual story. Girls in Eliza's

position had very few avenues open to them, even those who, like her, were fortunate enough to have some degree of education or training. 'That must have been very difficult for you.'

'It was horrible,' Eliza said bluntly. 'But, it could have been worse. Mrs Brown, the woman who kept the place, made sure we had good food and there was always medical care if any of the girls needed it. She told me her clients were very particular about that kind of thing and that she couldn't afford to have any of her girls getting sick.'

Anna nodded, knowing how miserable the lives of girls forced into prostitution could be. Even for those who had the good luck to find an establishment where the abbess cared about their welfare, a girl's worth diminished with every year that passed. As her looks faded, so did her value. 'Were you there long?'

'No. I met the Colonel…the gentleman I mentioned…on my first night. He was a kind man. I think he knew how frightened I was and he was…very gentle with me,' Eliza said, avoiding Anna's eyes, though two bright spots of colour stood out on her cheeks. 'Afterwards, he asked me about myself, where I'd come from and if I had any family. I told him I'd been born in Leeds, but that I'd moved to London after my parents died. I explained that I'd been a lady's maid and told him why I'd had to leave. He was quiet for a bit, then he asked me if I might consider working for his wife. Apparently she needed a maid; when I reminded him that I didn't have any references, he said it wouldn't be necessary and that I was to present myself at his house at ten o'clock the following morning.'

'And you were given the position?' At Eliza's nod, Anna said, 'You were exceedingly fortunate.'

'Yes, I was. Of course, there was one small…additional requirement,' Eliza added, again avoiding Anna's eyes.

'That you become his mistress?'

Eliza nodded. 'He said he and his wife hadn't shared a bed in years due to her being so poorly. He asked if he could see me, and when I said I didn't like the idea of him coming to me in the attic, he told me he'd be careful. It was all right for a while, but I think his wife saw the way he looked at me and knew what was going on, so she asked me to leave. She wasn't mean about it. She said she knew her husband kept mistresses, but that she wasn't willing to live with one in her own home.'

That was fair enough, Anna thought. She couldn't imagine *any* woman being happy about seeing the face of her husband's mistress in the mirror every morning as she brushed out her hair or fastened her gown. 'What happened after that?'

'The Colonel felt so bad about my having to leave that he said if I was willing to…continue with the arrangement, he'd put me up in a nice little house and buy me clothes and make sure I had everything I needed. Since I liked him well enough and thought it would be an easy life, I agreed.'

'Yet you left him.'

Eliza began fidgeting with the edge of the bedsheet. 'It was never my intention to be somebody's mistress, my lady. Even though the Colonel wasn't demanding, I didn't feel right about…what I was doing. So one day, I looked through a newspaper he'd left on the dining room table and happened to see an advertisement for a lady's maid. I thought I didn't have much of a chance, but I desperately wanted the position, so I put on the nicest of the gowns he'd given me and wore new gloves and a bonnet so I would look respectable.'

'And you went to see the baroness?' Anna said.

Eliza nodded. 'She was ever so nice. She didn't seem to care that I had no references. She said she liked the way I looked and that I had a nice way about me. She told me what the wages were and said I could start right away. And I did, as Miss Eliza Smith. I thought it would be best to start with a clean slate. I left the Colonel's house that very day.'

'Did you tell him about the position?'

Eliza shook her head. 'I didn't have the heart to. But I only took one of the dresses he bought me, apart from the one I wore to the interview.'

'So you didn't leave the Colonel because of my brother?'

'Oh, no, my lady!' Eliza said quickly. 'The first time I saw Edward was just before the baroness's dinner party. I was on Bond Street, picking up some things for her ladyship when I saw him walking towards me. I remember thinking I'd never seen a more handsome man in my life. I saw him twice more after that, and each time I did, my knees would go weak and I'd feel all quivery inside, as if I was filled with feathers. I'd never felt that way about a man before. Then when he turned up at the baroness's dinner party and I saw him with that other gentleman, I thought I was going to faint dead away.'

'But you didn't,' Anna said drily.

'No. Mr Hansen told me to be off and I had to go. But I was that upset, I couldn't settle to anything, so I went into the study to tidy up. Edward must have seen me and followed me. Then when you came in—' Eliza broke off, her face turning bright red. 'Well, you know what happened.'

Anna did, aware that the sight of her brother and Miss Smith locked in a passionate embrace would stay with her for the rest of her life. 'So you became Edward's mistress,' she prompted.

The girl nodded 'I lived for those moments, my lady. They were the only thing that kept me going. Please don't misunderstand, it wasn't just about *being* with him. Or about the fact he was a gentleman. It was just that…no one had ever made me feel the way he did. No one had ever said…they loved me before.'

Anna felt her heart go out to the girl. Poor Eliza. She was no different than Mercy Banks or Cynthia Wicks…or herself when faced with a man who made her bones melt. Reason and logic flew out the window when rational thought was banished by irrational desire.

Because love wasn't logical. The mistake was in trying to make it so.

'When did things begin to change?' Anna asked, her gaze touching on the bruises.

'After I took the necklace,' Eliza said in a dull, flat voice. 'That's when he stopped talking about us being together. He stopped treating me like a lover—and started treating me like a whore.' She looked up and Anna saw the hopelessness in her expression. 'That's when I saw him for what he really was.'

Anna nodded and resolutely got to her feet. 'You can't stay here any longer, Eliza. It will be safest if you come away with me now.'

'I can't!'

'Yes, you can. Obviously the relationship isn't going to continue if this is how he treats you. Besides, I need you to tell someone the truth about the necklace.'

Eliza's lips were pressed tightly together, her head going from side to side.

'Listen to me,' Anna said firmly. 'There's a rumour going around that my father stole the baroness's necklace. A rumour I have every reason to believe my brother started. And if nothing is done to correct it, my father's reputation *will* be destroyed.'

'I know,' Eliza said miserably. 'I felt terrible when I heard that. I asked Edward about it, but that's when he turned on me. He said it was none of my business and that I wasn't to talk to anyone about what really happened. He said if I did, he'd hurt Justine.'

Anna frowned. 'Justine?'

'My sister,' Eliza said, her eyes filling with fresh tears. 'Edward said he'd…make it worse for her if I stepped out of line. That's why he told Betty I wasn't to have any visitors—or to be let out.'

Anna stared. 'You're not allowed to go out at all?'

'Not unless he's with me,' Eliza said. 'I have to do as he says or he'll hurt her. And I couldn't bear that, my lady. Justine's younger than me and she's never been as strong. I've spent the last two years looking after her. That's why I was willing to do whatever I had to in order to get money. I promised our mother I'd take care of her.'

Anna sat back, struggling to come to terms with this disquieting piece of news. Her brother was keeping one girl a prisoner and threatening another with physical harm? What kind of monster was he? He obviously had no conscience at all…

'…and Justine's been so happy working for the baroness.'

'I beg your pardon?' Jerked from her thoughts, Anna said, 'Your *sister* works for the baroness, too? But you were the one I saw—'

And then the penny dropped. Of *course*. Eliza was the girl Anna had *first* seen at Julia's house, but she wasn't the *same* girl who had served her tea on several occasions after that. *That* had been Justine. And if you didn't look closely, it would be all too easy to mistake one for the other. Both girls had the same dark hair and the same elfin face, but where Eliza's eyes were a deep, clear green, Justine's were a pale misty blue.

'Eliza, did Sir Barrington question *you* about the theft of the baroness's necklace, or your sister?' Anna asked shrewdly.

'That was Justine,' Eliza said sheepishly. 'She didn't

know anything about the necklace, so when the butler told us someone was coming to ask questions about its theft, I asked Justine to work in my place. And because she knew nothing, she was able to be convincing when the gentleman questioned her.'

'So you and your sister have been sharing the job without the baroness knowing?'

A guilty flush suffused Eliza's cheeks. 'I didn't think she'd mind, my lady. I was nervous the first time Justine stood in for me, but she said everything went well and the baroness didn't question me about it when I went in next, so we carried on.'

'And none of the baroness's other servants questioned the arrangement?'

'None of them knew. There was only myself and the tweenie on that floor and she wouldn't say boo to a goose. Cook had quarters downstairs and Mr Hansen's room was on a separate floor. And Justine and I were very careful about our comings and goings.'

'But why did you do it?'

'To give Justine the training she needs to become a maid,' Eliza explained. 'I realised I wouldn't be able to look after her all the time, or make enough money to support the two of us, so we decided she would learn the skills necessary to go into service. I gave her as much time as I could when we lived with the Colonel—'

'Justine *lived* with you in the Colonel's house?' Anna interrupted. 'Did he *know* that?

'I made sure he didn't,' Eliza said. 'I had no choice, my lady. Justine had been working as a nanny to a man who worked at a bank. When he started trying to get her alone, I knew I had to get her out of there before it was too late. So I told her to leave and had her come live with me. The Colonel never knew,' Eliza assured her. 'I was the only one who went to him. Justine stayed in the kitchen whenever he came round. She knew what I was doing and she wasn't happy about it, but neither of us was in a position to complain.'

'Where is Justine living now?' Anna asked.

Eliza blushed deeply. 'At Mrs Brown's.'

Anna gasped. 'Your sister's staying at a *brothel*?'

'Only until I can make other arrangements,' Eliza said quickly. 'I couldn't leave her at the Colonel's, but I didn't want to bring her here either, so I let her use my room at the baroness's house until I gave notice. Then both of us had to leave. I couldn't afford to have Edward know where she was.'

'But to arrange for her to stay at a brothel—'

'It's the only place I could afford, my lady, and she's not working,' Eliza said. 'Mrs Brown promised me that. She's letting Justine have a small room in the basement, well away from the other girls. But I have to get her out as soon as I can.'

'Then we shall do so this very afternoon.' Anna abruptly got to her feet. 'You and your sister need to disappear until this situation can be satisfactorily resolved.'

'But Edward will come after me,' Eliza whispered. 'And Justine, too, if he finds out where she is!'

'He won't get the chance,' Anna said resolutely. 'I'm going to take you to the home of a good friend, then go back for Justine. Together we'll work out how to keep both of you safe until someone I know can get to the bottom of this.'

Anna saw how desperately the girl wanted to believe what she was saying, but she also saw the depth of her fear. 'I'd like to believe you, my lady, but—'

'Believe me, Eliza. I won't let Edward hurt you or your sister. Now, pack your things and let's be off.'

'You'll have to get past Betty first!' Eliza whispered. 'And

that won't be easy. She knows Edward will make it the worse
for her if she lets me go!'

'Then I'll find a place for Betty as well,' Anna said, aware
that matters were getting more complicated by the minute—
but she had no choice. She refused to see these women's lives
made worse as a result of their association with her brother.
She opened the wardrobe and took out the girl's tiny valise.
'What will you take?'

Eliza glanced at the array of dresses hanging in the closet
and shook her head. 'Nothing. I don't want anything he
bought me, because he never really wanted me, did he, my
lady? Only what I could steal for him.'

Anna wasn't sure how to answer that. What could she say
that wouldn't destroy the poor girl more than she already had
been? 'You must forget what my brother has done, Eliza,'
Anna said gently. 'When you leave here, you'll have no reason
to see him again.'

'I'd like to believe that,' Eliza said again, 'but he won't
take the blame for the theft of the necklace. He'll tell people
I took it, and once that gets around, I'll be arrested.'

'That's why you're not going to stay in London,' Anna said
firmly. 'I know people in the country. Good people who will
be only too happy to give you and your sister positions. My
brother will never find either of you.'

'But the necklace—'

'The necklace has been found and will be returned to the
baroness without her ever knowing how it came to be stolen.
Now, come along. We have much to do before this day is
over.'

Removing Eliza Smith from her brother's house was one
of the easier tasks Anna had to do that day. She hustled her
down the narrow staircase and after checking to make sure
that Betty was nowhere in sight, opened the front door and

pointed her in the direction of the waiting carriage. Then, telling the driver to wait, Anna went back in search of the housekeeper, knowing the poor woman had to be made aware of the situation.

Betty didn't have to be told twice. Aware that her employment would be terminated as soon as Edward learned of Eliza's escape, she threw off her apron, grabbed what few personal belongings she had, and left the house at the same time as Anna and Eliza, with two more of Anna's guineas jingling in her pocket.

'Can we stop and pick up Justine?' Eliza asked when Anna gave the driver the direction of the Park Lane home of the Marquess of Bailley.

'There isn't room,' Anna said. 'I'll go back for her once you're safely out of sight.'

Arriving at the Marquess of Bailley's house, Anna walked up to the front door with Eliza at her side and knocked on the door. It was answered in moments by Hilton, the family's long-standing butler. 'Good afternoon, Lady Annabelle.'

'Good afternoon, Hilton. Is Lady Lydia in?'

'She is, my lady. In the rose salon.'

'Thank you. Would you be so kind as to take Miss Smith down to the kitchen? She would be most grateful for a cup of tea.'

The unflappable Hilton didn't bat an eye. 'Of course, my lady.' Signalling a maid, he told her to take the young lady downstairs. Once that was taken care of, Anna made her way to the rose salon and within minutes, she was giving her friend a terse though somewhat abbreviated version of all that had happened.

'You wish me to keep Miss Smith and her sister *here*?' Lydia asked at the conclusion.

'Only for a little while,' Anna said. 'For obvious reasons, I can't risk having either of them stay with me. And I promise it will only be for a few days. I'm going to see Sir Barrington right now and tell him everything that's happened.'

'He's not going to be happy when he hears that you've involved yourself in this,' Lydia warned.

'Why not? He should be delighted that I've solved his case for him,' Anna protested.

'Not when he learns that you put yourself in harm's way to do so!'

'I was hardly in harm's way,' Anna said drily.

'You think going to Edward's house and kidnapping his battered mistress isn't going to spark a reaction?' Lydia demanded incredulously. 'I shudder to think what he would have done had he arrived and caught you in the act.'

'He would have been angry and told me to mind my own business, but it's silly to suggest that I was in any kind of danger,' Anna said. 'He is my brother, after all.'

'That doesn't absolve him. Edward is a wicked man and wicked men are capable of anything. Have you forgotten what happened to Sarah Wentworth?'

Anna's jaw tightened. How could anyone forget what had happened to that poor woman? Her husband had mistakenly believed her guilty of having an affair and had had her committed to an institution, even though it was clear to anyone who saw her that there was absolutely nothing wrong with her mind. Nevertheless, she disappeared one night and it was months before someone happened to see her in the asylum and made a complaint to the lady's father. Even then, it had taken considerable effort on her family's part to have her released and the resulting scandal had been horrendous.

'Please help me, Lydia. Will you keep Eliza and her sister here? It won't be for long,' Anna said. 'I shall write to a very good friend of mine this very night and see about sending both of the girls to her. Edward would never even think of going there. She runs a small school near York and her sister married well and has a very large house. I'm sure one of them will be able to give the girls some sort of employment.'

'You don't have to convince me, of course they can stay,' Lydia said. 'I shall put them in the room next to mine. In fact, their arrival has solved something of a problem in that my own maid asked for time off to visit her ailing father. If anyone asks, I shall simply say I hired them on a friend's recommendation. And I shall be sure not to send them out of the house on any errands.'

Anna pressed a kiss to her friend's cheek. 'Thank you, dear friend. I'll just go back and fetch Justine—'

'Oh, no, you won't.' Quickly getting up, Lydia went to the writing desk and took out parchment and quill. 'I refuse to see you venture alone into that part of town. It's dangerous; besides, someone might see you and start asking awkward questions.' She wrote a few words on the paper, sanded and folded it, then rang for a servant. 'I'll have John take the carriage and retrieve Miss Smith. A male servant going into that kind of place won't arouse any suspicions. And he can drop you at Sir Barrington's on the way.'

Touched by her friend's willingness to help, Anna gave her a hug. 'You are too good, Lydia. I promise I shall make it up to you.'

'Just get this mess straightened out,' Lydia said grimly. 'That will be thanks enough!'

Barrington had forgotten what a restful sleep was. For five nights in a row, he'd ended up pacing the drawing room because, for five nights in a row, he'd been unable to think about anything but Anna. She'd kept him awake—and aroused—into the wee hours of the morning. He couldn't explain why. He had trained himself to ignore what he couldn't have, to resist temptation in all its wide and varied forms. He couldn't be bought, bribed, or browbeaten. God knew, enough men had tried and failed. Yet when it came to her, it was as though he had no will at all. He became as docile as a kitten. And like a kitten, he craved her touch. He wanted to wrap himself around her, to immerse himself in her warmth and to lose himself in her body.

Knowing he couldn't do any of those things was driving him mad. Even now, as he sat at his desk, staring out the window instead of reviewing papers concerning a complicated case, all he could think about was Anna. Remembering the expression on her face during their last meeting—

'Sir Barrington…'

Recalling how angry she'd been at his refusal to abandon his pursuit of her father, her misplaced belief that he assumed the earl guilty—

'Sir Barrington?'

Her—

'Sir Barrington!'

'Yes, what *is* it, Sam?' Exasperated, Barrington turned to see his secretary standing in the open doorway, and right behind him—'Anna!' He leaped to his feet, sending a flurry of papers to the floor. 'That is…Lady Annabelle!'

She stepped in front of the younger man, hesitation and uncertainty written on her face. 'I hope I haven't come at a bad time?'

'Of course not. Come in. Sit down.' He stared at her greedily, devouring the sight of her, wondering how it was possible for a woman to grow more beautiful by the day. 'Thank you, Sam, that will be all.'

The door closed with a quiet click. Anna came towards him. 'Are you sure this isn't a bad time. You seem…preoccupied.'

'I am.' *With you.* 'I was going over the details of a case.' He glanced briefly at the papers on the floor and then walked around to the front of his desk. Leaning back against the edge, he crossed his arms over his chest and tried not to notice how the sunlight danced on her hair, turning it a warm, honeyed gold. Her complexion was as smooth as alabaster, her mouth a bright red berry, ripe for the taking—

Desire exploded, hardening him where he stood. And with a degree of resolve he didn't know he had, he forced it down and away. 'You look like a woman on a mission.'

'I am. I came here to tell you that I know who took Julia's necklace. *And* how it came to be in my father's wardrobe.'

His eyebrows lifted. 'Indeed.'

'My brother's mistress took it.'

'Elizabeth Paisley?'

He said the name without thinking, and watched as a delicate line formed between her brows. 'No. Eliza Smith.'

'Your brother's mistress is a girl by the name of Elizabeth Paisley,' Barrington said. 'I know because I was asked to find her by a gentleman who was…concerned about her welfare.'

'A gentleman by the name of Colonel Tanner?'

Barrington raised an eyebrow. 'How did you know?'

'Eliza told me about him. And I remember you speaking to a gentleman you referred to as Colonel that night at the Billinghams' soirée. I suspected they might be one and the same.'

Hiding his surprise, Barrington inclined his head. 'Elizabeth Paisley was originally Colonel Tanner's mistress. When she disappeared from his house, he began to worry so he asked me to see if I could find her. Initially I was afraid that foul play might have been involved, but when I learned through my visit to Madame Delors that someone else was paying for her clothes, I realised she had simply transferred her affections.'

'Madame Delors?' Anna said, wide eyed. 'Is *that* why you went to see her?'

'Of course. A good modiste dresses a wide range of women and sends the bills to their husbands or protectors. It seemed the logical place to start. Why? Did you think I had some other reason for going?'

Anna coloured, but firmly shook her head. 'No, of course not. Go on.'

'Because I knew the Colonel had ordered clothes for Miss Paisley from Madame Delors, I hoped she might be able to tell me what had become of her. After some careful prompting, she kindly provided me with your brother's name.'

'So you *knew* about Eliza's involvement with Edward.' Anna abruptly sat down. 'Why didn't you tell me?'

'Two reasons. One, because I was investigating her in confidence for another client, and, two, because I was afraid you might ask Edward what his involvement with her was.'

'And so I should! Eliza was the one who took the necklace!'

'Not possible,' Barrington said. 'The baroness's maid said she saw your father take the necklace.'

'That's right. Eliza *was* Julia's maid.'

'Wrong,' Barrington said. 'I interviewed all of the household help. No one matching Miss Paisley's description worked there at the time of the robbery.'

'That's because Eliza wasn't there the day you questioned the staff. Her sister, Justine, was.'

'But I didn't interview a Justine Paisley,' Barrington said. 'The baroness's maid was a girl by the name of Eliza Smith.'

'Exactly. Eliza Smith *is* Elizabeth Paisley,' Anna said patiently. 'She changed her name when she went to work for Julia. And she asked her sister, Justine, to stand in for her on the day you went to interview the staff because she was afraid that if *she* spoke to you, her nerves would give her away. Justine knew nothing of what Eliza had done so Eliza knew she would be entirely convincing.'

'Are you telling me the baroness didn't know she had two different girls working for her?'

'Not when the only difference between them was the colour of their eyes,' Anna said triumphantly. 'Justine and Eliza are twins.'

There it was. The missing piece of the puzzle. Barrington hadn't been able to trace Elizabeth Paisley because she had changed her name to Smith and because she and her twin sister were pretending to be the same person.

He picked up the crystal paperweight and turned it over in his hand, the sunlight sending shards of silver dancing around the room. Elizabeth *and* Justine Paisley. Damn.

'So it all started,' he said slowly, 'when Edward saw Elizabeth Paisley…or Smith as she was then, at the baroness's dinner party.'

'Actually, it started a little before that, but I suspect they first became lovers that night. Eliza told me she spotted Edward the moment she walked into the dining room and he must have noticed her because I saw them together later that night.'

'Where?'

'In the study. After you and I…parted company on the balcony, I went back into the house through another door and came upon Edward and Miss Smith.'

He watched the colour spring to her cheeks and his eyebrows rose a fraction of an inch. *'In flagrante delicto?'* When her colour deepened, he couldn't help smiling. 'That must have been awkward.'

'Apparently more so for me than for Edward,' Anna said ruefully. 'A few days later, I overheard him telling two of his friends that he had installed a new mistress at his house. I put two and two together.'

'So she went to him willingly,' Barrington said.

'Oh yes. Eliza said that while Colonel Tanner had been good to her, she wasn't in love with him.'

In love with him. So, his hunch had proven true. 'Is that how Edward convinced her to steal the necklace?' Barrington asked. 'By telling her he loved her?'

'Of course. He told her she would be doing it for them, so they could be together.'

'And she was gullible enough to believe it,' he said wryly.

'A woman in love is all too ready to believe anything she's told,' Anna pointed out. 'Edward made her believe that selling part of the necklace would provide the money they needed to start a new life together. And Eliza was too much in love with him to see how impossible a reality that was.'

'Of course. We always think the best of those we love,' Barrington murmured. 'Only to discover that love blinds us to the truth. Eliza was no different.'

'Until she found out it was all lies. When she threatened to leave, Edward realised she had the power to expose him and his method of persuasion took on a more…physical form.' Anna looked at him and Barrington saw the anger in her eyes. 'That's why I had to take her away.'

He froze, hardly able to believe what she'd said. '*You* took her out of his house? Dear God, Anna, do you realise how dangerous that could have been?'

'The only danger would have been to Eliza if I'd left her there!'

'And what if Edward had arrived whilst you were helping her to escape?' he said.

'He likely would have been angry and put a stop to it.'

'He might have done a damn sight more than that.'

'Why does everyone insist on believing that Edward would hurt me?' Anna asked in exasperation. 'He's my brother, for heaven's sake!'

'He's also a man with a grudge and guilty of having plotted a serious crime,' Barrington retaliated. 'He attempted to destroy your father's reputation and apparently had no qualms about using violence against Miss Paisley or her sister. Speaking of which, we have to find the other sister as quickly as possible. Once your brother discovers what's happened, she won't be safe.'

'I know. That's why a carriage is on its way to pick Justine up now and take her to the Marquess of Bailley's house,' Anna said. 'I asked Lydia if the girls could stay with her until I've had a chance to contact some friends of mine in the country who might be able to provide positions for them.'

'Good girl,' Barrington said approvingly. 'While I don't like involving anyone else in this, Lady Lydia's house is probably the safest place in the short term. Your brother would never think to look for Miss Paisley or her sister there.' He turned away from her, dragging a hand through his dark hair. There was still much to be done, but when he thought of what Anna had already endured, and what could have happened… 'I'm sorry you had to get involved in this, Anna. I would have spared you, if I could.'

'I know,' Anna said softly. 'But none of this is your fault, Barrington. Edward's turned out to be the villain. I would never have believed him capable of such treachery, but it seems I didn't know him *or* Peregrine as well as I thought.'

'You can't know what people don't want you to. That's what makes this such a dangerous business,' Barrington said, walking towards her. 'Please don't do it again.'

His voice was soft, barely above a whisper, yet it reverberated through her with the force of a hurricane. 'You don't have the right to tell me what to do,' she whispered back.

'No, but I'm going to regardless. And do you know why?'
He came to a halt in front of her, so close that he could see
the pulse beating beneath her skin. 'Because if something
were to happen to you, I would never know peace again.' He
raised his hands and placed them on either side of her face.
'If I never had the chance to kiss you again, I would slowly
go insane. Much as I'm doing now...'

He waited for her to pull away, but when she leaned into
him and closed her eyes, Barrington knew there was no turning back. He took her face between his hands and angled
her mouth to his, desperate to feel the softness of her mouth
under his.

It was more than he expected. Her lips, sweet, soft, and
maddeningly erotic, wiped every thought from his mind but
how much he wanted her. He touched his tongue to her upper
lip, heard her breath catch and felt his world shift when she
opened her mouth to him.

The taste of her nearly drove reason from his brain. The
warmth of her in his arms, the hunger he tasted in her kiss,
were all that mattered. And when her arms came around him
and her fingers pressed into his back, urging him closer, he
knew he couldn't let her go. With a groan, he slipped one
hand around to cup the nape of her neck, tilting her head
back, exposing her throat. She smelled like heaven and, like
a starving man, he feasted on her, savouring the scent and the
taste of her skin. Her breasts were warm and heavy against
his chest, rising and falling as the tempo of her breathing
increased.

He reclaimed her mouth, his kiss no longer gentle, his
tongue exploring the shadowy recesses of her mouth. He
kissed the pulse beating at the base of her throat, and when
she groaned and arched against him, he cupped one breast,
feeling the nipple harden through the slight material of
her gown.

Anna moaned, a whisper into his hair, and he went as hard as iron. God, he needed her. Needed to peel away the layers of clothing until they lay skin to skin, to caress her until they were both aching with desire, to hear her cry out his name as he claimed her for his own...

'Anna,' he whispered against her throat. 'Oh, my love...'

He spoke without thinking, the endearment slipping naturally from his lips. He no longer cared if she knew how he felt. All he wanted was to be close to her, as though, in this intimate embrace, all the reservations he'd felt had suddenly evaporated.

But something was different. Anna was pulling back. Her arms fell away, leaving him cold where he had been hot. Empty where he had been full. And when he looked at her, it was to see tears rolling down her cheeks. 'What's wrong, my love?'

'Don't *call* me that,' she protested, her voice tremulous. 'Don't talk to me of love when, by your own admission, you have none to give me.'

Her words stabbed at him like the point of a rapier. 'You know why I said that. I told you of the risks—'

'But you kissed me as though you cared—but you don't.'

'I do! Just—'

'Just not enough to marry me, yes, I know,' she threw at him. 'Then why torment me like this, Barrington? I won't be your mistress.'

'I would never ask that of you,' he said, aware that his own heart was thundering in his chest. 'But neither will I be the cause of you putting yourself in danger. You've already seen what I bring to your life: Rand's life in shambles; your father held up for ridicule; and you, forced to speak out against your brother and forcibly remove a woman from the prison he was holding her in. Do you not see the dangers of being involved with me?'

'What I see,' she said huskily, 'is a man trying to put right what others have put wrong. A man who chooses to expose the weaknesses that turn good people bad and which destroy families along the way. You did not *ruin* Peregrine's life, Barrington. He did that by involving himself with Lady Yew. And you certainly didn't hold my father up for ridicule. That was all Edward's doing.'

'And what of the dangers from Edward now? You've seen what he's capable of,' Barrington said. 'And while you might not want to believe it, *all* men are capable of violence. All it takes is one spark to ignite the fire.'

'Does that include you?' she asked.

He swallowed hard as an image of Hayle raising his hand to her appeared in his mind. 'If it came to the possibility of your being hurt by another, yes, I would most definitely be capable of violence.'

He had no idea if it was the answer she expected, or even the one she wanted. But it was the only one he could give and he knew that she was shaken by the intensity of his declaration.

'I have no wish to inspire such behaviour,' she said in a low voice. 'It has always been my desire to bring out the best in people, not the worst. And violence of any kind can only be the worst.'

'That's why I need you to be careful,' Barrington warned. 'Your brother is guilty of having tried to implicate your father in the theft of the necklace. If he suspects you of going public with that information, how do you think he's going to react? His standing in society means a great deal to him. He won't look kindly upon anyone who exposes him for what he really is.'

'Maybe not, but how *can* I expose him, Barrington? He's

a member of my family. Think of what it would do to my father. How disloyal it would be—'

'Did Edward consider loyalty when he asked the Marquess of Yew to persecute Rand over the affair?' Barrington said brutally. 'Knowing it would cause Rand public humiliation and disgrace?'

She blanched. 'Edward *asked* Lord Yew to bring charges against Peregrine?'

'Yes. The marquess is actually quite proud of his wife's ability to seduce younger men. He doesn't care that she slept with Rand, and neither did Edward. All your brother wanted to do was humiliate Rand in the eyes of society.'

'But why?'

'Because he's jealous.'

'Jealous! Why on earth would Edward be jealous of Peregrine? He's heir to an earldom, for heaven's sake! Peregrine is merely my father's godson—'

'No, Anna. Edward hates Peregrine Rand because he *is* your father's other son—'

'What?'

He'd gone too far. The moment he saw the look of disbelief on her face, Barrington knew he'd said too much, because contrary to what he'd believed, she hadn't worked it out. As astute as she was when it came to analysing and fixing relationships between other people's families, she was blind to the truth when it came to her own. 'You didn't know,' was all he said.

'Didn't *know*?' she demanded in a tortured whisper. 'How could I possibly have known? Papa introduced Peregrine as his *godson*. I had no reason to believe he was anything else.'

'What about the physical resemblance between them?'

'I thought it barely noticeable. Even Edward doesn't resemble my father all that much. Or are you going to tell me he's not really my brother either?'

Barrington heard the tension in Anna's voice and, though his first instinct was to apologise, he knew silence was the better choice. It was too late for apologies now. The damage was done. Anna hadn't moved an inch from where she stood, but she was as distant from him as the moon was from the earth. 'It was never my intention to hurt you, Anna.'

'Then why would you say such a thing to me?'

'Because I know it to be the truth. I did some digging into your family history,' Barrington said, not bothering to mention that it was Lord Richard Crew who had discovered the truth about Peregrine's background. 'It was all there, in the parish registers.'

Anna didn't move, but her eyes grew suspiciously bright. 'So that's why Edward hates Peregrine so much,' she whispered. 'He worked it out as soon as Peregrine arrived.'

'I suspect so, yes.'

She was silent for a long time, her expression one of mute despair. Barrington didn't say anything either, knowing it was better that she work matters out for herself. Anything else he said now might only make the situation worse.

Finally, she spoke. 'Why didn't Papa tell us? Surely we had a right to know.'

'Perhaps he thought to spare you the hurt you're suffering now. And while it pains me to say it, he wouldn't be the first nobleman to father a child outside marriage.'

'How *dare* you!' she cried. 'My father *loved* my mother. He was faithful to her until the day she died! How do I know *you're* not the one telling lies? You could be making this all up!'

'Why would I do that?'

'I don't know.' Anna wrapped her arms around her chest, as though to stop herself from shattering into a million pieces.

'You once told me that people lie to protect themselves or someone they care about, but we both know those aren't the only reasons. People lie to influence others, or to make them feel better about themselves. They lie to inflict hurt.'

'So you believe I'm deliberately trying to hurt you by lying to you about your father's relationship to Peregrine Rand?'

Anna shook her head. 'I don't know what you're trying to do. All I know is that my father is an honourable man. He would never have done something like that. It would have destroyed our mother. And he would *never* bring a child he'd had with another woman to live under the same roof as Edward and me. It would be too painful for all of us.' Her chin came up. 'If Peregrine *is* my father's child, he would have told us. I *know* he would.'

Barrington said nothing. What could he say? She was a daughter defending the father she loved. She trusted him, as she'd trusted her brother, believing that she knew the ways of the world. The ways of love.

Yet she didn't know how love could twist and warp until it was unrecognisable to anyone who saw it. She didn't know how it could wound with a single word, or destroy with a single glance. For what was jealousy but love without trust? What was obsession but love without reason?

Hayle was jealous of Rand because he was the product of his father's love with another woman. Elizabeth Paisley had stolen for the man she loved because she believed it would strengthen their bond and allow them to start a life together. And the earl had lied to his family in an effort to protect them from a devastating truth. He probably *had* been faithful to his wife while he was married to her, but Peregrine was his child by a woman he'd met *before* he married Isabel. Likely before their marriage had even been arranged or the two of them had met.

Sadly, none of that mattered now. Anna was looking at

him as though *he* was the serpent in the Garden of Eden. As though he was the source of all the rumours and lies. There was nothing he could do now but finish his investigation and walk away. Out of the case, out of her life.

'I will call upon your brother this evening, Lady Annabelle,' Barrington said quietly.

'Not at home!' she gasped.

He shook his head. 'Lord Hayle spends Thursday nights at his club. I shall speak to him there.'

'What will you say?' she asked, not looking at him.

'That is between your brother and myself. But when the interview is over, I shall send word to your father of the outcome.'

'And what about me, Barrington?' Anna said, finally raising her eyes to his face. 'What would you say to me?'

He stared down at the blotter, knowing there was only one thing he could say. 'I will say goodbye. Because after what's happened between us today, I can't imagine there possibly being anything else appropriate.'

Chapter Fourteen

Contrary to what he'd told her, Barrington did not find Hayle at his club that evening. He called in at White's on his way to another society event, only to be informed by the manager that the earl's son had not yet put in an appearance.

Thanking him, Barrington left and climbed back into his carriage. Where did he go next? There were any number of hells to which Hayle might have gone, but it would take the entire night to investigate them all. Had he gone to see his mistress? Possible, Barrington reflected. And if so, he would have found the house in darkness and Eliza gone. How would he react to such a development? With anger? Or with fear? Would he suspect Eliza of having revealed the part he'd played in the theft of the necklace and realise that information now existed that could connect him to the crime, thereby exonerating his father?

The likelihood of that was even more possible; afraid of what that might mean for Anna, Barrington gave his coachman the direction of Regent's Park. He intended to keep a close eye on Hayle for the next few days. Anna might like to think her brother was guided by family loyalty, but having seen what loyalty meant to him, Barrington decided it was best to play it safe. Any man that twisted by jealousy and anger was a danger to anyone he came into contact with—and that *included* his only sister.

The carriage pulled into the darkened street a short while later. Barrington knew the number of the house, but even from this distance he could see that there were no lights on inside and that neither a private carriage nor a hackney stood outside. If Hayle had paid the house a call, he hadn't bothered to wait around.

So where was he now—and in what state of mind?

Abruptly, Barrington remembered something Crew had told him during his last visit. As well as providing him with the surprising but very useful information regarding Cambermere and his relationship to Peregrine Rand, Crew had informed him that Hayle had taken to spending time with Lord Andrews. Apparently they were often seen heading in the direction of Andrews's favourite hangout, a disreputable tavern close to the Thames, down a dark alley most decent men knew better than to travel. A place known to opium users needing a place to hide.

Barrington thumped the roof of his carriage and gave the driver the address. Whatever he was going to say to Hayle had to be said tonight. And if that meant following him into the mouth of hell, that's what he'd do. But he'd go in prepared. He reached under his seat and pulled out the ebony cane. If he was to take Hayle on in an unfriendly atmosphere, the cane might well save his life. In places like the Cock's Crown, he was only going to get one chance.

Anna walked listlessly into the drawing room as the clock on the mantel struck nine. She and Peregrine were expected at Lady Bessmel's for cards, but the thought of having to spend an entire evening making light-hearted conversation and acting as though nothing was wrong was far from welcome. She perched on the arm of a high-back chair, only to get restlessly to her feet a few minutes later. She felt cold though the room was warm and even an extra shawl couldn't banish the chill, nor was it likely to given the source of her distraction.

Was Peregrine truly her half-brother? Barrington certainly thought so. He would never have made the comment to her otherwise. But the only person who could give her a definitive answer to that question was her father and he had gone out earlier in the day. And even if she knew when he was coming home, would she have the courage to ask him such a question?

How did one go about enquiring if the young man now living with them, a man who had been introduced to them by their father as his godson, was, in fact, their half-brother?

Her father's bastard.

No. Definitely not the kind of question a daughter asked. Because if Barrington was wrong, her father would be devastated by her questioning of his honesty. Indeed, of his very honour. And if he wasn't wrong?

Anna closed her eyes, retreating from the thought.

Unfortunately, Barrington didn't make mistakes. Everything he'd said to her from the moment they'd met had been proven true. What reason had she to doubt him now? His approach to everything he undertook was logical, unemotional and based purely on fact. Sentiment didn't enter into it, whereas with her, *everything* revolved around emotion. People didn't make mistakes because they were logical. They made them because they allowed their emotions to get the upper hand. Emotions like anger and jealousy and hate.

Having to listen to such accusations made against the members of her own family was horrible—but having to agree with them was even more so. It called into question the degree of loyalty she owed her family. A responsibility she'd never questioned until now—and Barrington was the one who was making her question it. Was it any wonder she had no desire to see him again?

Yet she *did* want to see him. Desperately, because he had become the only constant in her life, the one person she could count on. He consumed her every waking thought. Not an hour went by that she didn't think of him. Not a minute passed that she didn't remember every exquisite detail of the moments they'd spent together: the heady sensation of his hand caressing her breast; the warmth of his mouth on hers; the incredible eroticism of his body pressed intimately against hers.

But what was all that worth if love and tenderness weren't present as well? Intimacy without love was the reason men went to prostitutes. Barrington might not be able to deny the strength of the attraction between them, but he was still reluctant to encourage anything more. He used the charges he had laid against the men in her family as proof of the destructive force he brought into her life.

How was she to tell him that she didn't care about that any more? That all she cared about was loving him and of finding some way of getting him to love her in return?

How on earth did she tell a logical man something so thoroughly illogical?

'Anna? Are you ready to go?'

She looked up to see Peregrine standing in the doorway— and the sight of him caused her heart to turn over all over again. Peregrine Rand. Country gentleman—or unknown half-brother? It was impossible not to wonder in light of Barrington's stunning revelations.

And yet though she stared hard at Peregrine, she still couldn't find the confirmation she was seeking. The knowledge that he truly was her father's son by another woman…

'Anna? Are you all right?'

'Hmm? Oh, yes, of course.' *Don't think about it. It won't help you get through the evening.* 'Are you sure you want to go to Lady Bessmel's tonight?'

Peregrine's mouth twisted and, suddenly, there was no mistaking the hesitation in his eye. 'I'm quite sure I *don't* wish to go, but I can't hide in the house for ever. I'll have to show my face in public at some time.' He walked into the room, hands thrust into his pockets. 'If it was only the affair, I could bear it. But knowing that people are whispering about what I reputedly did to your father is a thousand times worse.'

Anna looked at him and saw how deeply he was suffering. The colour had gone from his face and his eyes were shadowed with despair. Even his attire was subdued: his cravat simply tied, his waistcoat plain, his collar points of moderate height.

'I know you didn't start the rumour about having found the necklace in Papa's possession, Per,' Anna said softly. 'You wouldn't have done that to him.'

His laughter had a hard, bitter edge to it. 'Then you're one of the few who believes it.'

'How did you find out what people were saying?'

'Lord Richard Crew was good enough to inform me.'

Hearing the name of the well-known lady's man, Anna raised an eyebrow. 'I'm surprised *he* would be the one to tell you, given his own less-than-sterling reputation. Did he happen to mention whether or not he believed it?'

'He didn't say and I didn't ask,' Peregrine replied, his expression bleak. 'Frankly, I didn't want to know.'

'Oh, Peregrine,' Anna said, coming to stand beside him. 'This really hasn't been a very good visit for you.'

'No, it hasn't, but much of it's been my own fault,' Peregrine said ruefully. 'Making a fool of myself over Lady Yew wasn't the best way to start and this has certainly made matters worse. But I can't believe people would think I would betray your father like that. Yes, I saw the necklace in his wardrobe. We both did. But I would never say so in public. Your father's been good to me, Anna. He brought me to London and let me live here. He made it easy for me to enter society when my background lends nothing to my being there, and he even forgave me for the débâcle with Lady Yew.'

'He did?'

'He said it was the right of every young man to sow his wild oats.' Peregrine gave her a lopsided grin. 'I just picked the wrong field in which to sow them.'

In spite of the situation, Anna was actually able to laugh. 'Yes, well, I suppose everyone must be forgiven one mistake.'

'Would that it was only one.' Peregrine said. 'I wish I was more like you, Anna. I doubt you've ever done anything stupid or irresponsible in your life. You would never let yourself be compromised by your feelings.'

'Oh, Peregrine,' Anna breathed. 'I am no more sensible than you when it comes to matters of the heart.'

'Nonsense. You're never out of humour. You don't allow familiarity from gentlemen and you act with moderation at all times.'

Except when in the arms of the man I love, Anna wanted to tell him. *Waiting for him to say the things I so desperately want to hear...and probably never will.* But all she said was, 'The young ladies I counsel would think me a poor example if I didn't follow my own advice. Besides, we both know how destructive unbridled passion can be. Surely it is better to love moderately than to lose oneself completely.'

'Perhaps, but I would never wish that for you. Or for myself. When I fall in love, I want it to be without reason or logic. I want to feel light-headed over it,' Peregrine said. 'Giddy with the excitement of it all. I want the woman I love to be all I think about—my reason for getting up in the morning and the motivation for everything I do during the day. I want her to be my queen. My Guinevere.'

Anna smiled. 'You're a poet and a dreamer, Peregrine, but I have no doubt that you *will* find your Guinevere one day.'

'And what about you, Anna? Do you think you'll ever find your Lancelot?'

Anna stood up. She already had…and his name was Barrington Parker. But he was lost to her, the bitter words they'd thrown at one another severing the tenuous connection that existed between them. 'I doubt it. There just aren't that many knights in shining armour left.'

As expected, walking into the Cock's Crown was like descending into the dungeons of hell. The dimly lit room was thick with smoke, the cloying scent of opium burning the eyes and addling the brain. Pictures both dark and disturbing hung from the walls and there was a sense of desperation and despair about the place.

It took only a moment to locate the figure of Viscount Hayle. Sitting at a table in the corner, he appeared to be well into his cups, though in truth, he was in better shape than many of his companions. Lord Andrews was sprawled out on the table next to him and a younger man Barrington recognised as the heir to a dukedom lay face down on the floor. The humid air was rank with the smell of booze and fear.

Hayle looked up as Barrington approached. His eyes were bloodshot and, in the dim light, his skin had a decidedly greyish tinge. 'Well, well, if it isn't the admirable Parker,' he drawled. 'A little out of your area, aren't you?'

'It's not one of my favourite haunts,' Barrington said,

resting his hands on the knob of his ebony cane. 'But something told me I might find you here.'

'And why should you wish to *find* me?' Hayle said, enunciating each word.

'You and I have business to discuss.'

'Really? I can't imagine what manner of business would be so important that you would need seek me out here. As you can see, I am with friends, and friends would resent me speaking to you on matters that do not concern them.'

It was hard to tell if Hayle was foxed or drugged, but either way, Barrington knew it was going to be a difficult conversation. 'Your friends can listen if they wish, but we *will* have a conversation.'

'I think not.' Hayle closed his eyes and rocked back on the legs of his chair. 'You take yourself far too seriously, Parker. You should learn to relax and enjoy life, as I do.'

'What, by viewing it through a veil of opium? Thank you, but I prefer reality to hallucinations.'

'Obviously, you've never tried it.'

'No, but it would no more be my idea of fun than forcing a helpless young woman to do my dirty work, then hold her prisoner for fear of her exposing me,' Barrington said contemptuously.

Hayle's eyes opened, the chair slowly righting. 'What the hell are you talking about?'

'I think you know. I'm sure the name Elizabeth Paisley rings a bell.'

'Eliza?' To Barrington's surprise, Hayle actually laughed. 'I'm not holding her prisoner. She came to me willingly. She loves me, don't you know.'

'She may believe herself in love with you, but you and I both know it was fear that kept her from running away from you.'

Hayle's smile slowly disappeared. 'And I suppose I have

you to thank for her unexpected departure. And for that of my housekeeper?'

Not even the most unholy of tortures would have prompted Barrington to tell Hayle it was his sister who had orchestrated Eliza's escape. 'The young lady was too afraid to leave on her own, so it was necessary that I assist her in that regard,' he said quietly. 'Once I realised she was the one who'd stolen the baroness's necklace and given it to you, I had no choice but to speak with her.'

'Gave the necklace to me? What a bizarre notion. And entirely wrong, of course.' Hayle unsteadily picked up his glass. 'My *father* is the thief, Parker. Surely you've figured that out by now. The much revered Earl of Cambermere stole the baroness's necklace and it was none other than his *godson*, Mr Peregrine Rand, who made it known to society. Were you aware that it was Rand who found the necklace amongst my father's things?'

'I did hear something to that effect,' Barrington remarked, 'though it seems a bit strange that you would ask him to fetch something from your father's room…a watch, I believe… when you were the one who was supposed to take care of it.'

The man gave a non-committal shrug. 'My father asked me to attend to it, but I was busy, so I asked Rand to do it for me. I thought him competent enough to undertake a trifling matter like that.'

'So you had no idea he would find the necklace lying right next to the watch when he went in search of it,' Barrington said blandly.

Again, the shrug. 'Had I known, I would have gone myself. I have no desire to see my father humiliated in the eyes of society, Parker. Or to see our family name tarnished by such a dishonourable act.'

'No, I'm sure you do not,' Barrington murmured, impressed

by the man's ability to lie so convincingly when under the influence of the drug. 'And, of course, it makes no sense that your father would steal anything from the woman he has asked to marry him.'

It wasn't the truth, but it got the response Barrington was hoping for.

'He hasn't asked her to marry him,' Hayle snapped. 'Julia would have told me!'

'You wouldn't have heard it from your father first?' Barrington probed.

'My father doesn't confide his plans to me any more. He hasn't for some time.'

Barrington heard the note of resentment in Hayle's voice and knew the loss of his father's confidence, and perhaps his respect, rankled. 'Still, it can't come as a great surprise that he wishes to marry her,' Barrington went on. 'He's made no secret of his affection for the lady. Your father is, in all ways, an honourable man. If he was in love with the baroness, he would naturally offer her marriage.'

'Oh yes, just like he offered Rand's mother marriage,' Hayle said contemptuously. 'But he didn't, did he? He married my mother and ignored his bastard for the first twenty-seven years of his life. Hardly the behaviour of an *honourable man*.'

'It's possible your father didn't know of Rand's existence,' Barrington said. 'It may have been brought to his attention only a few months ago.'

'He knew he'd bedded Rand's mother,' Hayle said with contempt. 'And the consequences of *that* are all too easy to predict.'

'As I said, the relationship may have ended without his knowledge of there being a child,' Barrington said reasonably. 'Rand is older than you, so the association between your father and his mother was an early one.'

'I don't give a damn when he had the relationship or what they were to one another!' Hayle burst out hotly. 'What bothers me is that the moment my father learned of Rand's existence, he brought him to London without so much as a by your leave.'

'What did you expect him to do?'

'He could have asked me how *I* felt about it. I *am* his legitimate son and heir, after all!'

'Perhaps he didn't think it concerned you. Rand is his son by a woman you don't even know. It's hardly surprising that he would be suffering feelings of guilt—'

'If my father was stupid enough to rut with a woman of low birth and then have feelings of guilt, he should have gone to the country, made his apologies to the family and left it at that,' Hayle bit off. 'He should *never* have brought his bastard to London and tried to pass him off as his *godson* so I might be made a laughingstock in society!'

'And that's what really bothers you, isn't it, Hayle? That you have a brother you never knew anything about and whose existence is an embarrassment. A brother who shares your bloodline—'

'He is nothing to me! Less than nothing!'

'He is your half-brother. And because you sensed that the moment he set foot in your house, you set out to humiliate Rand *and* your father by showing them both in the worst possible light,' Barrington said mercilessly. 'You had your mistress steal a necklace from the woman your father loved and then you tried to pin the blame for the crime on him, knowing that by exposing him, you would be humiliating your father as deeply as you felt he had humiliated you.'

If Barrington was hoping for a confession, he was destined for disappointment. 'I don't know what you're talking about, Parker. All I know is that the baroness's necklace was found in my father's possession and that he must bear the consequences for his actions.'

'And Miss Paisley? Would you see her hang for a crime she didn't commit?' Barrington pressed.

'Why should I care? She's a whore. She made her interest in me plain enough the first time I saw her and I wasn't about to pass up the invitation. Unlike you, I have hot blood running through my veins,' Hayle sneered.

Ignoring the slight, Barrington said, 'So you expect me to believe that you didn't take her as your mistress simply because she worked for the baroness and you knew that, through her, you could get your hands on the necklace.'

'That's right.'

'You'd also like me to believe that you didn't feed Miss Paisley a parcel of lies about how much you loved her, telling her that if she could steal the baroness's necklace, the two of you would be able to start a new life together.'

'Most certainly not.'

'Nor did you tell her that you actually wanted the necklace so you could set up your father to look like a thief.'

'You really have got the wrong end of the stick, Parker.'

'Have I?' Barrington shook his head. 'I think you planned the entire affair as a way of getting back at your father. You seduced Miss Paisley and then persuaded her to steal the necklace for you. You planted the necklace in your father's things and made sure Rand would be the one to find it, then *you* started the rumour that he was the one who named your father as the thief. Everyone knew that relations between Rand and your father were strained as a result of the affair with Lady Yew, so you reasoned it wouldn't come as any great surprise if Rand took an opportunity to get back at your father. But the fact is that Rand would never do something like that because, unlike you, he has a conscience.'

'A conscience!' Hayle threw back his head and laughed.

'You have the gall to say that after he slept with another man's wife?'

'Ah, but you laid the groundwork for that affair, didn't you, my Lord?' Barrington said. '*You* told Rand about the state of the Yews' marriage and *you* made a point of introducing him to her, knowing full well that she had a passion for younger men. Then, you made sure her husband found out and you asked him to go after Rand in public, knowing how furious your father would be when he learned what Rand had done. And by doing that, you thought you were giving Rand a reason for revenge against your father. It really was very well thought out. By trying to implicate your father and Rand, you attempted to destroy *both* their reputations at the same time.'

'My God, Parker, you really should be writing lurid Gothic novels for love-struck young females. Either that, or the opium has already got to your brain,' Hayle said derisively.

Barrington smiled. 'Pleading innocence won't wash, Hayle. I *know* what you're guilty of. That's why both Miss Paisley and her sister are safely beyond your reach. And if *you* know what's good for you, you'll confess to the part you played in this whole ugly affair.'

Again, Hayle laughed, but there was a nastiness to it that warned Barrington to be careful. 'Why should I? It's all supposition on your part. You don't have a shred of evidence. And even if I was guilty, it's not something that's going to put me in jail.'

'No, but it would make living in London intolerable and I think to a man like you, that would be almost as bad. When society hears what you've done, they *will* turn against you. No one will receive you and your reputation will be in shreds.'

Hayle's eyes darkened with hate. 'Get out!' he snarled. 'Get out before I forget I'm a gentleman and thrash you to within an inch of your life.' As if to make good on his threat, he rose unsteadily to his feet and took a lurching step forwards.

But Barrington merely stepped back and raised his cane. 'I'd advise you to think again, Hayle. This isn't the typical gentleman's walking stick. It doesn't break when it's brought down with force on a man's head. I know because I've done it before. And my reactions haven't been slowed by the numbing effects of opium or alcohol. I guarantee that if you take me on now, you *will* lose.'

Eyeing the lethal-looking cane, Hayle hesitated, but his voice was rough with emotion when he said, 'You won't get away with this, Parker. By God, I'll make you pay.'

'No, my Lord,' Barrington said. '*You're* the one who's going to pay. Because if I have my way, you won't be getting away with anything.'

It was nearly two o'clock in the morning when Barrington left the Nottinghams' soirée. He'd had enough of glittering society for one night. He was tired of the games he was called upon to play, weary of the desperation he saw in the eyes of so many. When had it all begun to lose its lustre? When had moving in society become a chore rather than a pleasure?

He remembered how it had been when he'd first come home from France. How surprised he'd been at the extent of society's welcome. Within days of his arrival, invitations to select gatherings had begun to roll in, as had sponsorships to the right clubs from gentlemen who had seemed genuinely interested in his welfare. He had been told which families to befriend and which to avoid in the same breath as he'd been told which tailors to patronise and which to ignore.

Then, of course, had come the ladies. All of them beautiful, many of them titled, a fair number of them married. They had shamelessly flirted with him, some in the hopes of eliciting a proposal of marriage, others in the hopes of prompting a very different type of proposal. Had he chosen to partake, he could have had a dozen of them lining up to warm his bed.

But he hadn't accepted their come-hither looks and it wasn't long before the rest of the pleasures had begun to pall as well. A brief affair with the widow of one of his father's friends, though sexually fulfilling, had left him feeling curiously dissatisfied, much like a hungry man who, having sat down to a magnificent buffet, discovered that the wine was bad and the food tasteless.

But the final blow had come during the investigation of the two men his late father had trusted and done business with. Men with whom Barrington had socialised and for whom he'd felt admiration and respect. Men who had turned out to be nothing more than parasites on the flesh of society. Greed had fuelled their quest for power and money and once their masks of civility had been stripped away, Barrington had seen them for the monsters they were.

The discovery had come too late to be of help to his father, but from that night on, Barrington had done what he could to make sure that other decent men were not so foully put upon. He'd begun listening to conversations, and when he heard something he didn't like, he'd started asking questions. Quietly. Unobtrusively. Always careful not to raise suspicions in anyone's mind. But he'd asked the questions he'd needed to get the answers that mattered.

He'd also started cultivating different friends. Friends not as highly placed in society. Friends who put more stock in a man's worth than in his title. People he found himself able to trust. He also stopped putting faith in a person's appearance. A lovely face could hide a heart of stone, just as an ugly one could disguise a generous and giving nature. He'd stopped basing his decisions on emotion and gut feeling and turned to uncovering facts, doing whatever he'd had to in order to get at the truth.

It hadn't always made him popular, but he hadn't done it to win friends.

As the soirée wasn't far from his house, Barrington decided to dismiss the carriage and walk home. He needed time to think through his situation with Anna. They hadn't spoken since their last conversation and Barrington was beginning to think they never would again. Of all the disagreements they'd had, this was by far the worst…because he'd found her vulnerable spot and struck it hard. He had called her father's honour into question. He had accused him of having a child with another woman and of not telling his legitimate son and daughter the truth.

And she, loyal to a fault and believing wholeheartedly in her father's integrity, had retaliated by accusing Barrington of being a liar and completely insensitive to her father's feelings. When he had tried to make her see her brother for what he was, Anna had told him he'd had no right to criticise and had steadfastly refused to believe that she was in any danger from Edward at all.

Unfortunately, Barrington had absolutely *no* doubt that Hayle was capable of violence and it infuriated him that Anna still tried to see the good in him, believing that his role as her brother would prevent him from visiting upon her the cruelty he so freely visited on other people. So it was up to him, Barrington realised, to keep her safe. Until Hayle could be dealt with, his priority had to be in keeping him away from Anna.

But apart from that, there was the other far more emotional situation between them: the one concerning their feelings for one another. Growing slowly but steadily, his had changed from simple liking and admiration to a deep and abiding love. Thoughts of Anna filled his days with longing and his nights with hours of sleepless frustration. He wanted her in his bed. In his heart. In his life.

But the life he offered was not one most well-bred young ladies would wish for—and it certainly wasn't what Anna deserved. For one thing, she would be settling for far less than was her due. As the daughter of an earl, a marquis or a duke wasn't out of the question; given her incredible beauty, Barrington knew she would have no trouble attracting either. And yet she remained single, professing to want *him*. She'd told him as much in the way she'd kissed him, in the way her body had melted into his, in the way her arms had closed around him and drawn him close. She was a passionate woman with a heart that beat for those she loved and she would defend them to the bitter end, Peregrine Rand being a case in point.

So how did he go about resolving this mess? How did he change her opinion of him without hurting her—or convince himself to marry her despite all the reasons he should not?

More importantly, how was he to go on living, if he was unable to do either?

He was passing a small copse of trees when he heard it. The snap of a twig. The sound of laboured breathing. Someone hiding in the bushes, waiting to spring. But even as he jumped to the left and drew the sword from its ebony holder, Barrington knew it was too late. His enemy was upon him, the sudden, sharp pain in his right shoulder proof that the danger was much closer than he'd anticipated.

Clamping his teeth against the pain, Barrington whirled and saw the man standing behind him. Darkness hid the contours of his face, but he had no need of lamplight to know who his enemy was. The hatred emanating from Hayle was a tangible force. And when he lunged again, Barrington knew it was in the hopes of finishing him off.

Fortunately, this time, the lethal blade missed its mark.

'The opium must have muddled your brain,' Barrington said, switching the sword to his left hand, knowing his right was now useless. 'A skilled fencer wouldn't have missed an opportunity like that.'

'I didn't miss with my first strike,' Hayle growled. 'Shall I take pity on you and finish you off quickly, Parker? Or are you as good with your left hand as you are with your right?'

Barrington shifted his weight to compensate for the change in fencing arm. 'I am, by nature, a right-handed fencer, but I learned to use a sword in my left so I might be doubly prepared.'

'Then we shall see how well you were taught,' Hayle cried, lunging again.

The sharp clang of blades echoed in the night, but Barrington knew better than to look for help. No sensible person was abroad this time of night and the watchman was likely asleep in his box. Hayle had chosen the time and place of his attack well.

'I must have caused you considerable alarm,' Barrington said, the edge of his blade gleaming dangerously in the moonlight, 'to provoke you into coming after me.'

'You said enough.' The earl's son aimed a deadly blow at Barrington's right side, obviously hoping to worsen the damage he'd already inflicted. 'I don't intend to let you or anyone else humiliate me again and I certainly don't intend to let you expose me.'

Barrington skilfully deflected the attack, but Hayle was fighting like a man possessed. While his skills were inferior to Barrington's, his anger and fear combined to make him a dangerous adversary. Fortunately, with that much opium in his system he couldn't hope to last long in a sustained fight. 'Killing me won't change the situation with Rand,' Barrington threw out. 'He'll always be your father's son.'

'His bastard, you mean!' Hayle shouted. 'And I'm damned if I'll let him take what's rightfully mine.'

'Don't be stupid, Hayle. Your father won't leave his estate to Rand. You're his legitimate son and heir.'

'But he *likes* Rand,' Hayle spat contemptuously. 'He wishes I was more like him. But I'm not and I'm never going to be. Rand's a spineless interloper who's going back to the country as soon as I can make it happen.'

Barrington felt a sudden wave of light-headedness. He must be losing more blood than he thought. And the pain in his right shoulder was a constant reminder of his carelessness…

'Feeling the strain, Parker?' Hayle taunted. 'It's all well and good to put on a fancy show in front of others, but we both know *this* is what it's all about. The fight to the death.'

Barrington took a deep breath. He *was* getting weaker, which meant he had to change his strategy. If he hoped to survive, he had to convince Hayle that he was failing. Lull him into believing that he could close in for the kill at any time.

Fortunately, Barrington had a feeling his opponent wasn't looking to make this a quick kill. Hayle was the kind of man who enjoyed prolonging the agony. By doing so, he would unwittingly give his opponent the advantage he needed.

Barrington let his arm fall, as though weakening. 'What do you hope to gain by killing me, Hayle? Freedom from persecution?'

'You could say that.' Hayle withdrew a few paces, but kept his fighting arm extended, the point of the blade level with Barrington's chest. 'With you dead, there will be no one to challenge my father's guilt. He won't go to jail, but he will be ostracised. And Rand will go back to the country where he belongs and I'll see to it that Anna is married off to some harmless bumpkin who prefers life in the country. Maybe

I'll push her in Lord Andrews's direction. She'd do nicely for him once he has knocked the spunk out of her.'

Fighting down rage at the thought of Andrews getting anywhere near Anna, Barrington took a step, exaggerated a wince and made sure his opponent saw it. 'You've thought of everything.'

'I always do. It's taken a while, but it's all come together,' Hayle said. 'Rand's humiliation, Father's disgrace and, eventually, my marriage to the lovely baroness. And with it, an end to all my financial worries.'

'So that was the final part of your plan.'

Hayle inclined his head. 'I've already told her it was my father who stole the necklace. She didn't believe me, of course, but she won't have a choice once it all comes out. And I have been very careful in my addresses to her. I am, of course, in utter despair over my poor father's circumstances. But if a man cannot bring himself to act according to the law, he must suffer the consequences. Julia will see that and, in time, she will agree to be my wife. I have expensive habits and they need constant feeding. I intend to make damn sure no lawyer puts her money beyond my reach.'

It was shameless, Barrington reflected, but he couldn't fault Hayle's strategy. Through careful planning, he had removed each of the obstacles that stood in the way of his getting what he wanted. Barrington saw the anticipation of victory on the other man's face and knew he believed success lay within his grasp, confident it was only a matter of minutes before it was his.

But he'd reckoned without his opponent's equally fierce determination to prevent any of that happening. Barrington let his arm fall another inch and saw the smile break out on Hayle's face.

'Well, I think it's time to bring an end to this. Goodbye, Parker. I hope your skills with a foil serve you better in hell than they did here.'

Chapter Fifteen

Anna stared through the window of the carriage as it made its way home from the card party. Peregrine was dozing quietly beside her, but even though the hour was late, she was far too wide awake to sleep. She had hoped an evening with friends might help her forget her concerns about Barrington and her family, but not even the constant chatter about balls and betrothals had been enough to do so—because she couldn't stop thinking about Barrington. She couldn't stop remembering everything he'd said to her. Everything he had come to mean to her.

And in remembering all that, Anna knew she had no choice but to tell him she loved him and dare him to turn her away! She would suffer the embarrassment of being spurned, take whatever chances she had to, but she was *not* going to let him walk out of her life without having made one last effort to get him to stay. She had no intention of spending the rest of her life alone, knowing she had no one to blame but herself if that's how it ended up.

They were passing the end of the park when she saw a flurry of movement in the trees. Two dark figures—then a shimmer of silver in the moonlit darkness. Swords! She sat forwards and pressed her face to the glass. 'Peregrine! Wake up!' She thumped on the roof of the carriage. 'Stop!'

'What's the matter?' Peregrine said, groggily coming to.

'There's a fight,' she said, throwing open the carriage door. 'In the park.'

'Anna, wait, are you mad?'

She ran across the grass, deaf to his cries. Some sixth sense warned her that this was no ordinary fight. She hadn't seen her brother or Barrington the entire evening, but Lord Richard Crew, appearing late at the home of Lady Bessmel, said he had been at a hell earlier in the evening and that both Barrington and her brother had been there and that neither of them had looked happy. Had Barrington gone to confront Edward about his conduct with Eliza and been met with threats of violence?

Those words echoed in Anna's ears now as she ran towards the two men. One of them was tiring. He was staggering backwards, hunched over, his right arm hanging limp at his side. The other man raised his sword for the killing blow and she felt the scream build in her lungs. *'Barrington!'*

A split second before he heard Anna scream, Barrington straightened. With deadly intent, he lunged, moving at incredible speed and catching Hayle completely off guard. He stabbed him first in the left leg to disable him, then in his right shoulder to render his sword arm ineffectual.

The earl's son screamed in pain as the sword fell uselessly from his hand. As he sank to the ground, Barrington saw the look of disbelief on his face. He hadn't expected that final rally. Hayle had been preparing himself for victory, readying his blade for the killing blow, his wounded opponent all but vanquished.

Instead, he was the one now down on the ground, blood flowing freely from wounds in his leg and his shoulder. He would live, but he would never fight with that arm again. Only then did Barrington turn and see Anna flying across the grass towards him. Anna, her eyes wide, her face white with fear. 'Barrington! Oh, dear God!'

And then she was in his arms, heedless of his blood soaking into her gown. He gasped at the pain her embrace caused, but there was no way in hell he was going to push her away. Not now when he felt the wetness of tears on her face. He closed his eyes and held her close as his knees finally gave way and he sank wearily to the ground.

'Barrington!' she cried, falling with him.

'I'm fine, Anna,' he whispered. 'Fine. I just need to...sit down.'

Seconds later, Peregrine came running. 'What the hell's going on?' He looked in horror at Edward lying on the ground, and then at Barrington bleeding in Anna's arms. 'What in blazes—?'

'Lord Hayle and I had some...unfinished business,' Barrington murmured over Anna's head. He handed his sword to Peregrine with the instruction that he watch Hayle, then he tipped Anna's face up to his. 'It's over, love. Everything's going to be all right now.'

He stared down into her eyes and saw everything that mattered to him. Everything that ever would matter. She was now his and for always. And he was never going to do anything to risk losing her again.

That was his last thought as he slipped into darkness and the pain in his shoulder mercifully disappeared.

It was a tense party that gathered in the Earl of Cambermere's library just over an hour later. Barrington, his shoulder bandaged and wearing a clean shirt lent to him by Peregrine, held a large glass of brandy in his good hand and Anna sat next to him wearing a new gown, her previous one having been liberally stained with his blood. Peregrine sat in the chair in front of the fireplace, looking deeply upset by all that had gone on, and the earl sat behind his desk, looking equally troubled as he nursed an even larger glass of brandy.

Only Edward was absent, his injuries being tended to upstairs by the surgeon his father had called in immediately upon the party arriving home.

A few minutes later, the door opened and the surgeon came in. Instantly, the earl was on his feet. 'Well?'

'Your son will be fine,' Mr Hopkins said with a weary smile. 'I've stitched the wound and given him a sedative for the pain. I doubt he'll wake up for some time.'

'How serious are his injuries?' Anna asked.

'The injury to his thigh was superficial, but he won't have much use of his right arm.' The surgeon glanced at Barrington. 'I suspect the only reason he's still alive is because you knew exactly where to strike.'

'It was never my intention to kill him,' Barrington said quietly. 'Only to prevent one of us from being killed.'

'Then you have my congratulations on a job well done. I've left some laudanum on the table by the door for you, Sir Barrington. It will help ease the pain.'

Barrington nodded. 'Thank you, Mr Hopkins.'

'Yes, thank you, Hopkins,' the earl said gruffly. 'Good of you to come so quickly.'

The surgeon smiled. 'I'll add it to the bill. Goodnight, all.'

Cambermere waited for the surgeon to leave before saying,

'Now would someone please tell me what in God's name happened tonight?'

Barrington glanced at Anna, but realised she was still too shaken to talk about it. Given that Peregrine didn't look much better, Barrington said, 'I think it falls to me to explain, my Lord. And as much as I regret some of what I am about to say, I'm afraid you need to hear it all.'

The earl grimaced. 'Say what you must. I shall bear it as best I can.'

So Barrington told him, beginning with Hayle's taking up with Elizabeth Paisley, followed by the details of his plan to have her steal the baroness's necklace and finally his reasons for placing the necklace in his father's room. He purposely made no mention of the conversation he'd had with Hayle regarding his feelings towards Peregrine, knowing it would reveal more than he—and likely the earl—wished to, but what he did say was damning enough.

At the end of the lengthy telling, the earl abruptly stood up, his face devoid of colour, his brown eyes deeply troubled. 'Why?' was all he said. 'I've never been hard on Edward. Never forced him to do anything he had no wish to do. And I gave him everything he asked for.'

'I'm sure you did all that and more,' Barrington said. 'But when you invited Peregrine to come and stay with you, everything changed. It's time, my Lord,' he said softly. 'You can't keep this a secret any longer.'

He felt Anna stiffen on the sofa beside him, but knew the time for deceit was over. She had to hear the truth and she had to hear it from her father's lips.

Cambermere obviously knew it, too. 'You're right, of course,' he said finally. 'It was naïve of me to think I could keep the secret for ever. A man's past is never truly past.' He looked at Anna and sadly shook his head. 'I'm sorry, my dear. I should have told you the truth straight away. Before Peregrine even got here. But I was afraid you would think badly of me.'

'I could never do that, Papa.'

'You might over something like this.'

'Like what?'

The earl sighed. 'The fact that Peregrine *is* my son.'

Barrington heard Anna's muffled gasp, but it was to Peregrine's starkly white face that his gaze was drawn. 'I'm *what*?'

'It's true,' the earl said. 'I met your mother when I was nineteen. We fell madly in love and it was my dearest wish that we be married. But my father wouldn't allow it. Olivia wasn't well born and I was heir to an earldom. So while my parents didn't object to our friendship in the beginning, they did once they saw it getting serious. When I told my father I was in love with Olivia, he forbade me to see her ever again.'

'Oh, Papa,' Anna said softly.

'We were both heartbroken,' the earl said quietly. 'At that age, love is so keenly felt, as was the pain of our enforced separation. But I had no choice. I had duties and obligations. Responsibilities to my name. So I made the decision to break it off. I never saw Olivia again.'

'But what about Mama?' Anna asked. 'Did you not love her?'

'Yes, but not in the way I loved Olivia. I'm sorry, my dear, but you may as well know the truth. My marriage to your mother was arranged and the love we came to feel for one another developed over time. But what I felt for Olivia was entirely different. Something that only comes along once in a lifetime. Peregrine is the result of that love.'

'But how could you just leave her like that?' Peregrine

asked in a harsh whisper. 'You got her with child and then just…walked away?'

'I never knew she was increasing,' the earl said, the sadness in his voice reflected in the bleakness of his expression. 'I was sent away to Europe. When I got back, it was to find the preparations for my marriage to Isabel already underway.'

'How did Mama feel about the marriage?' Anna asked.

'We liked each other well enough. Your mother was high born and beautiful, everything a man could ask for, and we were married a few months later. The problem was, I was still in love with Olivia.'

'But you never saw her again,' Peregrine said grimly.

Cambermere shook his head. 'I went looking for her when I got back, of course, but she was gone. And I had no idea there was a child until two months ago when the man you believed to be your father wrote to tell me about you.'

'But how did he know?'

'Apparently, Olivia fell ill not long after I was sent away. When she found out she was…dying—' the earl's voice caught, but he forced himself to go on '—she gave you to her sister, Mary, to raise. But she made Mary promise not to tell *anyone* who your father really was. Mary kept that promise until the night before she died. Only then did she tell her husband who you really were and that it was only right I be contacted and made aware of your existence.'

It was a shocking story and Barrington wasn't at all surprised that no one in the room spoke for a few minutes. They all had much to come to terms with. The knowledge that Cambermere had been in love with another woman before he'd met his wife. The fact there had been a child from that ill-fated love, and the fact that only three people had known the truth about Peregrine's existence.

'So, Peregrine really *is* my half-brother,' Anna said, the first to find her voice.

'Yes, my dear, he is,' her father said. 'And I hope you will believe me when I say that I was as deeply shocked when the letter arrived telling me about him as you are now.'

Anna nodded, her eyes heavy with regret as she glanced at Barrington. 'I'm so sorry, Barrington. I should never have doubted you.'

'It doesn't matter.'

'Yes, it does.' Anna turned to glare at her father. 'You should have told us the truth, Papa. As soon as you found out.'

'I know. I thought you might have realised it the first day Peregrine arrived,' Cambermere said. 'Edward saw it straight away.'

Anna shook her head. 'I wasn't looking. You introduced him as your godson. I had no reason to suspect otherwise.'

'But if you knew who I was when you wrote to me,' Peregrine said slowly, 'why didn't you tell *me* when I first arrived in London?'

'Because I wanted the three of you to get to know one another without any kind of prejudice standing in the way,' the earl explained. 'Perhaps that was naïve of me, but I thought it would be easier for you to become friends if you didn't know about the connection. Wrong, I know now, but that was the decision I made.' He glanced at his daughter, his eyes pleading with her to understand. 'I knew it would be difficult to explain my having a child with another woman. You loved your mother deeply and I feared you would see it as a betrayal of her that I had been with another woman, even if happened before your mother and I were introduced. I didn't want you to hold that against Peregrine. It wasn't his fault.'

'But it mattered to Edward,' Anna said sadly. 'He knew who Peregrine was and he wanted nothing to do with him.'

'It was worse than that,' Barrington said. 'Your brother wanted to humiliate Rand, the way he felt he'd been humiliated by your father's bringing Peregrine to London. Edward was convinced that if *he* knew Peregrine was your father's son, so would the rest of society.'

'And did they?' Anna asked.

'I'd be lying if I said there hasn't been speculation about it. Nevertheless, it was Edward's intention right from the start that Peregrine should fail.' Barrington said. 'He introduced him to Lady Yew, knowing her penchant for younger men, and made sure that Peregrine knew the truth about the state of the Yews' marriage. He encouraged him to become Lady Yew's lover, and he used that to try to set your father against Peregrine, and perhaps against you as well.'

'That's why he tried to make it look as though I'd stolen the necklace,' the earl said sadly.

Barrington nodded. 'He knew you wouldn't go to jail, but that your standing in society would be hopelessly compromised. That's what he was counting on. He also planned on courting the baroness in the hopes of eventually marrying her. He felt that by showing you in such a bad light, and himself in such a good one, she would eventually transfer her affections to him.'

'Dear God,' the earl whispered. 'What did I do to deserve such hatred from my own son?'

'He didn't hate you, Papa,' Anna said sadly. 'He was just eaten up by jealousy.'

'And by his fears, irrational as they were,' Barrington said. 'Perhaps he was afraid you might have made Peregrine your heir.'

'No,' the earl said firmly. 'Whatever my feelings for

Peregrine, Edward is my legitimate heir. The title must devolve to him.'

'But what of his future now, Papa?' Anna said. 'He cannot stay here. Not after what he did to you and Peregrine. To say nothing of the fact that he tried to kill Barrington tonight.'

'My lord, if I may...?' Barrington interjected.

The earl nodded. 'Of course.'

'It might be in everyone's best interests if Edward were to...go away for a while.'

The earl frowned. 'Go away?'

'To the Americas, perhaps. Or Australia. A man can do well in such places if he applies himself and your son is far from stupid. He is simply a victim of his own insecurities. This could be a chance for him to make something of himself. More importantly, it would get him away from London and give the rest of you time to work matters through. And, hopefully, to put all of this behind you.'

Anna nodded. 'I think it's an excellent idea. I don't see how any of us would be able to carry on as normal, given what's happened.'

'No, I don't suppose we would. But what about you, Parker?' the earl asked, his voice laced with regret. 'There's no getting around the fact that my son would have killed you. You would be perfectly within your rights to have him brought up on charges.'

'Perhaps, but I have no intention of doing so. I would never wish that kind of grief on your family. Your son acted out of jealousy and fear. He is tortured enough by his demons. There is no need for me to add to his suffering,' Barrington said.

All eyes turned to the earl, who seemed to be considering the suggestion. 'Are you sure you would be amenable to seeing him walk away? You may never wield a sword with that arm again.'

Barrington shrugged. 'Since I am able to fence with either hand, it is of no real consequence. It is enough that Edward experience life elsewhere. Perhaps it will force him to take a closer look at his life and to rethink his priorities.'

'I sincerely hope so,' the earl said heavily. 'A man's son is said to be a reflection of himself. I hate to think that in some way I inspired that kind of belief system in him.' He glanced at Peregrine, who was sitting quietly in the corner, and said, 'And what about you, sir? What have you to say about all this?'

Peregrine looked up, still clearly in shock. 'What *can* one say upon learning that the man he has always believed to be his father is not, and that a man he never knew existed until a few weeks ago is.'

'A shocking revelation indeed,' the earl agreed.

'Also, that I have a half-brother and half-sister I never knew, and that one of them hated me enough to wish his own father grievous harm.' Peregrine shook his head, his eyes troubled. 'It is a great deal to come to terms with.'

'Indeed it is,' the earl said quietly. 'But it is my sincere hope that you will stay here and get to know us better while you are endeavouring to do so. However, if you feel you cannot stay under the present circumstances, you are free to leave. Perhaps you will wish to return to the family you left behind.'

'Actually, I would rather stay in London,' Peregrine said slowly. 'One of the reasons my father…that is, the man I thought was my father wrote asking you to take me, was so that I might have a chance to experience life beyond the farm. I think he knew I wasn't cut out to be a farmer. And while they were good to me, I doubt going back there now would be in anyone's best interests.'

'Then you are welcome to stay,' the earl said. 'If Anna has no objections?'

'None whatsoever,' Anna said immediately. 'I don't like Peregrine any the less for having found out he's my half-brother. In fact,' she added with a smile, 'I like him a great deal more.'

'Good. Then the decision is yours, Peregrine. If you wish to stay in London, we will be happy to have you. And if you do not wish to live in this house, you may choose another,' the earl said. 'I shall see to it that you *are* taken care of and that you are acknowledged as my son.'

Peregrine stared. 'You would do that?'

'Why not? I'm not ashamed of you. Far from it,' the earl said softly. 'You are all I have left of Olivia and I loved her with all my heart. I see so much of her in you and I deeply regret that you did not have a chance to know her. She was... an exceptional woman.'

'Perhaps you could tell me about her,' Peregrine said slowly. 'I would like to know who she was.'

'I would be honoured,' the earl said. Then, roughly clearing his throat, he got to his feet. 'Well, it's late and I think enough's been said for now. Parker, my carriage is at your disposal. Or, you are welcome to stay here if your injuries are such that you would rather not travel.'

'Thank you, my Lord, but I would like to return home.' Barrington stood up, wincing slightly. It was one thing to pretend his injuries weren't serious; it was quite another to believe it. 'You have enough to contend with here, I think.'

'I'll see you out,' Anna said, quickly getting to her feet.

They walked to the front door in silence. Barrington was very aware of Anna beside him, but the situation was too fraught with emotion to speak of important matters now. The embrace they had shared in the park, the passionate words they had exchanged, would all have to be addressed, but not tonight. 'May I call upon you in a few days' time?' he asked as they stood together at the door. 'There are things that need to be said.'

'Of course,' she said, her expression faltering ever so slightly. 'Are you sure you're well enough to drive home, Barrington? You've been through so much tonight.'

He gave her a weak smile. 'We all have. Given that I won't be the one driving, I'll be fine. But I am in need of rest.'

'Yes, of course.' She looked at him then, and to his surprise she stood on her toes and kissed him full on the mouth in a long, intimate kiss that left his head spinning. 'Sleep well, my love,' she whispered against his lips. 'And thank you from the bottom of my heart for everything you did tonight.'

Incredible. As much as his body ached, the touch of her mouth instantly aroused him. 'I did nothing.'

'You let my brother live,' she said. 'But, more importantly, *you* lived. I wouldn't have liked having my brother's death on my hands, but I fear that's what would have happened had you died at his tonight.'

Barrington wanted to believe she was joking, but the look in her eyes told him otherwise. 'You would have destroyed your life.'

'It wouldn't have mattered,' she told him. 'If he had killed you, it would already have been destroyed beyond all hope of repair.'

As expected, over the next few days, Peregrine and the earl spent a great deal of time talking through their unusual situation. There were twenty-seven years to make up for and a lot of ground to cover. And though, at first, the words were slow in coming, it wasn't long before they were flowing freely, bringing the two back on an even keel. Peregrine was anxious to hear about his mother and Cambermere was delighted to talk about her. Given that he'd had to keep the truth about Olivia bottled up for so many years, it was a relief to finally be able to talk to someone about her—especially when that someone happened to be her son. And in learning of his true parentage, Peregrine seemed to mature into the man Anna knew he wanted to be. Lady Yew was never mentioned again.

As for Edward, he had been happy to go away. Aware that his future in London was in jeopardy, both because his family knew what he had tried to do and because it was quite likely society would find out at some point, he elected to go to California, where he'd heard stories that it was possible for a man with a good head on his shoulders to acquire vast tracts of land and make a fortune into the bargain. If there was one thing Edward wasn't lacking, Anna acknowledged wryly, it was confidence in his own ability to succeed.

As for Julia, she was thrilled at having her necklace safely returned to her. So much so that, when she learned the truth about what happened, she decided not to press charges against Miss Paisley and even offered the girl her position back.

'Why ever would she do such a thing?' Lydia asked as she and Anna walked their horses along Rotten Row a few days later. 'Miss Paisley has proven herself anything but trustworthy.'

'I know, but if you could have seen Eliza's face when Barrington told her she wasn't going to be charged and that the baroness was willing to take her back, you would understand. Eliza hasn't had an easy life,' Anna said. 'She told me the happiest she's ever been was during her brief time with the baroness and she apologised to Julia so sincerely that I actually saw tears in Julia's eyes. Eliza said she was willing to do whatever the baroness asked and that she could check her jewellery every night to make sure it was all there. She was just that happy to have a second chance.'

'Well, I'm glad it all worked out for Eliza, but what about Justine?'

Anna laughed. 'I was able to find a position for her and you will never guess with whom.'

Lydia looked blank. 'Who?'

'Miss Mercy Banks. Or, as she will shortly become, Mrs Giles Blokker. I think they will suit admirably.'

'How marvellous! And your father? This must have been a very trying time for him.'

'It has been dreadful,' Anna admitted. 'Learning about the existence of a son he never knew he had and finding out what kind of man Edward was were very hard on him. But some wonderful things have come out of it, too. He has acknowledged Peregrine as his son and Peregrine is delighted that he doesn't have to go back to the country. He's promised us all that he'll forget about sowing wild oats and stick to his papers and archaeological investigations.'

'And what of your father's hopes with regard to Julia?'

Anna slowly began to smile. 'In spite of my brother's best efforts, Julia never believed that my father was guilty of stealing her necklace. She didn't understand Edward's sudden interest in her and says she found it rather sad, since it was obvious he didn't love her the same way Papa did. I believe he will ask her to marry him once a suitable time has passed and the memory of all this has faded.'

'So,' Lydia said with a smile, 'your father and Peregrine are settled and Edward has been banished to the Americas. It would appear that matters have worked out splendidly for everyone…except you.'

'Nonsense, I am perfectly happy.'

'Has Sir Barrington spoken to you?'

Anna felt her cheeks grow warm. 'Not yet, but he did say we had things to talk about.'

'And do you wish to talk to him about these matters?'

'Yes, though there really is no hurry,' Anna said, knowing it for the lie it was.

But Lydia just smiled. 'Perhaps not on your part, but I believe the gentleman is quite anxious in that regard. No doubt that is why he is approaching us now with such a determined look on his face.'

Anna gasped and, lifting her head, saw that Barrington was indeed riding towards them. 'Oh, no, I'm not ready!'

'I don't think we ever are for moments like this,' Lydia said with a wink, 'but they come along regardless. And in case you're wondering, this isn't a chance meeting. Sir Barrington sent a note asking me if we would be riding in the park this morning. I told him we would.'

Anna felt her pulse begin to race. He had planned this? He'd wanted to see her that badly?

'Good morning, Lady Annabelle. Lady Lydia,' he greeted them, resting his hands on the pommel. 'Lovely morning for a ride.'

'It is indeed, Sir Barrington, and I think I shall take advantage of it,' Lydia said, gathering her reins and smiling at Anna. 'I shall return in a little while.'

In the silence that followed, Anna turned to study the face of the man watching her and realised her heart was beating so hard she could barely speak. 'I could say this is a surprise but I understand it was planned.'

Barrington gave her a wry, fleeting smile. 'It has been my experience that important matters are best not left to chance. I wished to speak to you in private, which meant not at your house or at a society gathering. So, I had to arrange for some other meeting place and I thought this the most suitable. I did ask Lady Lydia to stay close by so there could be no question of impropriety.'

Anna looked up and saw that Lydia was still within sight, having stopped under the shade of a large tree just beyond. 'You appear to have thought of everything.'

'I try,' he said quietly. 'Though when it comes to you, I find myself constantly falling short of the mark.'

Anna bit her lip so as not to smile. 'I can't imagine why you would say that. You always seem so completely in control of yourself, no matter what the situation.'

'Because I am used to dealing in logic and reason. Yet all of my dealings with you involve emotions, and rather strong ones at that,' he admitted.

'And emotion clouds judgement so as to totally obscure the truth,' she teased.

'I should have known you would use that against me,' he said wryly.

'It wasn't intended as a slight. I would never knowingly hurt you, Barrington.' Anna's smile faded, her fingers tightening convulsively on the reins. 'You look…much better than you did when last I saw you.'

Clearly intent on setting her mind at rest, Barrington grinned. 'I have fully regained my strength and the surgeon is very pleased with my shoulder, though my valet has been heard to complain that I have, at times, been a rather difficult patient.'

Anna laughed, a welcome relief from the tension she'd been carrying for too many days. 'I was so afraid, Barrington. That night, when I ran across the park and saw you and Edward fighting…when I saw all the blood…I was terrified I was going to lose you.'

'There was really never any danger of that,' he said quietly. 'Your brother was too far under the influence of the opium to be a real threat.'

'But he wounded you all the same.'

'Yes, because I was careless,' Barrington admitted. 'I lowered my guard. Preoccupied with thoughts of you, I wasn't expecting the attack. But he only managed to get in one thrust.'

'One good one,' she whispered, glancing at his arm, still in its sling. 'You may never use that arm again.'

'Not to fight to my previous standard, perhaps, but it is perfectly capable of doing other things. Like holding you close,' he murmured.

Anna closed her eyes, feeling the warmth of his words pierce her heart. 'Is this where you tell me again about the risks involved in loving you?'

She opened her eyes and caught his gaze. A minute passed, and then he slowly began to smile. 'No. It's probably what I *should* say, but I'm not going to. What I feel for you isn't rational, Anna, but I'm not willing to fight it any more.'

'Good, because love isn't rational,' Anna said. 'Elizabeth Paisley did what my brother asked because she loved him and thought he loved her in return. Just as Peregrine lied to me because he thought Lady Yew had deep feelings for him. Love excuses all things and forgives all things.'

'Do you honestly believe that?'

'No. It's a pretty sentiment, but it doesn't justify lies or deceit. Peregrine's belief that Lady Yew wasn't in love with her husband didn't make it right for him to enter into an affair with her. Just as being in love with my brother didn't justify Miss Paisley's stealing Julia's necklace.'

'So you're saying that truth and emotion will always clash,' Barrington said.

'Probably. I suspect men will always do bizarre things in the name of love.'

'Which brings me back to our ongoing conversation.' At her look of confusion, he said, 'The one we started the night we met at Lady Montby's and that we have been having ever since. The one concerning...us.'

Her pulse accelerated. 'I wasn't sure there *was* an us.'

'Oh, there most definitely is an us,' Barrington replied. 'I've spent the last few weeks trying to deny it, but finally realised I'm fighting a losing battle. And you know why.'

Anna stared down at her hands. 'You have taken pains to tell me and on more than one occasion. But you must feel there is hope for us or you wouldn't have sought me out.'

'You're right. Because the idea of *not* having you in my life is one I can no longer contemplate. You *are* all I think about, Anna,' he said quietly. 'And a man cannot be effective if his mind is constantly engaged upon something or someone he believes...unattainable.'

'I have always been attainable...for you,' Anna said, her voice husky. 'It was *you* who chose to believe otherwise. And I don't care if being with you involves risk. I would rather take the risks than live without you.'

'Even if it endangered your life?'

Anna suddenly felt wise beyond her years. 'You said yourself that life is never entirely without risk and you're right. But I like to think I demonstrated that I am not some witless female prone to running away at the first sign of danger.'

'No, you're not.' His mouth lifted at one corner. 'You have proven that most admirably. But would you allow yourself to become intimately involved with a man like me? Knowing that what I do might always put you in danger.'

Anna shook her head. 'The greatest danger to *both* of

us thus far has been from my own family. I couldn't be any closer to the source of the danger if I tried.'

'In that case…' Barrington dismounted and, crossing to her side, held out his hand. Anna placed hers within it and allowed him to help her down from the saddle. His hands lingered on her waist and they were so close she could feel the warmth of his breath on her face. 'I haven't spoken to your father, and if you say you have no desire to *be* my wife, I will not do so. But if you consent to marry me, Anna, I'll make you a promise here and now that there won't be any more risks to either of us, because I won't take on any more assignments.'

Her eyes widened in shock. 'You would do that for me?'

'I would do whatever it took to keep you safe,' Barrington said softly. 'I love you, Anna. There's never been a woman in my life for whom I've felt a deeper or more powerful passion. I love everything about you. Your enthusiasm for life, your unstinting concern for others, the genuine goodness that is so much a part of you. If you refuse to marry me, I will go on, but only because there won't be anything else for me to do. If you accept, you'll never have to worry about your happiness again.'

'Or yours,' Anna said. 'My brother almost killed you, Barrington, and I suspect there are others who would no doubt like to try. A man doesn't make friends by exposing other men's deepest, darkest secrets.'

'That's what I've been trying to tell you.'

'Nevertheless, someone has to try to stop them, and as I've been trying to tell *you*, I don't want you to give up what you do. I love you. There's no doubt in my mind about that. And, yes, I'll be afraid for you, but what you do is part of who you are. I couldn't ask you to give that up for me.'

'You don't have to ask. I've given a great deal of thought

to what I would be giving up and it doesn't compare to what I would be gaining. I want you as my wife, Anna,' he told her fervently. 'I want to hold you in my arms and tell you every day how much I love you. I want to cover your body with kisses and hear you cry out my name when we make love. And I want to see your beautiful eyes in the faces of our children. Marry me, sweetheart, and I'll spend the rest of my life not only telling you how much I love you, but showing you.'

His smile was slow and sensual, filling her with a giddy sense of pleasure. 'Good, because I *am* saying yes, Barrington, so you'd better be prepared to make good on your promise.' Uncaring as to who might be watching, Anna walked into his arms and tilted her head back, her eyes glowing. 'As far as I'm concerned, you can start telling me *and* showing me, just as soon as you like.'

* * * * *

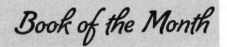

MILLS & BOON®
Book Club

2 Free Books!

Get your free books now at
www.millsandboon.co.uk/freebookoffer

Or fill in the form below and post it back to us

THE MILLS & BOON® BOOK CLUB™—HERE'S HOW IT WORKS: Accepting your free books places you under no obligation to buy anything. You may keep the books and return the despatch note marked 'Cancel'. If we do not hear from you, about a month later we'll send you 4 brand-new stories from the Historical series priced at £3.99* each. There is no extra charge for post and packaging. You may cancel at any time, otherwise we will send you 4 stories a month which you may purchase or return to us—the choice is yours. *Terms and prices subject to change without notice. Offer valid in UK only. Applicants must be 18 or over. Offer expires 28th February 2012. **For full terms and conditions, please go to www.millsandboon.co.uk/termsandconditions**

Mrs/Miss/Ms/Mr (please circle)
_____

First Name
_____

Surname
_____

Address
_____

_____

Postcode
_____

E-mail
_____

Send this completed page to: Mills & Boon Book Club, Free Book Offer, FREEPOST NAT 10298, Richmond, Surrey, TW9 1BR

Find out more at
www.millsandboon.co.uk/freebookoffer

Visit us Online

0611/M1ZEE

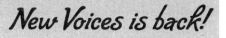